SPECIAL MESSAGE TO READERS

THE ULVERSCROFT FOUNDATION
(registered UK charity number 264873)
was established in 1972 to provide funds for research, diagnosis and treatment of eye diseases.
Examples of major projects funded by the Ulverscroft Foundation are:-

- The Children's Eye Unit at Moorfields Eye Hospital, London
- The Ulverscroft Children's Eye Unit at Great Ormond Street Hospital for Sick Children
- Funding research into eye diseases and treatment at the Department of Ophthalmology, University of Leicester
- The Ulverscroft Vision Research Group, Institute of Child Health
- Twin operating theatres at the Western Ophthalmic Hospital, London
- The Chair of Ophthalmology at the Royal Australian College of Ophthalmologists

You can help further the work of the Foundation by making a donation or leaving a legacy.
Every contribution is gratefully received. If you would like to help support the Foundation or require further information, please contact:

THE ULVERSCROFT FOUNDATION
The Green, Bradgate Road, Anstey
Leicester LE7 7FU, England
Tel: (0116) 236 4325

website: www.foundation.ulverscroft.com

Matthew Griffin is a graduate of Wake Forest University and the Iowa Writers Workshop. Born and raised in North Carolina, he worked for several years at Tennessee's Highlander Research and Education Center, a renowned hub of grassroots organizing for social justice throughout the south and Appalachia. He currently lives with his husband and too many pets in Louisiana, where he is a visiting professor at the University of Louisiana at Lafayette. *Hide* is his first novel.

You can discover more about the author at www.matthewgriffinwriter.com

HIDE

Wendell and Frank meet at the end of World War II, when Frank returns home to their North Carolina town. Soon he's loitering around Wendell's taxidermy shop, and the two come to understand their connection as love — a love that, in this time and place, can hold real danger. Cutting nearly all ties with the rest of the world, they make a home for themselves on the outskirts of town, keeping a string of beloved dogs for company . . . When Wendell finds Frank lying outside among the tomatoes at the age of eighty-three, he feels a new threat to their careful self-reliance: as Frank's physical strength and memory deteriorate, the two of them must fully confront the sacrifices they've made for each other— and the impending loss of the life they've built.

MATTHEW GRIFFIN

HIDE

Complete and Unabridged

CHARNWOOD
Leicester

First published in Great Britain in 2016 by
Bloomsbury
An imprint of Bloomsbury Publishing Plc
London

First Charnwood Edition
published 2016
by arrangement with
Bloomsbury Publishing Plc
London

The moral right of the author has been asserted

A catalogue record for this book is available
from the British Library.

ISBN 978–1–4448–3033–0

Published by
F. A. Thorpe (Publishing)
Anstey, Leicestershire

Set by Words & Graphics Ltd.
Anstey, Leicestershire
Printed and bound in Great Britain by
T. J. International Ltd., Padstow, Cornwall

This book is printed on acid-free paper

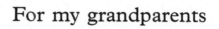

For my grandparents

1

Lord knows how long he's been lying out there: flat on his back in the middle of the vegetable garden. I see him through the smudged window over the kitchen sink as I'm carrying the groceries to the counter, the day burning bright all over him. I wasn't gone but an hour. I set down my bags and hurry out the back door. I've got two more waiting in the car.

'Frank,' I yell. 'Are you all right?'

He doesn't say a word, not until I'm looming right over him, my shadow draped across his chest and following the wrinkles in his plaid shirt before falling flat onto the dirt. He looks up at me, not even squinting against the sun. Three or four of his tomato plants are crushed underneath him, their silver-furred vines curled about his arms and knees like something that wants to pull him into the earth. He's broken a stake in trying to haul himself up, and ripped two more from the ground, torn cuts in it clotting with dark soil.

'I'm fine,' he says. 'Just needed to lie down for a second.'

'In the middle of your tomato plants?'

'Just wore out from the sun,' he says. His speech is sloppy and slurred as a drunk's.

'Smile for me,' I say. One corner of his mouth twitches upward while the other stays still, pulls his face into a lopsided grin.

'Can you raise your arms?'

1

He lifts them both, but one drifts right back down just as soon as it's risen, pulled back to the dirt by an insistent, invisible hand. I squeeze the one reaching for me. The green smell of tomato leaves is on his fingers.

'Don't you move,' I say, and I get myself back in the kitchen quick as I can and call for the ambulance. The operator doesn't sound like she's in too big of a hurry, and I'm fairly sure she's eating doughnuts. Makes all her words sound fat. I pace the tile thin waiting for her to take down Frank's name and our address.

'And be quick about it,' I say. 'It's an emergency.'

'That's what they all say, sir.'

The phone's mounted on the wall. I leave it off the hook, swinging by its cord over the floor, in case they need to trace the call in order to locate us — I wouldn't be one bit surprised to find out she'd written our address wrong — and take Frank out a glass of water. I hold it to his lips, but then if only half of him's still working, he might not be able to swallow it right and choke to death before they get here to rescue him, and he's so heavy, I don't believe I could even roll him over myself. I yank the glass from his lips before he can take a gulp, but he doesn't seem to care, just looks at me with that same muddled expression. His old blue baseball cap's tilted backwards, nearly fallen off his head. He keeps that thing perched so high and loose any breeze might knock it away, and usually does, spends half his time out here picking that cap up from wherever the wind's taken and dropped it.

But he hates anything to squeeze his skull.

'Well,' he says, as if we've lingered here just a little too long after the conversation's run its course, and things have become awkward.

'Does anything hurt?'

He raises the one eyebrow he can. His cap rustles up with it. 'Half of me feels mighty strange,' he says. 'Like it ain't hardly there.'

I snatch the cap off his head. Sweat stains along the band have turned the inside pale green in a few splotches. I stand here in the bright heat and fan him with it, stirring the thick air into the measliest of slow-moving breezes, barely trembling the white wisps of his hair, for what seems like two hours of waiting while he stares up at me with a blank, lopsided grin. Gives me the creeps.

'Stop smiling like that,' I say. 'It gives me the creeps.'

The raised half of his mouth slowly slips down his cheek, toward his chin.

'It's too hot out here. You shouldn't have been working out here in the first place.' He's eighty-three years old, for heaven's sake. An eighty-three-year-old doesn't have any business being outside in the middle of the day like this. I'm sure there's some kind of heat advisory in effect, warning people to get their pets and their elderly inside, safe in the air-conditioning. And of course he's only got the sleeves of his shirt rolled halfway up his forearms: never an inch higher, even in the full heat of summer.

Sweat trickles down my back. I hate to sweat.

Finally the siren wails down the road, and the

ambulance tires grumble on the long gravel drive through the trees and up to the house. Sun's blazing so bad I can't even see the swirling red lights. They skate invisible over the leaves, over the house's white vinyl siding. I open the wooden gate to the backyard and lead the paramedics to him. Panic splashes across his face, running under his limp features, as they kneel over him.

'I feel fine,' he says, 'just wore out from the sun,' before they can even press the stethoscope to his chest and ask him what symptoms he's suffering.

'You can go on,' he says.

It takes the both of them a good couple minutes of heaving and hawing to peel him off the ground and lift him onto a stretcher. The earliest tomatoes are splattered like gunshot wounds all across his back. I pour the glass of water over the crushed vines and into the dirt. The dark stain of it sinks down and down and disappears.

'You coming along?' one of the paramedics grunts as they lift the stretcher into the ambulance. I'm not too keen on the looks of them. They've both got thick, scuzzy mustaches over their wet mouths, and I don't like close quarters like that anyway, everybody breathing their germs all over each other, and who knows what they've picked up from the seeping wounds and phlegm of this town's sick and injured.

Frank stares at me, wide-eyed and worried as his face permits, as they fit the oxygen mask over his nose and mouth.

4

'Hold on just a second,' I say.

My car door's still wide open, the alarm bell dinging and two plastic bags slumped in the backseat, waiting to be carried inside. I close the door and hurry back and let one of the paramedics help me up the ramp. Frank and I are careful not to look at each other too much. They close us up and speed down the drive, tires hissing ruts in the gravel, the siren stretching behind us, still wailing in the yard long after we've turned onto the road and the trees have blotted it from sight.

*   *   *

At the hospital, I tell the worn-out woman behind the desk I'm his brother. Saves us all the ugliness of some kind of scene. The first couple times I did it, I felt so jittery and nervous I was sure they'd catch me, but by now I hardly think about it. Sometimes I even enjoy it a little.

'I'll need to see your ID, please,' she says. She's wearing scrubs with dancing teddy bears printed all over them.

I reach for my back pocket and pretend not to feel the bulge of my wallet. My last name's printed clear as day on my driver's license, like it has been since the world got so many people in it you had to start providing photographic evidence that you haven't invented your entire identity or stolen somebody else's, but brothers have got to have the same last name. At least they used to, before a woman could have children by as many different men as she pleased

5

without her family disowning her.

'Oh my,' I say, and pat the other pockets of my trousers, dig through them good and frantic. 'Oh my, I'm sorry, I'm afraid I've — all the commotion — '

She heaves a heavy sigh. 'Someone'll come get you when he's ready,' she says. The befuddled routine usually works all right. Ladies who lack the couth not to demand an elderly gentleman's ID usually also lack the patience to endure his flagging faculties. She points me down the hall to a holding cell, where I sit and wait with people coughing and fretting and softly weeping on all sides of me. One family holds hands in a big circle while they take turns whispering some kind of ostentatious round-robin prayer. I hate hospitals. They're too full of piety and hush, and the air's cold and stale, and the smell of iodine smeared on all those papery yellow wrists is enough to make you sick if you weren't already. They won't let anybody just die in peace at home anymore. The only people who get to die at home now are the victims of violent crime.

I try to look through some of the wrinkled magazines they've got lying on the table, but the pages all feel so greasy, smeared with hand-sweat and moist from people's coughs, that I can't bear to flip them. At long last a doctor saunters into the room. From the looks of him, bright twinkling eyes and shiny hair he's clearly spent hours carefully crafting to look mussed, he couldn't be more than twenty years old. Everybody in the room stops what they're doing and looks up, hoping or dreading theirs will be the name he calls. The prayer circle lifts its myriad faces in beatific expectation.

'Mr. Clifton?'

I nod and push my way out of the chair. Takes me a minute to do it, too, I've been sitting so long.

'Hi there,' he says, with a little too much enthusiasm for my taste, reaching out to shake my hand. He looks like the sort of fellow who's used to everybody liking him. 'I'm — '

'How is he?'

'Well,' the doctor says, 'he's had a mild stroke.'

'I know that. How is he?'

'He's in stable condition, but we — '

'Was it the heat? I told him he shouldn't be out in that heat.'

'The heat probably didn't help. But from what I can tell, it was really just a matter of time before one of those arteries got clogged.' He says all this real bright and friendly, as if he's explaining it to a child. 'Anyway, we've got him hooked up to the IV and we're pumping him full of drain cleaner, so it ought to be cleared out soon. He'll need to stay in the hospital for a while, of course.'

'But he's going to get better?'

'Oh, definitely. For sure. Yeah, he'll definitely get better. It's a little too early to tell exactly how much better. But you got him here pretty quick, so.'

I wait for him to finish his sentence. He smiles a bland smile.

'How long have you been practicing medicine?' I say.

'We're also maybe a little concerned about his heart.'

'His heart? His heart's just fine. He just had a new valve put in a couple years back.'

He scribbles that down on his clipboard as if he didn't already know, when Frank's got a bracelet on his wrist that tells you all about it in tiny letters etched in silver, and a stack of surgical records thick as that same wrist from this very hospital.

'Has he suffered heart trouble before?'

'Of course he has. He had a heart attack. Why else would he have gotten a new valve?'

He scribbles this down, too, his head bent close to his clipboard. When he raises it again, he says, 'That makes a lot of sense. A *lot* of sense. We're going to need to run some more tests, just to — '

'You can run whatever tests you want,' I say, 'but his heart's fine. They fixed it. What you need to worry about is his brain.'

'All right,' he says, smiling to himself, highly amused by my ignorance, and taps his clipboard twice with his pen, like he's rapping a gavel to officially bring this meeting to a close. 'You can go in and see him now. Room 214, just down the hall and around the corner,' which actually means down the hall, around the corner, and through a labyrinthine series of doors and forks it takes me ten minutes and the condescending kindness of two nurses to navigate my way through. The hallway's lined with empty beds they've stripped of their linens and pushed against the walls, unplugged

8

electronic contraptions with blank screens still clamped to their rails, monitoring nothing.

Lying there in the bed, he looks so wrinkled and flat, his skin so colorless you can hardly tell it from the dingy hospital sheets folded neatly back from his waist, that I have to lean against the doorjamb. His cheeks are sunken in as if he's got no bones to hold them up, and every few seconds they quiver with his breath. His hand hangs limp over the edge of the bed, tubes running into the back of it, right into his knotty purple veins as if extensions of them, drawn out through slits in his skin.

I sit in a chair beside him and rest my hand on his forearm. The hairs on it feel dusty and dry. On the other side of the dull pink curtain that divides the room, somebody whimpers.

'I'm here,' I say, but Frank doesn't hear me. He sleeps and sleeps.

I sit here and watch him while the last of the sunlight fades from where it struck the other side of the curtain, and the gray fluorescent lights, which seem to slowly rise in contrast, sanitize the room. I switch the TV on to *Win, Lose, or Paw*, the game show that tests the bonds of pets and their owners. It's his favorite. But he doesn't stir, doesn't even turn his head to one side or the other, and that hand just dangles there, out in empty, open space, completely still.

A tall, skinny nurse, a colored woman, comes in to check on him. 'You want something to eat?' she says as she squints at the level of clear fluid in his IV bag.

'No, thank you.' I refuse to eat food that's

been inside hospital doors, and especially not that pureed stuff they bring you. She lifts his wrist and presses two fingers to it. Her lips count silent numbers as she studies the jumble of tattoos scrawled from his shoulder down to his forearm. If he was awake, he'd be scrambling to tug the sheet over them.

'You ought to go home and get some rest,' she says. 'You look about as exhausted as he does.'

'I'm fine,' I say. 'I need to be here when he wakes up.'

'They've got him knocked out good,' she says. 'He'll sleep all night.'

I don't know how she can count and talk at the same time, but she's the first person I've met all day that seems to actually know what she's doing. I nod at her fingers on his wrist. 'Doesn't the machine do that for you?'

'There's things the machine can't tell.'

I thought they'd be able to tell us everything by now. I thought the future would be nothing but robots, robots everywhere, doing everything, so you'd never again have to worry about or depend upon the messy, illusory phenomenon known as a human being.

She looks at the clock, lets go of his wrist, and writes his pulse and some hieroglyphics in red marker on a whiteboard on the wall.

'I'll stay a little while longer,' I say. 'Just in case.'

She nods. 'Just don't run yourself into the ground right off the bat, okay? You'll be here plenty for the next couple weeks.'

'Weeks?'

She lifts his other hand, the one dangling off the bed, and sets it on top of the sheet, tucked to his side.

'Thank you,' I say. Something bubbles in my chest, reaches cold up into my throat.

'Let me know if you need anything,' she says softly, and slips around to the other side of the curtain.

★   ★   ★

I wake up in my cot beside his bed at eight in the morning. My neck hurts, and everything around me looks bright and slow-moving, like it's happening through a sunny haze. Frank hasn't changed positions, hasn't even moved his arm.

A new nurse comes in to check on him. This one's red-faced and in a rush.

'He hasn't moved,' I say.

'He's resting,' she says.

'Is he in a coma?'

'No,' she says. 'He's definitely not in a coma.'

'Then why hasn't he moved?'

'He's resting.'

'I think he's in a coma. You need to have somebody come in and evaluate him. Shine that little flashlight on his eyeballs.'

She jabs a syringe into his IV tube. I lean real close so I can make sure she doesn't pump any air bubbles in.

On the other side of the pink curtain, a man groans.

'That man needs your assistance,' I say, but she starts fiddling with the plastic clothespin

11

they've got clipped on Frank's middle finger. 'It sounds like it's very bad.' I turn on the TV, bolted high on the cinderblock wall and looking every moment like it's on the verge of crashing down on us, to drown him out, and finally she stomps her way around the curtain. On the morning news, they're looking for an eight-month-old boy that's gone missing up in Virginia, just a couple hours north of here. His mother set him down in his bouncy seat while she went to run the water for his bath, and when she came back, he was gone. They keep showing the headline HAVE YOU SEEN LITTLE LARRY? in black on a band of yellow, like the caution tape police use to cordon off brutal crime scenes, underneath a picture of him wrapped up in a powder-blue blanket and looking like every other baby in the entire world.

The bouncy seat, the newsman says, was still quivering with his last bounce.

A hand lands heavy on my arm. I turn in my seat and Frank's eyes are open, bleary but conscious, looking all about him.

'Where are we?' he says, real slow.

'The hospital,' I say.

'Naw,' he says. 'That don't sound right.'

'Look around. Where do you think — '

'How long have I been here?'

'Since yesterday afternoon.'

'Did you water the garden?' he says.

'Of course,' I lie.

'Good. Don't let the weeds get ahold of it.' He pats my hand weakly and smiles, one corner of his mouth moving quickly, the other slowly catching up. He heaves a heavy breath and dozes off again.

I pull my hand from his.

'Nurse,' I yell. 'Nurse.'

★　★　★

Two days he's been here, and he's already getting antsy. They've taken him to run a bunch more tests, gotten him a private room, and barely have him propped up in the bed with his lunch tray pushed against his chest before he's asking me, 'When can I go home?'

'You can't even get your own self out of the bed,' I say.

'I feel fine.'

'That's what you said the other day, too. While all the blood was seeping out of your brain.'

'Be sweet to me,' he says, frowning. He's still slurring his words a little. They sound swollen. It's only the drugs that have him loosened up enough to talk in public like this. After his heart surgery, you'd have thought I was some monster come to terrorize him, the way his eyes roved to rest on every single surface in the room but me.

'There's too many old people here,' he says, peering suspiciously out the door. 'They kept wheeling them past my door, all night long.'

'How would you know? You were passed out on drugs the whole time.'

'The squeak of the wheels gets into your dreams,' he says.

His hands tremble on the white sheets, shake for the sheer terror of uselessness, and his jaw keeps chewing invisible cud. He doesn't seem to notice.

'The doctor's supposed to come by in a little bit,' I say. 'You need to eat your lunch.'

'I can't even tell what my lunch is.' Each compartment on his plastic tray is filled with a different color of mush. 'Ain't they already feeding me through one of these?' He paws the bundle of IV tubes. The colored nurse fastened them with a few straps of velcro to get them out of his way.

'It's just sugar water,' I say. 'Eat. You need to get your strength up. The sooner you do, the sooner we can go home. My rear end's permanently sore from sitting in these chairs all day.'

He looks put out, but he reaches for his spoon. His fingers shake so bad they have trouble closing around it. And that's the hand that still works right. The other one he can't even ball up in a fist yet.

'What are you scared of?' I say. 'The applesauce?'

He frowns at his fingers, as if he could whip them into stillness with just a stern look, and closes them, real deliberate and tight, around the spoon's handle. And he does get them under control, but it looks like he's squeezed their tremors up into his wrist: it rocks his whole hand back and forth so hard it dumps half the spoonful into his lap before he can get it to his mouth. I may have to request him a bib before it's all over.

I've got the TV on the court channel, where

14

Little Larry's mother is holding a press conference to unveil the police sketches of the strange man she kept seeing in the days before her baby disappeared — pretending to trim a bush in her apartment building's parking lot, leaning against the side of the soda machine at the laundromat, crouching in the third-story window of the abandoned cigarette factory across the street from her bedroom.

'Ooh,' Frank says. He pushes himself up in the bed to get a better look. He loves murders and kidnappings and things like that. The suspect's perfectly clean-shaven, and his hair is black and oiled and combed neatly back from his pale forehead and dark eyes, with a level-straight part along one side, the way I used to keep mine.

'She's the one that did it,' Frank says.

'You think?'

'Look how much makeup she's got on.' It's caked all over her face so thick you can see the line along her jaw where it stops, and the skin above that line is a whole different color from the skin below. She's got her blond hair done up in ringlets, sprayed stiff into place like she's going to a fancy party, and a tight blouse with the top three buttons undone so it's only by pure chance we can't all see her brassiere. Mascara runs down her cheeks in cloudy black tears, cutting through big swaths of rouge.

'If that's not the face of guilt itself,' he says, 'I don't know what is.'

'Please,' she says, 'if anyone watching has seen this man, call the police. And if this man is watching, please, bring my baby back. I'm begging you. Bring Little Larry home, please. I won't — I'll give you anything. Anything. All I want is my little boy. That's all.' Her face twists into sobs. She has to hold the podium to keen herself standing.

'Look how hard she's crying,' I say.

'You mean to tell me you believe that?'

'I sure do. Nobody that concerned about how she looks would come on national television and cry that ugly if she didn't have a good reason.'

He sighs. 'You never were very good at this sort of thing,' he says.

The sheriff puts his arm around her shoulders and leads her into a crowd of deputies. They shield her from the cameras.

'I don't think she did it,' I say.

'It's always the mother that did it. Who else but a mother would want to commit a crime against a baby? Nobody else cares enough about babies to commit crimes against them. They'll have her in jail by the end of the week.'

'You want to bet?'

'What do you have to bet that I would want?' he says. 'Not a thing.'

Another two bites of applesauce and he's asleep again. I watch continued coverage of the empty podium until a doctor knocks lightly on the open door. He looks like the one from before, only older and somehow, against all odds, even more pleased with himself, as if thirty years had passed during the night, each one of them further confirming his unwavering faith in his intelligence and skill. My neck hurts from leaning my head back to see the television.

'How's he doing?' he whispers, louder than if he'd just said it normal.

I get up and go to the door so we don't wake Frank. 'Shouldn't you be the one to tell me?'

He bestows a smug, benevolent smile upon the entire room.

'Who are you?' I say.

'The cardiologist.'

'I don't remember you. When did he see you?'

'He didn't. He saw the radiologist.'

'Then where's the radiologist?'

He gives me that same smile, this time all for myself.

'We've had a very in-depth consultation,' he says.

You can't have just one doctor anymore, one person who knows all there is to know about you. They keep dividing us up, down and down into parts too small for a knife blade, and then they go and invent an implement with a finer edge. You've got to have your heart man, your lungs man, your digestive man, your skin man, your brain man, until you're nothing more than an assemblage of organs they can split apart and divide among the needy if you check the right box on the form to renew your driver's license. The woman at the Department of Motor Vehicles tried to give me a real shaming look last time I told her no, I did not want to be an organ donor. I prefer to keep my organs to myself.

'What we're looking at,' the doctor says, flipping through a stack of charts and test results, 'is cardiomyopathy. Dilated cardiomy-opathy.' After a second of me staring at him in

17

anticipation of something that will pass the slightest scrutiny as an actual explanation, he adds, 'An enlarging of the heart. A weakening.'

'I already told that young doctor he's had a valve replaced. How can his heart be — '

'In one way,' he says, 'it's not as bad as it sounds. What we're really looking at is just the fact that his heart's wearing out. Wearing down.'

'He's getting old? That's what you're trying to tell me?'

'In one way,' he says, nodding encouragement.

'What's the other way?'

He presses his fat, shiny lips together and pumps air in and out of the skin around them for a moment, like a frog, while he ponders the best way to gild the information he's about to deliver. 'Between his high blood pressure and cholesterol and some narrowed arteries, that heart of his has to work pretty hard, and it's probably been damaged a little. This causes the muscles to stretch — to *dilate* — which then damages the heart's ability to — '

'I brought him here so you could fix his stroke. Not come up with a hundred more problems for us to worry about.'

'Well,' he says. 'It's all connected.' He holds out his interlaced fingers.

'How long does he have to stay here?'

'You'll need to check with the neurologist on that one.'

'And what's wrong with his hands? It looks like he's got some kind of palsy. Can you fix that?'

He scrunches his mouth into one corner of

18

itself, then the other. 'Here.' He pulls Frank's chest X-rays from a folder at the bottom of the stack. Against the black background, and inside a cage of ghostly, translucent ribs, his heart hangs like a stuffed sock from his breastbone. Back when we had Fancy, one of our beagles, he used to take an old white tube sock, stuff a couple other wadded-up socks inside it, down into the toe, and use it to play tug-of-war with her. After a few rounds, he'd let her have it to rip and shred, then spend half an hour with her on his lap, lifting her jowls and pulling the strings out from between her teeth and under her tongue. She'd just lie there and let him do it, didn't growl or nothing, and that sock would hang over the arm of his chair, torn up and sagging and sopping with drool: that's what his heart looks like in his chest.

'What we're looking at,' the doctor says, 'is his heart.'

'I can see that.'

'Well, as I'm sure you can also see, the problem here is that when the muscle stretches like this, it actually weakens the heart. Damages it even more. It's a sort of terrible cycle. The heart can't pump blood the way it should, and eventually, usually, it leads to long-term heart failure.'

'Can you do surgery? Get him a pacemaker or something, get him a new valve. Get him a heart transplant.'

'At this stage, surgery's not really what we want to be looking at. Especially open-heart. For now, we'll put him on some new medications, up his blood thinner, get him on some stronger statins. As long as he's careful, he could keep living for years.'

'Could?'

'I've seen worse,' he says. 'I have seen worse. But: I have also seen better. You really want to make sure he doesn't exert himself. The last thing you want to be looking at is him putting too much strain on this thing.' He taps the X-ray. 'We want him to stay active, of course. That's very important. Crucial. Keep him moving around as much as he can, keep the blood flowing. Just not *too* too much. Don't let him exert himself. Any other questions?'

Bronchi enclose his heart like bare, winter branches folded about it. I shake my head.

'All right,' he says, and slips me a business card from his pocket like it's an illicit substance. 'I'll need to see him in a month. Go ahead and make the appointment now. Before we get booked up.' And then he's strutting off down the hall to dole out his knowledge to another waiting customer.

I sneak back into the room. Frank lies sound asleep in the bed, his jaw working silently, while inside his chest, his heart slowly wears out. Can't say I blame it. It's worked hard, keeping the blood flowing through a man as big as him, and never once has it gotten a break. Even on the downbeat, when it felt beneath my hand like it had stilled in his chest, it was only opening itself to the blood, preparing to wring itself dry.

As the sun starts to go down, the colored nurse brings his supper and leaves it on the tray beside his bed. I promise her in whispers that I'll try to get him to eat. A breeze picks up outside, blows so steady that the silver undersides of the upturned leaves on the trees don't even flutter, look like they grow that way, pointing still and straight up. Around the horizon, the sky's as bright red as that woman's rouged cheeks. I open the window. I don't know if we're allowed to do that in here or not, but the warm wind feels good. This hospital's always chilly. When I shuffle back to his bed, Frank's sitting up. The breeze flutters the hem of his sheet. He looks out the window, confused for a minute, before he remembers where he is.

'Sailor's delight,' he says.

His hair's so thin you can see plain through it to his pale, spotted scalp. At the top of his chest, peeking out over the sea-foam collar of his paper gown, is the scar, the pale white line where they opened him up the last time and sewed him back together.

He frowns. 'What was supposed to be so good about a red sky at night?'

'I have no idea.'

'You ought to. You grew up around all them ships.'

'Eat some supper,' I say, and push his tray toward him: creamed spinach, creamed corn, and creamed potatoes, and jello red as the sky, with chunks of peaches and pears in it, and peeled, halved grapes that look like somebody's fingertips after they've been in the water too long.

'I hate the red kind,' he says.

'It's all ground-up horse hooves. What difference does it make what color it is?'

'I can taste the chemicals they use to get it that way.'

'You cannot.'

'I can. I can taste the chemicals.' He stares down at it, mounded up like the lump of his old, limp heart. 'Red sky at morning,' he says, and sighs.

'Sailors take warning.'

'Have you heard anything about Larry?'

'No. Though they have managed to talk for two full hours about the lack of new developments.'

'For such a little guy, he sure is a *big* story,' he says, raising his eyebrows jauntily on the word *big*.

'I should have asked if they can cure you of your terrible sense of humor while you're here.'

'I believe I may be a terminal case,' he says, chuckling. 'There is no cure.'

I rest my hand on top of the sheets, next to, but not touching, his leg.

'You mean to tell me you never once asked somebody to explain that saying to you?' he says.

'No,' I say. 'I did not.'

He makes a grumbling noise of disappointment at my lack of intellectual rigor. Then, with great concentration and effort, he flicks his jello with one big finger. Inside it, the pears and peaches and grapes, suspended, slowly sway.

2

I was wiping the blood off my hands when I saw him. I was twenty-three years old, and outside, the whole town, buildings and trees and the first green buds of tentative spring, was coated in a casing of ice from a late-winter storm like something in a museum, something fragile and important that had to be preserved, kept from all the grubby hands that would want to touch it. The power lines sagged beneath the weight, and the trees and streets and sidewalks held themselves tense, waiting for the snap. But in those last minutes of afternoon, as the trees darkened and flattened into silhouettes against the sky, the ice began to loosen, gathering slow into cold drops that hung so heavy and still it seemed they would never fall.

I was on my way to the window to flip my notice from OPEN TO CLOSED — though of course nobody'd set foot in the shop in the three days since the storm hit, and I'd been reduced to skinning squirrels out of sheer boredom — dragging a rag across my fingers so they wouldn't stain the sign, and there he was, standing on the train tracks that ran down the middle of the street to the depot on the corner, wearing an old coat a few sizes too small, the cuffs of which didn't even come down to his big, knobby wrists. He was about the tallest fellow I'd ever seen, with wide shoulders squeezed up and together by his jacket. He didn't have any gloves on, or a hat, and his cheeks were red and raw, his hair yellow, thin, and straight, all except for one curled forelock that rested on his brow like something wilted.

You could tell he hadn't been home long from the war. He stood stiff upright, as if constantly startled by the world around him, and he had that look, as he turned to survey its thawing landscape, of trying to find anything that seemed familiar.

It was getting dark, but the sky above the buildings was bright pink with light reflected off the snow. He lifted his hands to his lips, clasped them together, and breathed onto his fingers before shoving them as far as he could into the pockets of his coat. The glow of the street lamps filtered cold through the window, twice distilled by ice and glass.

I opened the door, and the noise was so loud I couldn't even walk into it. All around was the thud of snow clumps falling into snow piles, the groan of ice as it spread beyond itself, the crackle as it split apart.

'Excuse me,' I yelled. 'Were you looking for something?'

He turned, startled. 'Naw,' he said. 'Nothing in particular.'

'Oh.' I shoved the rag, stiff with dried blood, into my back pocket. 'I thought you might be lost.'

He shook his head and took a few steps toward me, ducking under the branch of an elm. The thin layer of ice atop the snow broke under his bootsole, and its jagged edges caught on his khaki pants, tugging them up from his ankle. He squinted at the hawk mounted on an ossified branch in the window, at the snake curled about the bough. They stared back, impassive. The collar of his coat was half bit away and unraveling, and the seams were pulled so tight over his shoulders you could see each stitch that barely cobbled them together as he held out his hand. It was enormous, with big, wide fingers, and knuckles the size of walnuts.

'Frank Clifton,' he said. Water dripped from an icicle, lashed the pile of shoveled snow at his feet.

'Wendell Wilson.' I shook his hand harder than I needed to, and wished I didn't have black crusts cupped in my cuticles. His sleeve drifted further up his forearm, where a dark scrawl on the skin barely slipped out from beneath the cuff.

'Pleased to meet you,' he said, smiling wide and earnest, and I thought I'd be struck down by it, the way it struck down mortals to behold Zeus in his full, blazing divinity, reduced them to ash, the painful glory of him. The branches shuddered off their casts of ice, and the power lines broke free of their insulation, snapped taut and scattered it over the street in pieces that still cupped the hollow channel where the wire had run. Icicles plunged from gutters and shattered on the sidewalk, sheets of snow slid from roofs. The din of it, the creak and thump and shatter, sounded like the world coming undone.

3

We're at the long-term care facility, a brick house-looking building on the bad side of downtown, where the mills and the denim plant used to be, with sallow nurses smoking out front all day long to make the place look even more like some sort of seedy rehabilitation center for homeless drug addicts than it already does. Two weeks we've been here now for physical therapy, more for those days he lay in the bed after the stroke than for the stroke itself. It's hard to get a body moving again once it's got used to stillness: atrophied, that's what the doctor kept saying. His muscles have atrophied.

And of course Frank has to go and make it as difficult for everyone to help him as he possibly can, gives those nurses so much trouble I'm surprised they don't give up and leave him there to waste away. You can tell he's about back to normal because he gets real aloof any time they come by, acts like I'm not even in the room. The nurses have got him sitting on the edge of the bed, with his metal-frame walker pushed right up to his knees. Each of them, one on either side, reaches a hand toward one of his elbows, and he knocks them away.

'All it is is walking,' he says. 'I don't need any help just to walk.'

He rocks himself forward, grabs the handles of the walker, and bears down so hard that the four aluminum legs, built in telescoping rods so you can adjust the height, wobble and bend like they're about to snap beneath his weight.

'Good,' the nurses murmur and coo. 'Very good.'

'Imagine that,' Frank says. 'A grown man able to raise himself up from the bed. A real miracle of modern medicine.'

The physical therapist, yet another young-middle-aged man with a yet more cheerful and firm belief in his own competence, strides into the room.

'Good afternoon, Mr. Clifton,' he says, but Frank ignores him — against all odds, he's come to despise his doctors more than I do — and shuffles across the room, the rubber feet of his walker scuffing and squeaking against the tile, with a grim look of barely-constrained malice on his face.

'And let's see you get a book from the shelf,' the nurse says. Frank reaches up to the warped piece of unfinished plywood they've got resting on long wood screws drilled halfway into the wall, pulls down one of the worn-out romance novels with dusty, soft-edged pages they have squeezed together there, and slaps it into her hand so hard she drops it.

'You want me to pick it up, too?' he says.

'I think,' the therapist says, sidling up beside me, 'Mr. Clifton's ready to go home.'

'Ready to go home?' I say. 'When?'

'I'd say as early as tomorrow.'

'Don't you think he needs more time? His hands are still — '

'He'll make more progress at home now than he possibly could here.'

'I think he needs more time.'

'I know it can be a daunting prospect,' the therapist says. 'But he won't really need that much taking care of. He's in pretty good — '

'That's not what I'm worried about. I just don't think he's ready.'

Frank pushes his walker back toward the bed.

'Do you need to use the bathroom first?' one of the nurses says.

'When I need to use the bathroom,' Frank says, 'I'll get up and use it.'

She frowns and glances at her clipboard. 'And when was your last bowel movement?'

'Mind your own damn business.'

The therapist gives me a significant look.

Through the window, the denim plant's red brick smokestack looks so impossibly tall and thin it shouldn't be able to stand, ought to have toppled a century ago. The word CONFEDERATION is set into it in darker brick, one huge letter atop another. Confederate Mills, it was called. Thirty-five years he worked there. Now all the buildings are empty, and the bricks at the top of the smokestack have crumbled and fallen in, and the windows are black and shattered. I wait for a shellacked hairline and dark eyes to rise above the jagged glass.

'Give me two more days,' I say.

'You've got yourself a deal,' the therapist says. He strides over to Frank, says, 'Great job!' and raises his palm for a high five.

Frank scowls at him, turns his back, and lowers himself into the bed.

★ ★ ★

I hold his elbow as he steps onto the porch. It's only one shallow stair, it's hardly up off the ground at all, but he has to hold on to the railing with one hand and my shoulder with the other to haul himself onto it, and then he leans so hard he nearly knocks me down. They still haven't got his balance right, have him canting to one side with every step. I let go of his elbow just for a minute to unlock the front door, and he walks down to the end of the porch and leans over to check on the camellias growing against the side of the house, sways like one of those skyscrapers they design to bend through storm winds and earthquakes, teeter back and forth so far you can't hardly believe they don't snap in two. Just watching him nearly gives me a fit.

'Come on,' I say, and he shuffles to the door, never breaks contact between his feet and the floorboards, holding the porch rail all the while. 'You need to use your walker.' The nurses even cut crosshatches into tennis balls and stuck them on its feet so they would slide across the floor easier, but he refuses to touch it.

'Why didn't they just give me a cane?' he says. 'With a cane you can at least look half respectable. That metal contraption makes you look like you belong in an institution. Walking up and down the halls in a daze.'

'Watch your step.' There's a little bump in the

doorway. He has to concentrate to lift each foot over it.

'And it's too short,' he says. 'I have to stoop so bad to hold on to it, I nearly fall over just from that.'

'That's not true. That is empirically not true.'

He lets go of the doorway. 'All it is is walking. And I can empirically walk just fine.'

The den's dark and stuffy, with deer poking their heads out of the wall over every doorway, and a quail caught in flight over the gas logs, and a raccoon peering around the old metal trash can where we keep the umbrellas. There's too many of them, really, too close and crowded together, but you'd be surprised how many people will bring you a perfectly splendid specimen to mount and then never come back for it. Most of them I sold to somebody else, but there were a few I could never get rid of, or got myself particularly attached to, and between them and all the dark wood paneling on the walls, it feels in here like you're a fugitive from justice, hunkered out in the wilderness, but he pats his thighs and says, 'Great day in the morning!' like he's never seen a more beautiful sight, and does his closest approximation of hurrying across the room to sit heavily down in his recliner. I open up all the blinds, let the sluggish afternoon light seep in, but it only seems to thicken the air, makes the whole place feel like it's caught in amber. Frank looks around and sighs contentedly.

'Great day in the morning,' he says again, quietly this time, just to himself.

He walks into the kitchen the next afternoon, wearing his dirty work pants and that same blue baseball cap, right as I'm pulling my jar of sourdough starter from the fridge to make us some yeast rolls. He loves a yeast roll. The kitchen's a whole different feeling from the rest of the house, big and bright and open, with white walls and a black-and-white tile floor and a whole bank of windows over the counter that look out over the backyard and the bird feeders hung from the eaves. He likes to watch the birds, has a feeder strung from every gutter and limb. He's partial to the real big, puffed-up bird royalty, blue jays and cardinals with their crests and ostentation, and to the goldfinches, for reasons I've never understood. I don't care for finches much myself.

I turn on the water to warm up while I pull my sugar and potato flakes down from the cabinet to feed the starter. It's a real good one, beige and murky like swampwater, with all sorts of stringy fungi swirling in its depths. I've kept it bubbling sweet for ten years now, even fed it while he was in the hospital. Frank makes a beeline, such as he can, for the back door.

'Where do you think you're going?' I say. He stops with his hand on the doorknob.

'To fix that garden.'

'Get back in the living room and sit yourself down. You just got home.'

'If we get it back in working order, we might

could plant some collards in time for the frost to hit them right.'

'You're not supposed to exert yourself. Working out in the hot sun like that's what gave you the stroke in the first place.'

'That was never definitively determined.'

He turns the knob. With the lights off and the curtains drawn to keep it cool in here, the open door looks like a blazing white rectangle, burning away the black edges of his silhouette as he surveys the land, hands on his hips, shaking his head in sorrow. His garden takes up the whole back half of the yard, long rows of staked tomato plants, and snap-pea vines twining around their trellises, and squash bursting out of mounds in huge open fronds. The watermelon vines are always strangling the cabbage. Every afternoon, he unwinds and pulls free the tendrils, curling and thin as razor wire, nudges them back over onto their black landscape cloth, and every morning they're wrapped right back around the cabbages' necks, trying to squeeze the life out of them. I don't know why he bothers with watermelon anyway. The ones he comes up with are never very good. They always turn out lumpy, like they've got warts, with mealy, desiccated flesh. It's all covered over with weeds now, stringy brown grasses so high you can't hardly see the stakes.

'Close the door,' I say. 'You're letting all the cold air out.'

'Looks like Guam out there. I may have to fish out my machete.'

'You weren't even in Guam.'

'You ought to've sprayed the weeds,' he says.

'You know how I feel about sweat.'

He makes to start through the door. I grab his elbow. Its loose-hanging wrinkles are rough and dry. Water hisses from the faucet. 'The doctor said — '

'I ain't going to exert myself,' he says.

'It's too hot. I'm exerted just from standing here.'

He tugs his elbow loose. 'You can stay cooped up inside all day long if you please,' he says, 'but I've got to grow us some food,' and lumbers across the yard, through the knee-high waving grasses, leaves me standing in the doorway in the hot sun. I'm already sweating.

I slam the door. The water rushing from the tap's so hot steam billows from the basin, and I have to turn it back cold to get it the right temperature. I open a little crack in the drapes over the sink so I can watch him slowly picking his way across the yard, swaying back and forth with each step and looking down at the dirt from a great height, while I measure out the sugar and stir it into the warm water, turn it cloudy. Stubbornest man I ever saw. All of twenty-four hours he's been home, and already he's trying to send himself back to the hospital. It'd do him right to fall and break a hip. Least then he'd be laid up, couldn't run around finding new ways to send himself quicker to the grave.

And instead of just spraying the weeds like he usually does, he leans over, with one hand on his knee, and yanks them from the ground by the fistful. I don't know if he's trying to prove that he's capable of doing it, or if he can't manage to walk the extra fifty yards to his shed for the weed killer or even a hoe, for heaven's sake, or if the stroke permanently damaged the part of his brain that knows the first thing about keeping a garden, but either way, it makes me so mad watching him I go back and throw the door open again.

'If you fall out there,' I yell, 'you can find somebody else to call you an ambulance.' He waves the shout away like it's a gnat.

I don't leave the kitchen the whole time he's out there. I stir the potato flakes into the water, pour it all into the jar with the starter, and set it on the windowsill to bubble in the sun, and then I pull myself up a chair to the back door and wait.

Thirty minutes later, he trudges back in, sopping wet, lets the screen door slam behind him with a loud crack. I hate when he lets the screen door slam. On the edge of the garden there's a big pile of weeds he's pulled, drying in the sun with all the soil shaken from their roots, but in the garden itself you wouldn't know he'd done a thing. Looks like there might — might — be a thinner, balding spot in the grasses near the tomatoes, but if you tilt your head to the left, even that little bit of progress vanishes.

He sets my jar of sourdough starter in the sink, pulls three pinkish tomatoes from his bulging pocket, and sets them on the windowsill to ripen. 'There were a few survivors,' he says. 'Despite you.'

With shaking hands, he fills himself a glass of water and chipped ice — the dispenser set in the freezer door sounds like it's grinding bone before it breathes out the little shavings — and drinks it down so fast I'm afraid it'll kill him. I saw a special on the news about marathon runners who sweated out so much salt and drank so much water it threw their systems out of balance and they died on the spot. The color drains from his skin, washed down by the water, and his Adam's apple rises and falls with each swallow, a stone rolled away by the flood. I press the back of my hand to his cheek, the way you're supposed to feel the wood of a closed door when you suspect there's a fire on the other side. It's warm and damp, which is at least better than cold and dry. Cold and dry means you're having heatstroke. I learned that from one of the many informational brochures the smiling doctors provided me.

He goes to set the glass on the edge of the counter and misses completely, drops it so it shatters on the floor, and then, as if this isn't bad enough, bends down and starts grabbing at the pieces with his bare hands, when you can't even tell the glass from the ice. I slap his elbow away, pull a dishrag from the drawer, drag the trash can and chair over, and sit while I pick up the splinters. Time shows real quick which is which: the ice shrinks, its edges soften and spread, but the pieces of glass stay sharp in their puddles. It all gets flung into the trash just the same.

I wipe the water in circles across the tile, spread what I can't soak up thin enough to evaporate. The wet spot dries into a paler, shinier gray than the rest of the floor. The whole house needs a good mopping.

He pulls down a can of chicken noodle soup from the cabinet. Why he'd want soup for lunch when he's already so hot is beyond me. Doesn't make any sense. He has trouble clamping the can opener on, can't steady his hands enough to get the little sharp wheel flush against the rim. He examines the can opener as if he thinks that's where the fault lies, winds the crank and watches the gears fit cogs into notches and slowly turn the blade. Before he decides to start tinkering with it and the afternoon ends with me having to go buy a new can opener, I snatch it out of his hands, open his soup, mix it with a can of water, and put it in the microwave. I don't say a word while I smear the mayonnaise on his bread for his tomato sandwich, and I don't say a word while he takes the last tomato from the basket, rinses it, and tries to slice it. After he cuts off the cap, all he manages to do is squash the whole thing until the juice and seeds come spilling out across the cutting board. He's using the wrong knife, but I don't say a word.

He takes his food to the living room so he can watch the court channel. I'm not hungry, but I piddle around in the kitchen for a while and wash some dishes real loud to make a point before I finally go in there to be sure he isn't keeled over dead from a sodium imbalance. He isn't, but he's hunched so far over his TV tray that he might as well be, and even across the short distance from the bowl to his mouth, his hands shake the chicken soup from his spoon. It splatters on the tray, and the broth runs in a stream over the edge and into a yellow puddle on the floor.

I stare at him, then at the puddle. The broth trickles loudly into it.

'It just kept happening,' he says, doesn't even look away from the screen. 'Thought I'd enjoy my lunch and clean it up when I was through.'

They've found Little Larry's body. It was inside a trash bag, stewing in a puddle in a highway ditch two hundred miles from his hometown. A skeletal lady with enormous bifocals and prodigious wrinkles found him when her radiator went haywire and started spewing so much smoke she had to pull off to the side of the road. Got out of her car, went to look under the hood, and there in the ditch was a black trash bag, shiny and wet from the rain, with a tiny, pale hand sticking out the open top.

'Just as soon as I saw that tiny, pale hand,' she croaks, 'I knew whose it was.'

The press is camped outside his mama's apartment building, waiting for a statement. She lives on the second floor, so all the cameras are on the ground, tilted upward. After a while, her door opens, and she's standing there in nothing but a ratty sweatshirt and some pink satin underwear that at some point long ago in its sad history was meant to be seductive. Her blond hair is wadded up and falling loose all around her head. Deborah Norris, that's her name. She takes one look down at the cameras with wide, empty eyes and shuts the door.

I drop the same soggy dish towel on the floor, rub it around with my foot, and leave it there for him to pick up. He can do it easier from the chair than I can from standing.

'You want the rest of my sandwich?' he says, staring at the wrinkled, shining black lump of the trash bag between the policemen's legs. 'This tomato's too dry.'

I turn around and leave the room.

★ ★ ★

After he's gone to bed, I sneak to the back door. Outside, the moon's light makes everything look like its surface, silver and barren. The trees rustle, full to bursting with sleeping birds. You see so many of them during the day, always moving as if there's some churning engine inside them that won't ever let them rest, darting solitary from branch to bush to power line, or wheeling in flocks so huge their movement against the sky looks like space itself spreading and collapsing, it's hard to believe they can settle so silent and still in the trees at night, disappear so completely.

I pull the door shut behind me, real quiet, and creep through the rustling weeds to Frank's shed, sagging on its cinderblock foundation. We built it ourselves, fifty years ago now, I guess. Dug out the dirt with a spade, laid the cinderblock and the plywood floor, built up the frame, even ran the electricity out, all of it by ourselves. We had to. Any time we had a repairman over, I had to close the shop and

38

pretend to be a neighbor who'd come to let him in while Frank was at work, a flimsy disguise at best given that nobody lived within a mile of us until ten years ago, and you never knew if the air-conditioning man might turn out to be a second cousin Frank had forgot about, or if the plumber was an old classmate who might take the opportunity to snoop around a little, so we learned to do most everything ourselves. Which is probably why the tiles are bubbling up and peeling away from the floor under the kitchen counter, and the power flickers with the slightest flutter of the breeze, and that shed sags like somebody broke its back.

The door's open. He never does close it, just leaves the screen shut to keep the bugs out. Anybody in the world could march right in and take whatever they pleased. The inside of it's hotter than it is outside, air's so stuffy and thick I can hardly breathe it in, and what I can smells of sawdust and mold. I yank a chain dangling from the ceiling to turn on the light. Saws and hammers hang from hooks in the cork-board walls, and his lawnmower sits smack in the middle of the bowed floor with an oil-stained towel draped over it. Beside it, red plastic gas cans with dingy yellow spouts are lined up, smeared with greasy cobwebs. I squeeze past them all — the floor's real long and narrow — and pick my way between buckets of stripped screws and rusty nails that he's never going to do anything with but still refuses to get rid of, to the far wall, where I have to stand on my tiptoes and hold on to a table to pull his pruning shears from their hook. They're nice shears, with sharp, curved blades, and long handles you barely have to squeeze together to snip stems away.

I shuffle back through the shed, careful and slow like he does, trying not to lift my feet from the ground for fear they'll fall right through a rotten patch of plywood or onto a rusty nail when I set them back down, and out to the garden.

I move along the rows and cut through the plants, one by one. The shears are long enough I don't hardly have to bend over at all, but it's still hard work, takes me a good thirty minutes. The tomato vines are so thick, some of them I have to twist the blades to tear through, and they twist right along, fibers pulling apart like a double helix uncoiling before they snap. Some of them I can't hardly get to for all the tangled weeds. I try to cut them off right where they emerge from the dirt, so they won't get the impression that I'm just pruning them and then grow back even worse.

The cabbage heads snip from their buried necks easy as the head of a bird from its body, and the tendrils of snap-pea and wax-bean vines are so slender I can't even feel their resistance through the shears. The squash are bad, though. The squash are the worst. I have to cut into the thick tentacles of their stems again and again before they finally sever, and I half expect two to regenerate for every one I lop off. I barely brush against one of them, and it scrapes my arm to bleeding with thorns so tiny you can't see them. The big leaves rasp against each other, give off a smell like buttered popcorn. A good sharp hoe might've been easier, I guess, chopped clean through them, but I don't have the strength in my arms for that anymore. The cuts itch with a warm, radiating feeling, like cat scratches.

When it's done, and I've replaced the shears, I slip back into the house, lock the door, and flip the light switch. The night crashes inward, rushes toward the bulb and snuffs it out. I feel better already. Slowly my eyes adjust enough to press the darkness against the shapes underlying it, and I make my way to the bed, settle into it beside him perfectly unnoticed, like the birds in their dark boughs, like a body inside a trash bag.

4

He tried to teach me the constellations once, out at the lake at Warren Park. It was the first time we'd been together outside my shop, and even then, after two agonizing months of him leaning real casual against my counter, telling me about the war and his family and asking trade questions I'd have thrown anybody else out for asking, I still wasn't sure exactly what he was after. He'd said he wanted to go out there and see the spot in the woods where some kids had found the headless body of a young woman earlier that week, to look for clues — 'Something the police might have missed,' he'd said, meaning primarily her head, which they still hadn't found — but the sun was already setting as he said it, and gone by the time we got there.

We laid our jackets on the ground and sat on the banks, with our backs against one of the big trees, our shoulders close but not touching. I tried to think of something to say. Spread out before us, the dark water was distinguishable from the rest of the darkness only by the way it shifted and rocked, so slightly you could easily fool yourself into thinking it wasn't there at all, that your eyes were inventing movement where there was none, the way they do when you stare at a thing for too long.

'There's Ursa Major,' he shouted helpfully. The cicadas shrilled so loud you had to yell over

42

them just to talk. Sounded like the bark itself buzzing as the trees trembled to hold themselves solid around some great pressure within their trunks.

'Ah,' I yelled back in my best approximation of interest. On the list of things I was interested in beholding, the constellations were fairly low.

He pressed a fingertip to the sky and carved out the lines that were supposed to hold the stars together, momentarily extinguishing each one he touched. 'The Great Bear,' he said. 'Or the Big Dipper.'

'Which one is it?' I said.

'Both.'

'How's it supposed to be a bear and a dipper at the same time?'

'Use your imagination.' He took his shoes off, rolled his pants up to his knees, and stretched his long legs out over the grass. I plucked a blade and split it apart, peeled fiber from fiber and laid them across my knee. Somewhere behind us, the moon rose bright and full, cast the faint, tangled shadows of the branches over us in a net and gave the water shape, held it down under a thin sheen of silver. I slapped my neck. I kept thinking I felt bugs crawl under my collar.

'You see any heads?' he said, squinting.

'No,' I said. 'No heads.'

He lit a cigarette, cupping his hand around the lighter's flame. It dug shadows into the deep creases of his palm.

'That's all the investigating you're going to do?' I said.

'It's too dark,' he exclaimed, as if this was a

situation none of us could have foreseen.

That girl getting murdered was the best thing that had happened to him since he got home. His daddy had been chief of police in the thirties, until he went and got himself killed rushing in to save somebody when the gas station on the corner blew up. Frank's mama insisted he start college in the fall, make good use of the GI Bill, but after that he was going to join the police force. He read detective stories and pulp novels all the time, and earlier that very same week had been complaining about how the only crimes that occurred around here these days were somebody getting too drunk in public, stumbling down the sidewalk for children to see, and teenagers stealing jars of pickles from the general store. He was always waiting restless for something worse, for the string of grisly murders that would give him the chance to prove his bravery and prodigious deductive powers, and to encounter the scantily-clad ladies who always managed to get themselves drawn into the seedy underworld of crime and knelt in bosom-heaving supplication on the covers of his paperbacks, of whom, in those days, I was still unsure whether I ought to be jealous.

'Anyway, they're good to know,' he said. 'In case you ever get lost.'

'I don't plan to ever go anyplace that would require navigation by stars to get myself out of.'

He grinned. The tip of his cigarette flared and faded with the breath he drew through it. As he reached to pull it from his lips, his sleeve fell toward his elbow, away from the dark lines on his arm. Carefully I pulled a filament free from another blade of grass. It stuck to the skin under my thumbnail.

'What are those?' I said, nodding.

He looked real hesitant, then took a deep breath of smoke, rolled his sleeve halfway up his biceps, far as it would go, and exhaled. It was hard to separate the markings on his skin from the shadows of the branches that overlaid them: they tangled from the middle of his forearm all the way up over his elbow and kept going under his sleeve, drawn in thick, clumsy black lines like the old woodcut prints you'd see in history books of villagers flinging plague-ridden corpses over their city walls and into heaps on the other side. There were so many of them so tangled together, I couldn't hardly tell at first what they were or one from another, had to wait for my eyes to adjust to the knotted chaos of his skin like they did to the dark before it sifted itself into some semblance of order. Everything on his forearm was underwater: a marlin and lobster and fish all crowded together and overlapping, and an eel insinuating itself between strands of seaweed that swayed with the muscles they were etched over as he tapped his fingers on his leg. Above them, a whale swam in choppy waves, and the waves broke on a stippled sandy shore, from which sprang thick clumps of grass where, on the tender skin inside his elbow, an oak tree's roots traced his veins. On his biceps, a buck was arrested in mid-leap, its antlers slipping under his sleeve as if to pry it up, and a dog of uncertain houndish breed and gangly limbs paused with one paw lifted, watching a squirrel and waiting endlessly for that one movement that would set it running. They were all drawn in those same thick, woodcut lines, and they weren't anywhere close to proper scale: the squirrel was near as big as the buck.

'We all went out and got them one night,' he said. 'A few days before we shipped off. It was supposed to be a sort of show of patriotism and solidarity, I guess. An eagle on the chest, right over the heart. Then I just kept going back every night and getting more.'

'Didn't it hurt?'

He nodded and pulled his knees to his chest. The soles and sides of his feet were smeared with dirt, and his calf was lashed by deep lines, the imprints of grass blades, like the creases a pillow might have left on his cheek while he slept. I watched his skin slowly start to fill itself in from underneath.

'We were strutting around so puffed up and full of ourselves, the rest of them probably didn't even feel it,' he said. 'I was the only one of us sober. Including the fellow who was doing it. Probably could have done a better job myself.'

'They ain't that bad.' Already I'd started to sound like him.

'They make me look like a criminal. I have to wear long sleeves the rest of my life. Even in summer.'

The cicadas' song smoothed itself out into one endless, pulseless drone, always on the verge of a crest but never tumbling over. He flicked the nub of his cigarette away — it faded from orange to

46

dark as it fell — and sat forward, the shadows of the branches sliding from his shoulders, down his arms and back and onto the grass, soaking into the dirt underneath. When he stood, his knees made a loud sound like paper crumpling, and he leaned against the tree. Its trunk trembled on the edge of unwinding.

'I tore them up,' he said, 'dropping to the ground so much.' He ripped a tender shoot from one of the low branches. Where it tore loose, the pale wood, twisted and splintered, looked exactly like the dried-out chicken I cooked before I knew any better, shredded apart under the fork. His legs were smooth again under their blond hair. Somehow I'd missed the moment, that last moment, when the imprint pressed flush again to the skin around it.

I followed him clambering down the bank, onto the large, smooth rocks they'd piled to stop its erosion, though the mud just ran right between them, out into the water, and the little waves carved the bank so concave you could stay dry from a rain if you huddled back in it, behind the rocks. The water that splashed against them was edged with a muck as thick and pliant as skin. It clung to the rocks when the rocking water lapped against them, and stretched as the waves subsided, and when the ebb finally managed to pull it down again, it left a shining residue on the stone.

Frank peeled the bark from the shoot, scraping it away with his fingernails, while he stared out at the water. The reflections of the stars blinked on and off atop it, their light alternately smoothed out and folded up into dark pleats.

'All those boys drowned when we landed at Omaha Beach,' he said. 'Every single one.' Just as soon as they jumped off the ramps, they started going under. They were too far offshore, and their packs were loaded down with equipment and supplies. They filled up with water, just soaked it in, and pulled the ones who weren't strong enough down under the waves. For a second or two they'd bob there, shouting and trying to push themselves up, tear foaming wounds into the water, and then they sank down, and the water, like a wound, closed over them in clots of reflected light.

'And that water was cold,' he said. 'It was the middle of summer, and still that water was so cold you felt like you'd just woken up. Like your entire life before that had been one drowsy sleepwalk.' He'd gone under a few times, swallowed a lot of seawater, but he and a couple boys from other companies made it to shore. The Germans were shooting down on it so heavy the sand their bullets kicked up looked like a fog gathered thick round the bluffs, but the other two were so excited to make it to land they crawled right up on it, even when he yelled for them to stay in the water, and into the line of fire. 'Turned them inside out,' he said. 'That's how it looked. Like they'd split open and burst out of themselves.' Then he did the only thing he could think of, which was wriggle back out into the water and lay under it, his pack against the sea floor, with just his face exposed, water slapping the sides of his nostrils, so the tide could carry him hidden toward the cliffs a little at a time.

He'd never told me about the fighting before, just the geography and weather and wildlife, as if each battle had been another stop on some luxury vacation cruise, each destination more restful and interesting than the last.

'All that was in the first five minutes, I guess,' he said. 'Time ran real funny. Seemed to stretch out forever. Like nothing would ever end.'

He stepped off the riprap and into the lake. His pale, bare feet warped in the churned water so drastically they seemed to fold in on themselves and disappear completely for a moment before opening again into thin, rippling approximations of their original shape.

'After a while, you couldn't really feel the water for itself no more. All you felt was this pressure. This hard pressure all over your skin, like the whole ocean was trying to break into you. Feeling you all over for weak spots it could split apart. And then there was this — some part of me buckled under the pressure, and the water and the cold just seemed to rush in, filled me up until I wasn't nothing but a tingling feeling. Like the kind you get when you sit on your leg and put it to sleep. Feels like dissolving. That's how I felt, all the way through.

'None of the boys from my platoon — a lot of the others washed up onshore eventually, but our lieutenant had got on us bad about strapping our packs on as tight as we could. Held them down on the ocean floor so the waves couldn't even wash their bodies where somebody could find them. They were just gone. That's how good the water swallowed them up.'

The branch was pale and bare as bone. He flung it out into the water. A heavier object would have flown halfway across the lake, hard as he threw it. But it was so light, it barely got anywhere. The water rippled in slow, shallow furrows that flattened as they moved toward the shore.

'The worst part,' he said, as we climbed back up the bank and sat down again, 'was warming up. Once I fought my way under the cliffs and found the boys from the other boats. Felt like every cell in your body closing in and crushing itself, every blood vessel bursting.' He rolled his jacket into a pillow, put it between his head and the tree so he could lounge back, and dug his hand in the grass between us, wriggled his fingers into the dirt. The waves on his forearm churned. 'Sensation coming back,' he said, shaking his head. 'You don't feel it at all when it disappears, but when it comes back, you wish you'd never feel another thing.'

He looked at me in the dark, and for a moment I saw on his face, like a reflection on a clouded pane, a kind of ache, blurry and diffuse; and like a reflection, so fragile any stone thrown might shatter it, any light turned on in the dark might wipe it clean, it slipped off the surface and was gone.

'There's Gemini,' he said, and leaned close, the space between us crushed hot and crowding against my ribs, to draw the lines between each of their stars in turn: the twins Castor and

Pollux, one mortal and one immortal, who loved each other so desperately that when Castor went and got himself killed in some battle, Pollux couldn't bear to live forever without him, so he begged his father Zeus until Zeus plucked Castor from the underworld and set the both of them as stars in the sky. At least that's how it went in one of the endings. Another one said that Pollux had to give up half his immortality to his brother, and then they shuttled together back and forth between Olympus and Hades, one day among the gods in paradise, the next crowded together in the cold grave, toward which they now were headed, the canopy tangled about their ankles and dragging them from the heavens.

It always bothered me how so many of those old myths had different endings. You'd read one version and think you were really something, think you knew what had gone on, the whole story, and then you'd read a different book and find out you didn't know a thing. As if the very same action could have five or six different outcomes, and you could never be sure which one you'd get, as if, even long after it was over, you could never be sure what a thing meant.

He leaned away again. The space between us slackened and subsided.

'That doesn't look anything like them, though,' I said. 'None of these things look at all like what they're supposed to.'

'They do,' he said, sounding personally offended. He burrowed his long, bony toes into the dirt. 'They do. You just have to let your eyes go a little fuzzy.'

'When I let my eyes go fuzzy, I can't see any stars at all.'

He laughed. 'Just try,' he said, and I did, but the stars had already drifted away from where they'd been only minutes before, and the sky had already filled the grooves his fingertips had carved into it.

5

I'm in the bedroom, up early and getting dressed to go to the farmers' market. They've got a big one now, off the highway on the edge of town, has every vegetable and fruit you could ever think of wanting, bins of them spilling over. You've got to go early, though. After noon, you may as well stay home, unless you're in the mood for split tomatoes and ears of corn with brown rings where bugs have eaten their way around the cob. We usually go out there a couple times a week, though Frank would have you believe that garden of his was the only thing saving us from imminent starvation. I drop him off at one end and start myself down at the other, and we rendezvous at the car, parked way out in the lot, far away from the others. We end up with lots of duplicates, but at least he lets us take the same car now. We used to have to drive separate, and not stray from our own designated territory of vendor stalls.

I'm belting my britches when he looms up in the doorway. His face is red, and the wisps of hair atop his scalp are smeared flat with sweat. I've kept more of my hair than he has. It may be white, but at least it's still there.

'Ready to go?' I say. I sit on the edge of the bed to put on my shoes. They could use a polishing; the toes are scuffed to matte.

Sunlight falls through the bay window and

53

across the placid shining sea of wood floor. He wanted to put carpet down, didn't want to set his bare feet on a cold floor first thing in the morning, but I refused to let him cover up the hardwood.

'Don't just stand there looking like a criminal,' I say. 'Go start up the car. Get the air going.'

He still doesn't speak, just watches me, his jaw clamped shut tight so it won't chew the air and ruin the effect of his glaring. I tie my shoelaces.

'You cut down all my plants,' he says. His voice is low and hoarse.

'I did no such thing.'

'I've been growing those plants since March.'

'It was probably some vandals,' I say.

'It wasn't no vandals.'

'And you think it was me? You think I'd do something like that?'

'You've got squash cuts all over your arm.'

'These aren't squash cuts.'

'Then what are they?'

'I don't know. I don't keep track of every single surface that abrades my skin.'

'I've picked enough squash in my life to know what their scratches look like.'

'There are all kinds of animals running wild out there,' I say. 'I heard coyotes — '

'Every single plant was cut off right at the bottom of the stem.' He crosses his arms. 'Nice and neat.'

I haul myself up by the bedpost. 'We don't need those plants anyway,' I say. 'That's what we've got the farmers' market for. Are you coming or not?'

His face turns hard and brittle. 'No,' he says. 'I might exert myself.'

'Well, at least you're *sounding* sensible for a change.'

I squeeze through the sliver of space he doesn't occupy in the doorway and head down the hall. He turns and watches me go, aghast.

'Five months of work,' he yells after me. 'How'd you like it if I went and sliced open all your deer?'

'I sure wouldn't act like such a big baby about it, I know that much,' I call over my shoulder. I step into the sunlight. Day's barely started, and already it's so hot the handle of the car door burns my fingers.

I don't see what he's so broken up about. It was just some plants.

* * *

While I'm out, I buy him everything he needs: big plastic cups with spouted lids that won't shake water down his shirt when he tips them to his lips or break when he drops them, thick plastic plates and bowls and forks and spoons big enough for him to get his fingers around without too much trouble, an extra-large remote control with extra-large buttons he'll be able to hit one at a time, even a cane, a fancy one with a gold wolf's head for the handle, looks real Victorian and distinguished. And when I come home, a veritable cornucopia threatening to spill forth from the trunk, he's in the bathroom at the end of the hall, with the door open and light pooling across the floor in slick, wet puddles, and the fan roaring, and him down on all fours, scrubbing the bathtub. He wears thick pads around his knees. In the hallway, outside the bathroom door, there's a vacuum I've never before seen. Comes up to my waist, gray plastic with purple handles and all sorts of hoses and gadgets and brushes and extension arms snapped and tucked into its sides, and in the middle of it all a clear, cylindrical chamber packed tight with dust and hair and layers of sediment compressed halfway to rock.

I stand in the doorway, and he pretends I'm not here. He's got an old toothbrush, and he's furiously scouring the scum that outlines the petals of the raised flowers on the rubber mat in the tub. They give you traction, keep you from slipping, but they do gather grime.

'This tub is filthy,' he says, looking pointedly at me. 'It's an embarrassment.' He says this like it's supposed to be some sort of accusation, some kind of impugnment of my own personal cleanliness.

'Of course it's dirty,' I say. 'You weren't around to scrub it.'

He scoffs, but he knows good and well that cleaning the house is his job. Always has been. He cleans the house, takes out the trash, keeps up the yard, and does the laundry. I cook and do the dishes and take care of our finances. That's how we do it. That's how we've done it for near to sixty years.

'I won't live in a filthy house,' he says.

'It looks plenty clean to me. Come on and get

up. You ought to rest.'

He laughs, as if to say he'll be the judge of what's clean and what's not, since my grasp on the matter is so obviously and woefully impaired, and keeps scrubbing.

'You're not supposed to do anything strenuous,' I say.

'I believe I've got enough strength left in me to wield a toothbrush.'

'Fine.' It's probably doing him some little bit of good to feel useful, at least. I don't think he'll give himself another stroke just from cleaning the tub. 'Where'd you get that vacuum?'

'The neighbors.'

'The neighbors gave you their vacuum?'

'They left it out on the curb with the trash. It ain't even trash day. It's *Saturday*.' He says that last part like we all, myself included, ought to be ashamed for not paying adequate attention to the municipal waste schedule. Until five years ago, they wouldn't even come out here; he had to haul all our trash out to the dump himself, pile the bags up in the back of his truck so high I thought they'd all fly off before he could get them there.

'That lady,' he says, with profound loathing of our neighbor, an unwed mother whose name he pretends not to know — he never has liked her, ever since she cut down all the trees on her property, right up to the line with ours, thinned out the woods so bad that some afternoons we can hear her bastard children screaming while they beat each other with switches in the yard, and all, as she explained in the letter she illegally deposited in our mailbox after Frank yelled at her from the car that she'd better not pry up so much as a single root that crossed into his yard or she'd be hearing from his lawyer, to *let a little light in around here* — 'that lady came out and told me it didn't work.'

He gapes at her idiocy as if it were floating, brazen and arrogant, right here in front of him. 'I said I'd be the judge of that.'

'She caught you going through her trash?'

'It was right out there beside the can. I just walked up and took it. Didn't have to dig through nothing.'

'She didn't mind?'

'She wished me 'the best of luck,'' he says, imitating the condescending sweetness in her voice.

'I wish she hadn't seen you scavenging. It looks bad. Low-class.'

'Nobody takes care of anything,' he grumbles. 'Look at it. It's a perfectly good vacuum.'

'It's probably full of spiders,' I say, looking in the chamber for spider eggs. You can see the different cleanings and different rooms, the passage of time, in the differentiation of its strata: a thick buffer of pure dust after they let the house go for too long, a pale, thin line of sawdust, a wavy band of white hair.

'Ain't room for spiders in there,' he says. 'They've crammed it too full.'

'I wish you hadn't brought it in the house. I don't want little baby spiders swarming all over everything.'

'I just told you there's not any spiders.' He

intensifies the force with which he saws the toothbrush against the edge of a rubber petal. The brush's bristles flatten and fan.

'I got us some peaches,' I say. 'A whole bushel of them. Real nice ones from Candor.' The best produce all comes from Candor. It's something in the soil. 'Thought I'd make us a cobbler.'

He makes some noncommittal grumbling noise to avoid sounding pleased. He loves a good peach cobbler. I carry the bushel of them into the kitchen, a couple pecks at a time. Maybe I shouldn't have gotten quite so many. I don't know how we're going to eat them all. But it's the height of the season; they don't get any better than this. You've got to enjoy them while you have the chance.

When I go back to check on him, he's still scrubbing away. The overhead light gleams bright on the porcelain.

'Don't you think it's clean yet?' I say.

'I'm almost finished,' he says.

'It's spotless.'

'I said I'm almost finished.'

'It's pure as the driven snow. I can't look straight at it or it would blind me.'

Something's wrong with his scrubbing. He's doing it too slow, almost absentmindedly, and his free hand holds the lip of the tub so it juts his elbow into an awkward angle behind him.

'You can't get up, can you?' I say.

'I can get up whenever I very well please.'

So I sit myself down on the commode and watch him clean for another ten minutes, pushing the bristles of the toothbrush into every cranny and bloom, until I start to hear a pulsing undulation inside the previously uniform roar of the fan, and finally he wedges the toothbrush into the drain — bristle side up, so it can dry out before he throws it back into his plastic cleaning caddy — and tries to stand, but his legs are too stiff, won't bend far enough underneath him, and his arms are too weak. They tremble, wobble, and give out, and he sags against the lip of the tub. Sweat drips down the back of his head and into the fold of skin where it meets his neck.

'They never should have let you come home this soon,' I say. 'I knew it. I knew they were just tired of dealing with you. I told them you weren't ready. Too weak. I told them you were too weak.'

'Stop crowding me. I just need some room.'

'What you need is some help. Do you want some help?'

'I want you to stop crowding me.'

I stand behind him with my hands in his armpits. He tries to shrug me off, but he doesn't try very hard, and then I strain to lift him while he strains to push himself up, and we succeed in moving him about three inches before he sinks against the tub again.

'I'm calling the ambulance,' I say.

'Don't call the ambulance. They don't need to come all the way out here just to help me get up. We'll rest a few minutes and try again. Bring me something to eat. We need to get my strength up.'

'How long have you been stuck down there?'

'Since you left.'

'I'm calling the ambulance.'

'They won't come. This ain't an emergency.'

'It's my taxes paying them, so I'll decide for myself what's an emergency.'

'Don't,' he says. 'It's bad enough you called them out here last time.'

'You'd rather I'd left you there?'

'I'd rather you go get me some food like I asked you to.'

I go to the kitchen and slice him a peach. It splits right open, its cloying smell curling thick out of the cut. The meat pulls easy from the wrinkled pit. I set the slices on one of our new plates, a bright green one, pour him some iced tea into a cup, and snap on the lid.

I sit on the edge of the tub, stab a slice with my fork, and hold it out to Frank.

'What's that?' he says, glaring at the thick tines.

'This,' I say, 'is a fork. And this here is a plate. And this' — I swirl his tea around — 'is what we call a cup.'

'You want me to eat with those?'

'I thought you wanted food. Didn't you just make a big to-do about how you wanted some food?'

He doesn't answer.

'They're easier to hold,' I say.

'They might be, if I were ever going to hold them. Which I ain't,' he adds, as if I didn't catch his implication. I don't know why I thought this would go any other way. I sure can't believe I expected him to be grateful.

'You won't have to worry about spilling things, or — '

'These are for children,' he says.

'No, they're not. The ones for children had princesses and castles and dump trucks all over them.'

'I don't need those. I don't need any of this.'

He stares into the tub. I pop a chunk of peach into my mouth and chew it loud, really let the juices squish around.

'What?' he snaps, real sudden and grumpy, as if I've said something provocative.

'I didn't say a word. I'm just eating my peach.'

'I worked on that garden all spring.' The look on his face is so sick, so broken-hearted, I nearly apologize. Instead I eat another slice. 'The watermelons were just now getting good and ripe.'

'Are we back to that again?'

'Back to it? We ain't ever left it.'

'Your watermelons are never very good anyway.'

'And how about my tomatoes? And my squash and peas and — '

'I had no choice,' I say. 'You left me no choice.'

'No choice?'

'You backed me into a corner.'

'What corner?'

'The doctor says — '

'I'm tired of having to hear every five minutes about what the damn doctor says. It ain't gonna kill me to work outside for half an hour.'

'It might,' I say. 'It very well might.'

'Well, I don't plan to turn myself into a shut-in invalid just because I had one little stroke.'

'One little stroke?'

'That's all it was.'

'And what about your heart?'

'That's a bunch of nonsense and you know it. 'Cardiomyopathy'? That's nothing. Nobody ever had 'cardiomyopathy' when I was a boy. They've made up that entire diagnosis just to sell more medicine, I'd bet you money. It's a racket. The only thing I'm suffering from is getting a little older. Stiff joints, that's all this is.'

'I saw the pictures,' I say. 'I saw your heart strung up in your rib cage like an old sock, limp and stuffed so full it was about to rip. So if living with me is so terrible that you can't bear it one more month, you just keep on doing what you're doing. Wear it right out. It won't take much. I just never realized I was so awful to be around that you'd rather — '

'You know that's not what I mean.'

'That's what it comes down to. You can either stay here and enjoy a few more years with me, or you can work yourself into the grave like some fool who didn't know any better, when I know you do. Leave me here to try and go on without you, all alone. All by myself. I don't believe I'd last very long.'

He hangs his head, eyes squeezed shut.

I have to admit, I'm a little impressed by how smoothly I've managed to turn all this around.

'If I can't clean,' he says, 'and I can't work in the garden, then what can I do?'

'Watch the birds. Read all those books you've got piled up. Collect something.'

He doesn't answer, doesn't move, just stares

into the tub, at the splash of light diffused across the basin, as if trying to divine the future in the shape of its glare.

'We could start playing cards,' I say. 'We could join a bridge club.'

He gives me a look that asks if I've lost my mind or if I've always been this stupid.

'We tell the hospital we're brothers. I don't see why we couldn't tell a bridge club the same thing.'

'Men don't play bridge,' he says.

'You want to play poker instead? Fine. I'd beat you at that, too.'

After a minute, he says, 'All right. I have a plan.'

His plan is that he stretches out one long arm, grabs on to the sink, drags himself over to it, and, with me heaving him up from behind in a bear hug, manages to get one foot under him, kneeling, and then hauls himself to his feet, pulling on the sink so hard the caulk splits and tears away from the wall. Nearly rips the plumbing out with it.

He leans against the doorjamb and waits for his legs to solidify. From the stricken look on his face, you'd think I'd violated him.

He limps to the den, snatches up the remote, and mashes the keypad with his big fingers. He does manage to turn it on, at least, then takes us to two channels full of static and one with a bunch of sweaty, half-naked young people cavorting to what's supposed to pass as music these days. He holds the remote close to his face and squints at it while a young woman with her

64

hair dyed in black and blond stripes like a raccoon's tail gyrates herself against the corner post of a boxing ring. I grab some scissors from the drawer in the hallway and cut the new remote out of its package. They seal these things so tight it's like they never want you to use it, nearly slice my thumb open on the plastic before I manage to get it out. I hold it up like it's a prize on one of his game shows. The thing's so wide I can barely grip it in one hand, and the numbers are each big as my thumbnail.

His lower jaw bobs up and down as if it were timed to a metronome. He concentrates hard and presses the tiny buttons again, the hand that holds the remote rocking back and forth so bad he's lucky he manages to hit even one of them. This time it takes us to the home shopping channel, where a woman extols the virtues of a gadget that scrambles your eggs inside the shell. All it is is a needle you jab into them, and it whirls their innards around.

'Then just crack the egg right over your preheated nonstick pan!' she exclaims. 'Instant scrambled eggs!'

He hurls the remote across the room. It hits the wall so hard the battery compartment breaks open and the batteries jump out. They roll loud across the floor. He stares at his palms, turned up in submission like dogs' pale, tender bellies.

Real slow and deliberate, just in case he might miss it, I pick up the remote with my brand-new mechanical arm, a long plastic stick with pincers on one end and a trigger on the other so you don't have to bend down or reach up to grab a thing, carry it to the trash can, and drop it in. He sticks a toothpick in his mouth, so it'll look like he means to chew, and sits there with his arms crossed, hands clamped tight in his armpits.

I hold the new remote out, right in front of him, turn to the court channel, and look real pleasantly surprised at how easy it was. The police are holding the mother in custody now. There's footage of them ushering her into the police station, while she holds a ragged teddy bear in front of her face so the cameras can't catch it.

He goes to the bedroom and closes the door.

★　★　★

He doesn't get up for dinner, or to use the bathroom, or to watch the news. He's still lying there when I wake up in the morning, so silent and still that for a second, before I hear the heavy rasp of his breath, I think he's dead. I open the blinds so the morning light slashes his eyes. He turns his back to it.

At lunch, I shake his shoulder and tell him it's time to eat. I set his medicine and a bowl of peach cobbler on the nightstand beside him.

'I'm too tired,' he says.

'That's because you're not eating. You need to eat.'

'I'm too tired to eat,' he says.

After I've cleaned the kitchen, I perch next to him, on the very edge of the bed. He's facing away from me. His ice cream's all melted, just some peaches and crust floating in a pool of cream and sugary ooze.

'Are you feeling all right?' I say. He doesn't answer, doesn't stir. His breathing is slow, with a sudden, sharp exhalation at the very end of each breath, the way it is when he sleeps. But he could be pretending. I put my hand on his arm. He doesn't pull it away, and he doesn't roll toward me. I shake him.

'I feel fine,' he says.

'You've got to get up.'

'Why? I can't do nothing.'

'Can't do *anything*. Can't do *nothing* means you — '

'I'm worn out,' he says, with such resignation I almost believe him. 'I need to rest. The doctor said so.'

'All you've done all day is rest.'

'I'm tired.'

'No, you're not. You're just doing this to get back at me. And you've succeeded in making me miserable and worried sick for the past twenty-four hours, so you may as well pat yourself on the back and get out of bed. Mission accomplished. Job well done. Use whatever remote you please.'

'Tell me one thing I've got to get out of bed for,' he says.

'To keep your muscles working. Before they atrophy.'

'Tell me one thing I've got to get out of bed for.'

He waits for me to come up with a reason. In the hall, the clock chimes the half hour in hollow, brassy tones. I hardly even hear it anymore.

'I'm just trying to keep you around,' I say. 'That's all.'

He tugs the sheet out from under me and pulls it up to his chin. I take his bowl back to the kitchen, scoop the wasted food into the trash, and load up the dishwasher.

Fifteen minutes later, the mattress springs groan as he slowly gets out of bed. All the energy his weight's coiled inside them unwinds and is gone, flung out in little bits of imperceptible heat that dissipate into the general coldness of all things. He walks into the hallway, his hair stuck out in all directions in damp, quivering shocks. Outside, squirrels rip the shriveled tomatoes from his vines; the land rises up quick in dandelions and stars-of-Bethlehem. His feet whisper across the floor as he makes his way to the bathroom, does his business, and goes right back to bed.

6

He came to the shop late, later than usual, sweaty and flushed and out of breath. I was at the counter, measuring a whitetail buck some yokel had driven over with his car and dragged straight there behind it, as proud as if he'd killed it with his bare hands, when Frank shouldered his way through the door. He smiled when he saw me, sweat running down his face. His nose and cheeks were sunburnt just the faintest pink, so he looked perpetually embarrassed. It drove me a little wild.

'Did you run the whole way here?' I said.

'Just wanted to stretch my legs a bit.' He looked all around the showroom, as if making sure nobody was hiding in the corners. He seemed strange, exhausted and frenetic at the same time, and distracted. He'd got a job painting houses for the summer, so he wouldn't have to bus quite as many tables in the campus dining room when school started in the fall, and he was plainly fatigued from twelve hours in the sun, but he kept bouncing on the balls of his feet like a child who'd been cooped inside all the glorious, free summer day, even after he folded his arms on the counter and peered with evident sorrow into the huge, ragged slash down the deer's belly where the yokel had tried to dress it, stretched and torn in spots as if the knife had run into resistance and he'd just gone ahead and used it as a crowbar, pried the deer open and pried him out — intestines and stomach, heart and lungs — into a glistening heap on the side of the road. His entire midsection was crumpled, the tire track smudged black across his snapped ribs, shattered glass glinting and ground into his fur. Frank ran a hand along his back, the skin torn away in some spots, rubbed bald and caked with gravel dust in the rest, as if to comfort him. He never could bear to see an animal hurt, sat on that counter with his legs swinging over the floor and wept the night he drove over a cat on his way to the shop and saw it rolling all around twitching in his rearview mirror, sat there and wept and made me walk down the road with my skinning knife to put the thing out of its misery. He always was the kinder of us. I never had the patience.

'That idiot thought he could still get a full-body mount out of this thing,' I said. ''Raised up on his hindquarters and ready to leap. Just like the Good Lord made him.' We'll be lucky if I can salvage him a shoulder mount.'

The antlers were wide and budding, still covered in gray velvet. The man had chained him by the neck and hooked the chain to his back bumper to keep them off the ground, keep them from tearing. When you squeezed them, you could feel through all the blood and soft tissue only the thinnest sliver of bone compressed at the core, barely begun to harden.

'And of course,' I said, 'of course he wants to keep the antlers. In *June*.'

Frank nodded. The bell over the door rattled

faintly from the tapping of his foot.

'I need to get the hide off,' I said. 'Before he spoils.' Already he was beginning to smell, with death's particular scent of sweetness allowed too much of itself, of fruit grown so tender and ripe it's split wide open and leaked out, liquid. I dragged him onto a rolling cart a couple inches shorter than the counter. The impact threw a cloud of gnats up from the gash, spreading outward for a brief moment before drawing themselves back downward, inward, to hide under the skin.

'Can I stay?' Frank said. He was studying the edge of the counter.

The eight o'clock train from Atlanta rumbled into the depot, trembling the floors with its cars full of hoboes and grain, flapping the pheasants' wings against the wall. I'd never let anyone watch, not even the dumb, earnest teenage boys with sunburnt necks who came in wanting to learn. Not even the handsomest of them.

'Only if you relax,' I said. 'You're making me anxious.'

He followed me into my workshop. It was about the size his shed is, cluttered and close and hot, even with all the windows open and the fans going. He had to squeeze his way between the big tubs of arsenic along the wall, dissolving inside them the living tissue from the skins of the dead, and the armatures of deer, their wooden bones awaiting wound excelsior muscle, grazing among the split and scattered pieces of the plaster mold of a mountain lion I was doing for the Natural Science Museum down in Raleigh

— legs halved lengthwise, belly sawn from back — shellacked and waiting to shape the layers of burlap and plaster and window-screen mesh into the form that would finally hold the skin.

I stacked the deer's hind ankles and pounded a nail through the bones. The knives on the table rattled and bounced. Frank shoved his hands in his pockets. He looked oversized and oafish standing there, the air and the quiet too thick to permit space for him, like he'd shouldered his way into it and now found himself wedged too tight.

'What's wrong?' I said.

'Nothing.'

'You're acting strange.'

'How?'

'You're being quiet.'

I pried the nail free. Frank pretended to be deeply engrossed in the novelty squirrels drying in whimsical tableaux upon the shelves: a squirrel orchestra, seated in tuxedos and playing tiny violins I'd carved from balsam; hayseed squirrels in overalls and no shirts lounging down by a blue-glass fishing hole, slender bamboo poles held in their curled toes, chewing blades of grass; a turn-of-the-century squirrel couple out courting, the young squirrel lady dressed in the finest tulle I could sew, a white lace parasol balanced in the crook of her arm, while her monocled squirrel beau lifted his dandy cane in greeting to some invisible squirrel passersby.

I always hated those things myself. Their hands, their fingers, always bothered me. They looked downright human, with their sharp little nails, greedy and grasping. But they sold like you wouldn't believe.

'You never talk about your family,' Frank said. 'Your life before — all this.'

'No,' I said, and started working a hook, on the end of a rope that ran up to a pulley I'd rigged on the ceiling, through the hole the nail had left behind. 'I don't.'

'Did you — do you have brothers or sisters?' He tried to sound real casual, as if he thought I might not catch his line of questioning.

I shook my head and yanked the hook, hard, to make sure the bone wouldn't split.

'What about your parents?' he said.

'What about them?'

'I don't know. Are they living?'

'I expect they are.'

'Expect?'

'I was sixteen the last time I saw them.'

'Oh.' He nodded several times, as if I was still talking and he was thoughtfully agreeing with each thing I said. I hauled down on the loose end of the rope. The stag's crushed ribs crackled as the cut along his belly pulled open and pulled them apart. Inside, the empty cavern of his chest was dark and dripping. Frank pulled his shirt over his nose.

'Don't look so astounded,' I said, between tugs of the rope. 'Living things are disgusting.'

'You mean dead things?' His voice was muffled by the fabric. The deer's head swayed at my chest. His knees tapped the edge of the table.

'The difference,' I said, tying the rope to its anchor on the wall, 'isn't very great.'

With a sewing needle I pricked the rounded tips of each antler, then clamped my thumb and forefinger around the burr in a collar I pulled tight along the length of the beam and down each tine, squeezing the soft tissue tight. Frank pressed close beside me, watching over my shoulder as little spots of blood bloomed on the tip of each branch, swelled, and ran together into a trickle that fell and splattered on the tile, spotting the toes of his boots. I wiped the blood from the soft fur — it was almost iridescent — and felt through the shriveled, empty tissue for the resistance of an artery, through the wall of which I eased the tip of a syringe and pumped it with formaldehyde till the antler was plump again, the artery turgid beneath the velvet. I squeezed that out, too, then filled it and emptied it, over and over, until the fluid ran clear.

It was too early in the summer, the tissue too young and unformed. In a few weeks it would shrivel and flake away, unravel the barely-knit bone inside, and the yokel would come in complaining until I replaced them with a salvaged rack, even though I'd already told him I couldn't save them. But I wanted Frank to think I could. I wanted him to think I could work magic, that I could resurrect the dead.

I dipped the syringe into the jar of formaldehyde, and, as I pulled back the stopper, my elbow brushed the loose fabric of his shirt, hanging away from his stomach as he leaned forward. I could feel him beside me, how rigid he held himself, the tension in his muscles it took to keep from backing away. He felt like an aching knot, a sore spot in the air. In a wide-mouthed jar on the next table, scavenger beetles filigreed the flesh from a copper-head's skeleton, stripping it clean and fine as the bared veins their herbivorous cousins leave quivering on the branch. I eased the needle into each artery and filled it one last time, slowly, watching the wrinkles as they filled and flattened, until the antler was heavy and swollen and taut, straining to hold itself in.

'What happened?' he said. 'To your family?'

I slipped the curved tip of my knife under the soft, white fur of the stag's chest, right at the bottom of his breastbone, and drew it in a circle over the shoulders. The skin split apart easy and clean. Didn't even try to hold itself whole.

'I left,' I said. 'Lived in boarding houses for a while. Sometimes I lived nowhere. Mounted what trophies I could, worked odd jobs while I saved up money, kept it all in a wad in my boot, that kind of thing. It's a bleak tale. Which is why I never tell it.'

'Sixteen sounds awful young to make a decision like that.' The very idea of it was impossible to him.

'I didn't have much choice.'

'Why not?'

I had to be sure, absolutely sure. I knew, by then, what happened when you weren't.

'It turned out,' I said, working hard to keep my hands steady, 'I wasn't any of the things my parents wanted me to be.'

I opened a line along the spine, up to the base of the skull, forked the cut, and drew a branch to

75

each antler; I peeled an edge of fur back from the shoulder blades. The skin was cool, but underneath it the buck had just the last little bit of warmth left.

'We're all disappointments,' Frank said. 'In one way or another.'

'Not like this.'

He watched me, waiting for some explanation. There was a sort of desperate brightness in his eyes, a restlessness, something of the wild and starving dog that keeps moving, pacing, to stave off the pangs of his hunger. The back of his hand was streaked with white paint. I took it wide and cool and trembling in mine; I slid his fingers into the cut. I thought it would tell him, somehow, all the things I couldn't say: my mother's magnolia perfume exuding from behind the heavy folds of her dress, so thick and sweet it made me sick to be close to her for too long, the dark shine of my father's hair, with its sharp part, shellacked so tightly to his skull he might as well have been bald, the bump and jostle as he drove us swerving over the dirt road, late at night, from one of their endless parties, the two of them drunk and laughing and leaning together as they stumbled onto the porch; the way, as a boy, I'd felt the passage of time with an acute pain, nostalgic for afternoons when I was happy, for beautiful spring evenings full of warm, wild wind, before they were even over, so that I'd start to cry in the middle of running through the grass with my cousins because I knew it would be over so soon, the way, when I was ten years old and the first booklet of the Northwestern

76

School of Taxidermy's nine-part correspondence course arrived in the mail, its thin pages, with their arcane diagrams and alchemical formulae, seemed so grave and profound, so full of the power to make the world finally stop for a moment, to stay as it was, that I carried it with me everywhere, though it was years before I was brave enough to try even the simplest of its rituals, my mother's voice murmuring though the wall as she suggested hopefully to my father that this might, after all, be a marvelous introduction to the art of medicine; all the plans they'd had for me, and the way I felt those plans torn away late one summer afternoon when I was fourteen as my friend Paul pulled his sweaty, dirt-streaked shirt over his head after an early-evening pickup game of baseball, and how I stood alone that night on the bridge where the Neuse and Trent Rivers joined, the setting sun reflected red on their waters so they looked like a branched vein rushing toward the sea's frantic, troubled heart, and thought about his skinny, bare chest, and about how easy it would be to fall: how quickly the water would draw you into itself, how one good breath would draw it into you; how many years after that I had been, in one way or another, alone.

Down there by the shoulders, where the skin's good and thick, it comes off easy, cleaner than you'd peel an orange. You don't even need a knife. Frank's whole arm was rigid and shaking as I worked our hands under the skin, gnats swarming at our wrists, and pressed his palm to the muscle of the shoulder, so he could feel its cabled fibers, its radiant, diminishing warmth. His fingers stayed stiff a long time before they relaxed and cupped the shoulder's curve. I covered them with mine.

The further up we went, along the smooth length of the neck, the thinner the skin became, and the more tightly it clung to the body. The membrane that joined it to the muscle snapped across our nails and wedged tight beneath them. I watched our fingers creep under it, a little bit at a time, along the warm, slick neck, all the way to the top of the spine, nearly to the skull, until the skin was so delicate and married to the muscle we could see it stretch across our fingertips, the hairs that covered it spreading apart to show the pale hide underneath. Frank's breath whistled in his nostrils. He looked like he was going to be sick. If we pushed any further, our fingers would tear through, out into the cold, thin air.

Formaldehyde leaked clear from the antler tips, one fat drop at a time, diluting the puddle of blood on the tile. Its edges trembled with surface tension as they stretched wide. Slowly, carefully, Frank pulled our hands out, back down the length of the neck. The skin fell in a curtain away from the muscle, a pale, dull pink webbed with white fat and gray sinew. The whole world felt raw and exposed.

He hurried to the sink, his hands shaking. He scrubbed them until they were pink, scraping away the blood, the dried paint. We couldn't look at each other. When he was done, he flung the water from his hands into the basin and looked around for a clean towel on which to dry them, but every one was soiled. He held his fingers dripping out in front of him, afraid to touch anything. A little paint was left at the bottom of his thumbnail. For his sake, I washed my hands too, the water so hot at first I had to yank them away while it cooled.

'I try not to think about them,' I said. 'My parents. We did our best to love each other. That's all anyone can do.'

I wiped my hands on my britches.

'Wendell.' His voice was low and hoarse, scraped raw by desperation, and shame, and by supplication. 'I — ' He shook his head, looked away, rested his hand on the counter. With one finger, I scraped the paint from his thumbnail.

He leaned forward, resting his forehead on mine, and breathed a long, heavy breath. It sounded like giving up. 'I'm sorry,' he muttered. The words broke across my cheek, hot and loud as thunder. 'I'm real sorry.'

I kissed his jaw. I kissed the pink razor burn across his Adam's apple. His stubble scraped my lips tender.

★　★　★

On his biceps, clouds unwound from a dark skein about the buck's antlers, scudding motionless along his pale underarm; they tangled into the tuft of damp hair in his armpit. Two of the other boys had had to hold his arm over his head so he couldn't yank it down, while another shoved a folded-up belt in his mouth so he didn't crack a tooth gritting them, left permanent marks in the leather. I lifted his arm and kissed him there, the clouds warm and wet on my cheek, I breathed in their muggy air. He shivered and tensed, his eyes squeezing shut. He smelled like the street right as it starts to rain.

On the other side of his arm, those same clouds twisted and piled into thunderheads that condensed black into the night sky itself, studded with pale stars of bare skin. 'It must have hurt,' I said, running my palm over it. It felt cooler and smoother than the rest of him, as though it really were the night. Every time I pulled back to get a better look, there on the bed in the hot, cramped efficiency where I lived above my shop, every time I stopped to ask him what something meant, or how it felt, he laughed with mild desperation and looked as though I'd sentenced him to death, and pulled me quickly against him again.

'It bled black for a week,' he said, his lips on mine. 'Soaked through my shirtsleeves.'

The sky stretched across his shoulder to his collarbone, from which a flock of birds of all kinds, swallows and sparrows, hawks and owls, bluebirds and red, emerged, their bodies and beaks overlapping, the sky's darkness fractured and furling into them, drawn into the curves of their wings and the feathers of their tails, dragged with them as they strained toward his breastbone. The blond hair on his chest blurred the lines of their bodies. Their wings beat against my lips.

Above his belt was a tiny, still-forming scar, shiny and tender as a plant stem, where shrapnel had grazed him just enough to split the skin. He leaned back as I worked my fingers underneath his waistband, he held his breath as I found it there, that warmest part of him, and pulled it free, barely curved like the branch of an antler, long and hard, the velvet just rubbed away from the bone. Its musk was unruly, wild, the kind that lingers on bark, marking to whom the land belongs. I felt the heavy pound of his heart inside it.

He wrapped his arms around my waist and dragged my hips to his; he pushed my legs up, my knees to my chest, but held himself just slightly above me, squinting a little, looking at me much longer and more closely than I was accustomed to, and in a way no one had ever looked at me before: as though he were seeing, all of a sudden, the answer to a question he'd been asking for a long, long time.

In the last thin film of evening light, he blushed, hives rising in patches up from his collarbone, dappling red the skin of his throat. And then he grinned, open and expansive, and in that moment he seemed happier, more animated, more alive, than anyone I had ever known.

He ran his thumb along my eyebrow. It had been years since a hand had touched my face.

The birds rode the ragged currents of his breath, rising and falling. Trembling, he rested against me all his heavy weight, and pressed his face into my hair, and gasped as he pushed slow and straining inside me, where he waited, rigid and pulsing and still, until my body believed he was just another part of itself.

7

I'm in the den, playing my solitaire video game — it's a little handheld thing they were giving away as a consolation prize on one of his game shows, lets you play solitaire without having to shuffle the cards, so it's easier on your knuckles — when a Special Breaking News Update comes on the television: the mother's finally confessed to killing her son. All the stations are playing the grainy video from the police interrogation. Somebody in the department leaked it, which they promise will be the subject of a thorough in-house review. It's taken from overhead in the dingy little interview room, so the only thing you've got a good clear view of is the part in her poorly-dyed hair, the dark roots creeping like fingers out of her scalp and into her blond curls, and her own hands flat on the table, fingers spread wide and painted nails chipped. The sound of the recording's real scratchy, so they've put captions on the whole thing.

'I didn't mean to do it,' she says. 'I didn't mean to hurt him. I was trying to give him a bath, and he kept crying. He wouldn't stop. And I was so tired. He cried all night, no matter what I did, he just kept crying, so I couldn't sleep. My apartment was so small, anywhere I went, I still heard him. I got earplugs and everything. I tried. But I just wanted him to be quiet, just for a second, that's all. Just for a second. So I held him under the water, I just dipped him, really, just for a second. Just to muffle the noise. It was only a second. And then I pulled him up again, I pulled him right back out of it, right back out of the water, and he wasn't breathing. It was only a second. I didn't mean to do it.' Her hands stay still the entire time.

'I was tired,' she says. 'I was just so tired.'

There's eight whole hours of interrogation, apparently, but they keep playing just the one clip, over and over. All the news stations are calling her Debbie Drowner.

I slap my knees, I'm so excited. It's about time something good happened. I hurry down the hall. That vacuum's still standing outside the bathroom, right where he left it. Hasn't touched it since the day he scavenged it, but every time I come near, with even just the formless, inchoate intent of possibly dragging it back down the driveway for the garbage truck, he twists himself around in the bed, as if he can sound even my murkiest wordless thoughts, and shouts through the door, 'What are you doing?'

'She did it,' I shout back.

'Don't you touch that vacuum.'

I throw the door open. 'The mother did it. Drowned him in his own bathwater.'

The bedroom smells like old socks. It's turning fall already, starting to get cool, but the house stays stuffy. Frank's kicked the sheets off.

'What?' he says. He looks so small, curled up there on the bed, his wrists and ankles swallowed

83

in their cuffs. He must have lost twenty, thirty pounds already. Maybe more.

'Little Larry,' I say. 'There's finally going to be justice for Little Larry.' That's what the shrill lady lawyer on the television keeps saying. 'You were right. I thought for sure I had you this time, but you were right all along.' I wait for him to make some acknowledgment of triumph. 'Now, what I want to know is why she reported him missing in the first place. After all that time. She had no reason to. She's estranged from his daddy, and from her own parents. She could have got away with it forever if she'd wanted to, just moved off and pretended to be somebody else, and nobody'd have been the wiser. That's the mystery now. A real mystery.'

Frank rolls onto his back and stares at the dust motes lazing through the light from the bay window.

'Probably for attention,' I say, cuing him. 'A sick need for attention.'

'Will you turn the air on?' he says. 'It's hot in here.'

The thermostat's right there on the wall over his nightstand. I walk over to it and flip the switch to cool. The walls rumble far away.

'They've got the actual footage of her confession,' I say. 'All the gory details, straight from her very own mouth. You know she drove around with his body in her trunk for weeks? Right up until the day she called the police. Said she 'couldn't bear to let him go.''

'Hm.' Looks like he's got fuzzy gray mold growing in the wrinkles around his mouth.

'You need to shave,' I say.

'Ain't worth the time it takes. Nobody cares what I look like.'

'I care.'

'But you're stuck with me either way,' he says grimly, as if with great sympathy for my plight.

'The police might recall the footage at any moment,' I say. 'There could be an injunction.'

He gives me a tired, resigned look, begging me not to start again. The dust floats into the hallway, gets pulled into the vent in the floor, through the long ducts of wrinkled silver foil inside the walls, and gathers in gray sheets on the filters. They gasp and wheeze as the air strains through. I walk back to the hall.

'Don't you touch my vacuum,' he says.

'Why? It's been sitting there for two weeks. It's an eyesore.'

'I'm fixing it.'

'With what? Prayers?'

'You leave it right where it is,' he says. 'I'll get to it as soon as I can.'

'What's preventing you from getting to it now?'

'I'm formulating a plan.' He turns his back to me.

'If you don't get out of that bed, I'm throwing the vacuum away.'

His voice is firm and grave, but detached, too, as if from some oracle warning, through wisps of narcotic haze, of something terrible in which he has no particular stake. 'Don't throw the vacuum away,' he says into his pillow.

I stand there a long time, longer than I should, staring at it, before I finally grab the handle and tug it behind me down the hall. The sheets rustle as Frank rolls over. I drag it out the front door and yank it down the step and onto the ground, good and hard so it makes a loud thud on each one. Frank yells something, but I can't hear it very well from out here. I stop and wait. I give him time to push himself out of the bed and shuffle down the hall, or to pound on the bay window and shake one big finger at me. I give him a chance.

Then I drag the vacuum all the way through the trees down to the road, where those three bastard children have crossed onto our property and are writing curse words and drawing pictures of oversized breasts in bright chalk on the curb. They scramble backwards into the street when they see me, all pale and blond and mangy, like they've spent every moment of their lives up to this one locked in a dark cellar.

'Hey,' shouts the oldest. He blinks slowly. 'That's our vacuum!'

'He's got our vacuum!' the middle one yells, as if it's his very own discovery.

The youngest, four or five years old, starts to cry at the sight of me and runs away.

'You get out of here,' I snap at the other two. The oldest throws a nub of chalk, but it bounces off the mailbox and lands at my feet, and they run away after their little brother. Don't even stop to gather up the tools of their vandalism.

I step on the chalk, one piece at a time,

grinding them into powdery neon smears across the asphalt. The feel of each one cracking apart, like an old, brittle bone under my heel, gives me a little thrill of joy.

8

We went to the beach together the end of that first summer, stayed in a little two-room shack with plywood walls so flimsy the sea breeze would have knocked them down on top of us if there weren't so many gaps between the boards for it to slip through instead of strain against. We slept for the first time in the same bed, so narrow he crushed me against the wall and had to peel his chest from my sweaty back just to roll over, but I rested better than I had in years. I loved how deeply he breathed in the night, how early and suddenly he rose in the morning, as though sleep were a thin covering you could throw back as easily as the sheets. I loved how he had to stoop every time he walked through a door.

He cooked breakfast, humming as he pushed scrambled eggs around a dented skillet on the hot plate and waited for the last gleaming bits of moisture to burn away, while I summoned the will to get up. Even at my happiest, it always took me a long time lying in the bed, half-awake, to convince myself the world was worth waking into. He had the loveliest voice, though, could have been a singer if he'd wanted. Every note sounded like a deep laugh.

'I didn't know you could cook,' I said, when the pop and sizzle and smell of bacon frying finally pulled me shuffling to the worn wood bench at the dining table. It barely fit between the walls. We had to climb over it to get from one side to the other.

'This is it,' he said. 'Bacon, eggs, and toast. Don't expect nothing else.' He'd learned it in the army. He was in his swim trunks already, and a white undershirt with yellow sweat stains creeping from the armpits. He scraped the eggs and bacon onto my plate and pressed two slices of bread into the greasy pan. Nothing I've ever cooked, in all these years, has ever tasted as good.

Afterwards, we walked through loose, hot sand that fell away from our feet and pulled us into lurching, uneven steps, down to where the waves solidified it into wet silt that held us up and held, for a few moments, the shape of our footprints. It was early still, maybe ten o'clock, and the light was hazy and soft, broken on the waves and blurred with salt. The breeze blew the loose sand in tumbling swirls toward our legs, then away, knotting together and blowing apart. There wasn't hardly anyone else on the beach, just clumps of families so far away they could have been piles of driftwood, or heaps of seaweed. They may have been. Realtors had only built the rickety bridge to the island a couple years earlier, and there was just the one ramshackle motel then, and some falling-down shanties like ours tucked into the dunes for solitary fishermen.

We took each other's pictures with the camera I'd bought to photograph my mounts for a newspaper ad. In them, he's standing with his hands on his hips like he's surveying the shore and not particularly pleased with what he sees, his brow jutted low to drape both his squinting eyes in shadow, the corrugated sea hammered out behind him. Just from the walk down to the water, he's already drenched in sweat, his shirt hanging in heavy folds, his hair stringy and flat with it. His bare legs are huge, his calves almost as thick as his thighs.

He tugged his shirt over his head and grabbed my hand, pulled me toward the water. His palm felt rough and smooth at the same time, like sandpaper caked with the dust it's ground away from wood, and his cheeks and shoulders and chest were sunburnt bright pink now, with dead skin peeling away in thin, papery scraps.

'You go on,' I said, taking his shirt.

'You can't swim?'

'I can swim,' I said. 'I don't.'

'Come on,' he said. 'It's no fun by yourself.'

'I don't trust water I can't see my feet through.'

He looked mighty disappointed.

I watched him wade out past the sandbar, where the waves crashed and foamed, until the ocean covered his shoulders and its rolling surface sometimes obscured him completely from view before it sank again toward the earth, and there he spread his arms, lay on his back, and floated as though a lighter man had never been born. I could hardly believe somebody of his size could float so effortlessly: palms upturned to the sun, head leaned back as on a cushion, legs lounging just beneath the water with their upturned toes breaking through it to point at the sky.

I sat just beyond the water's reach and wriggled my fingers and toes into the wet, gleaming sand at the furthest edge of a just-receded wave. I scooped up fistfuls of it, let it run between my fingers and over the edges of my hand. When I opened my fist and spread it wide, the sand cupped inside it broke open along the lines of my palm.

Frank waved at me as if I was an old friend he hadn't seen in years and couldn't believe his incredible fortune to come upon here, in this very place, his tattoos warping with the movements of his muscles like the shadow of a shifting cloud upon his skin. The waves built up and passed beneath him. Sometimes the water ran across and pooled in the hollow between his chest and stomach, but it never could push him under. I understood, then, how he made it to shore while all those other boys drowned, and I waved back, the wet sand trickling down my forearm, hardening as it dried into grainy, translucent rivulets that cracked and fell away. A wave spread itself across the shore as thin as it could without disappearing, then gathered itself up as it slipped backwards beneath the next, which unfurled forward and over it, as though the two were actually separate bodies, instead of twin fibers of the same heaving muscle. I marveled at that, how a single thing could move both forwards and backwards, in two directions at once.

You could do anything you wanted, I thought then. Anything at all.

He walked dripping out of the water. It poured

off him in streams that ran back into the ocean, where they gave up their edges and shape and became again indistinguishable, as if they'd never pressed against him. Sea foam clung to his ribs and knees before dissolving in the wind. He sat heavily beside me in the sand and kissed me, his wet lips salty, the hair on his legs burning gold in the sun. Its light fell full and hard down on him, burned away another layer of his skin. I loved to touch those tender, sunburnt spots: how he tensed against the twinge of pain, how my white fingerprints on his chest filled back in with red.

⋆   ⋆   ⋆

We're not together in any of the photographs. It was reckless enough just to walk out in the open and the sun like that without going and asking some stranger, who might not turn out to be one after all when you got close enough, to take our picture. But we've still got all of them, in a cedar box at the top of the closet, with his medals from the war and his mama's wedding rings, and as tenuously as they link us, they're the only real evidence that any of it ever happened, that we were ever even in the same vicinity. The rest we got rid of, if it ever existed at all. We never wrote each other love letters, anything someone might find, and he never came to my shop at the same time two days in a row, or by the same path through the downtown streets and alleys. Once I went to throw some carcasses in the trash can out back — the big noticeable ones I had to haul off myself, but the smaller ones, squirrels and possums and owls, I tossed in the trash can and nobody was the wiser — only to find him crawling on hand and knee down the alley to stay below the line of sight of some poor tenement family eating their gruel in the window above.

'So nobody can establish a pattern,' he said, real gruff and clipped, looking up at me from the ground.

He was the most worried about his mama. He was the only one she had left, after all — his older brother Harvey and his baby sister Iris had both died from consumption when he was a boy. It's strange, now, to think about how many and often people died when we were children. It was happening all the time. Everybody had brothers and sisters, more than one, usually, who never saw their tenth birthday. So many people survive these days. Everybody lives so awfully long.

She was always trying to send him courting some girl she'd just met, and talking about how empty that old house felt, and how she sure would like to have some grandchildren someday to fill it back up. She was supposedly not in the best of health, had dizzy spells and heart palpitations and 'the vapors,' she called it. I was never convinced that was anything but a ploy to keep his attention.

But I didn't blame him. For protecting her, for protecting himself. He'd lost enough already, felt enough pain. I didn't want him to know how it felt to fumble for an excuse, to stammer and redden and try to explain without explaining the compromised position in which he'd been found;

I didn't want him to see the change in his mother's eyes as the stain of understanding spread through them, seeping back through every memory and forward into every hope, so that no matter which way she looked, every sight of him was tinged with filth and soaked in sorrow.

I'd never met her, never even seen her from afar, but I felt her pull on us all the time, every minute we were together, even lying there on the beach in the hot sun. It wasn't something we argued or even talked about, but a fundamental underlying force, like all forces invisible, that shaped our every surge toward each other and our every drifting apart, as if she was some enormous, distant mass so far away you couldn't see it but so heavy and dense it warped all the space around it, curved it so sharp that by seven, seven-thirty every night, he started to look down at his feet, and out the window at the darkening sky, and every straight line I tried to pull him along into the hot night, no matter how fast and sure, bent into an arc that carried him back to her in time for dinner at eight. And so the closest any of those pictures come to showing the two of us together is my blurred fingertip, creeping in at the edge of one of them like the first dark sliver of the moon, invisible in the bright sky until just that moment, beginning to pass across the sun.

★   ★   ★

A storm blew up that night, a pretty bad one out of the east. I could feel it building all afternoon, slowly knotting the air into a bruise out over the waves, the ocean turning back on themselves the river waters that were supposed to run into it, and as the sun set Frank sat in the worn rocking chair out on the sagging front stoop of the shack, smelling like salt and sand, his hair ruffled with it — I loved the way his hair smelled when we came in from the beach, never wanted him to shower — and with his clasped hands pressed to his lips watched the storm clouds muscle their way through the drowsy evening light. He was always real funny about the weather. He wouldn't take a shower during a storm, wouldn't even wash his hands, thought the lightning would travel through the pipes and pour out the tap, crackle pink and branching all over him. His mama and her people had taken some kind of religiously-inspired pioneer trek to the Midwest when she was a girl, before they ran into a pack of unneighborly Indians and some mild cyclones and retreated back to God's Country, having decided that they'd misinterpreted the previous signs and that it was, in fact, His Country after all. When he was a boy, she made them all huddle in the closet any time she heard a rumble of thunder. He was always watching the sky, even on the brightest of days, waiting for clouds to curdle green.

I pulled him inside, and we sat in our swimsuits on either side of the table and played gin rummy while the clouds scraped across the stars. He stretched his legs under the table and propped his feet on my lap, cold as the other side of the pillow when I flipped it in the night. When

I got hot, I held them to my chest to cool me down. I pressed their soles to my cheek.

Each individual drop of rain resounded on the tin roof, sounded like someone dumping an endless truckload of gravel down on top of us, and thunder rattled the window glass. The little shack shuddered and swayed. You could feel the wind itself every now and then, big whistling gusts blowing right between the boards. I was just a turn or two away from laying my whole hand on the table in victory, when suddenly he set his cards to the side and his feet on the floor and wiped his sweaty hands on his bare thighs.

'Let's stop,' he said.

'Stop what?'

'This game,' he said, amazed that I could even consider such an activity at such a time. 'We'll probably need to make a run for it.'

I couldn't help laughing. He looked highly insulted.

'A run for what?' I said.

'For anywhere but inside this rickety damn house. Before it falls in on us.'

I loved to hear him curse. He was always so wholesome.

'It's just a storm,' I said.

'Just a storm? The whole house is swaying back and forth.'

'It's supposed to sway,' I said. 'It's on little stilts.'

'It's going to collapse.'

'It sways so it won't collapse. That's the whole point of the swaying. And even if it did collapse, these boards are so flimsy it probably wouldn't hurt.'

'We ought to evacuate,' he said.

I laughed and clambered over the table, to the one window that looked toward the ocean. Rain ran down the glass; the clouds billowed and crumbled. Light peeled them back from a bright crack in the sky, as if day were breaking through night, before darkness closed over and sealed the wound.

'Get back from there.' His voice was high and strained. 'Didn't anybody ever teach you to stay away from windows during a storm?'

I loved his nervousness, I loved his fear. I loved the way his bare foot bounced nervously on the floor, as if barely restrained from running away.

'Come here,' I said. He shook his head. 'I don't know how you ever made it through a war like this.' And, as if being dragged by an invisible, overpowering force against his will, he took the two steps from the table to the wall.

He wrapped his arms around me from behind, rested his chin in my hair. 'My mother would kill me,' he said, 'if she knew I was exposing myself to the elements like this.'

'You sound like somebody's mother right about now,' I said.

He squeezed me tight against him. Sand, caught in the hair on his chest, ground against my back.

Rain dripped through a leak in the ceiling and onto the table. The roar of the wind was indistinguishable from the roar of the waves, as if they were crashing against the walls, closing over the roof. It blew through the room in a cool current. The floor shook.

'This house is about to come apart,' he said.

Lightning ripped the clouds open and sewed the clouds shut. I leaned us against the sill, so he could feel the wind: how it passed through the boards of the house and between our bodies and kept on its way, how the storm moved right through us without disturbing a thing.

9

I've decided to get us a dog. We used to have one or two all the time, a couple purebred beagles, and a big, black German shepherd who dragged herself onto the porch one night as a puppy, ragged and so starved you could see her ribs plain through even that thick, downy undercoat, big chunks of which had been torn out. Fancy was the last one, another beagle, and it must have been twenty years ago she died. Frank wanted to get another one after her, but I couldn't do it. She was real jealous, real possessive, and I just knew she'd be furious if we ever replaced her. But it's rainy and gray outside, and the water's running down the windows, and Frank's lying in the bed, and the whole house is so quiet I can't stand it, and a situation like this even she might make an exception for, so I leave him lying there and take myself down to the animal shelter. That's where they say on TV you're supposed to get your dogs anyway, so I'm feeling pretty good about that, thinking I'm doing the public a mighty fine service, my civic duty, until I actually get there. It's about the most depressing establishment I've ever entered, all gray cinderblock walls and concrete floors with drains in them and water standing over the drains because they're clogged up with dog hair, and the whole place divided into prison cells with chain-link fencing, and all the dogs howling in sorrow or barking at nothing at all. The people who work here look just about as miserable and trapped. They all drift around in a sort of shell-shocked daze.

The only creature in the entire building who isn't keening and crying, the only one with a little equanimity about her, is some kind of basset hound mix — she's got the basset's long ears and stocky body, but some other blood's pulled her face a little tighter so it doesn't sag completely off her skull — sitting in the corner, as far from the others as she can get, silent and slumped against the fencing so her soft belly pushes through the open diamonds. Her head's stooped low as if under some terrible shame, and her tail's bent two thirds of the way down, at a perfect right angle, so its tip points upward. Some little boy, I bet, like one of those bastards next door, took it in his hand and snapped it.

The soiled sheet of paper clothespinned to the fence says her name is Daisy. And she's already spayed and house-trained, which is what we need. I'm not too keen on scrubbing stains out of the carpet these days, or trying to keep a thing from chewing the stitches on her belly so it doesn't spill wide open.

'Daisy,' I say.

Without raising her head, she casts her weary eyes up at me.

'I'll take her,' I tell the skinny boy with rotten teeth following me around. He's probably doing this is as community service, in penance for some minor crimes. He scoops her out of her cage and hooks a thin leash to her collar.

'Twenty-five bucks,' he says. Doesn't even make me fill out any paperwork.

She curls up on a towel in the back seat, looking bored, but when we pull up to the pet store she whimpers with excitement and thumps her broken tail. She must be able to smell it from out here. I take her in to help me pick out her food and biscuits and bed, walk her up and down the aisles and let her sniff the bags of kibble until she pauses at one and starts nibbling the corner in her tiny front teeth, leaves it all crinkled like crepe paper. I only buy a small bag of it, even though you save a whole bunch of money when you get the bigger ones. I can't carry a fifty-pound bag of dog food around anymore. Plus you want to make sure it agrees with her stomach before you go and buy a lifetime supply.

The bed aisle looks like some kind of luxury condominium resort. They've got dog beds that have a mattress and box spring, dog beds with silk duvets. One even has a wrought iron frame, complete with headboard. The checkout girl gives me a look of muted surprise and condemnation when I dare to buy one that's just an oversized pillow.

At home, I lead her across the yard. The clouds are starting to thin out, the rain diffused into drizzle. The house is quiet when we walk in. First thing she does is pause in the doorway to stare at the raccoon that's always creeping around the umbrella can. She waits a good while, transfixed, doesn't move a thing but the bristling hair on her back and the pulsating sides of her nostrils, trying to close around and grip the long-faded smell of it.

'Come on,' I say. 'You'd better meet Frank.' She keeps staring over her shoulder at it as we go.

He's still in the bed, lying on his back with his shoulders drawn up, hands folded atop his chest like a damn corpse in the coffin. His eyes are closed, and his face is pinched tight, watching something painful in his dreams. It's no wonder he has to sleep so much, if that's the kind of rest he's getting when he does.

'Wake up,' I say, prodding his shoulder.

'I'm all right.' He doesn't open his eyes. 'I'm fine. I'm just tired.'

'I've got a present for you.'

'I don't want any presents.'

'You'd better. It ain't going away any time soon.' I pat the bed beside his legs, and Daisy promptly hops right up and sits there, staring at him with the kind of solemn nobility you don't expect in such a stumpy animal. Frank opens his eyes and stares back at her a long time in a parody of her graveness. He props himself up against the headboard, which rocks back and taps the wall where it's scraped a feathered line into the paint. She sits nestled against him.

'There she is,' he says, scratching her under the chin. Her jowls pool in his hand, and she licks his wrist with a sideways swipe of the tongue. 'Hey there, Fancy.'

'Fancy? Fancy's been dead twenty years.'

He frowns, and his forehead wrinkles into thick, ponderous folds.

'She doesn't even look like Fancy. She's mostly basset.'

'I guess you're right,' he says grudgingly. He gathers up the loose skin on the back of her head, pulling it taut over her face, stretching her eyelids back until they're almost closed, and lets go, chuckling quietly as it sags.

'No guessing about it. I just picked her up from the pound. Name's Daisy.'

He grimaces. 'That's an awful name.'

'I didn't come up with it. But it's too late to change now. She's four years old. We'd give her an identity crisis.'

She roots around the sheets, snuffling loudly, then turns in a clumsy circle three times on his lap, her paws continually slipping off his legs, and lays herself down.

'Well,' he says, 'I think we might get along all right anyway.'

'She probably needs some dinner. Lord knows what they were feeding her in that prison.'

'Stale bread and water,' Frank says.

I start for the door. Frank swings his legs over the side of the bed. His feet are swollen, and their tops are mottled purple. Daisy leaps down.

'I'll do it,' he says.

Of course: no matter how I beg or plead, he won't get out of the bed for me, but he'll do it for some dog he's just met. If I'd known it would be that easy, I'd have got us one three weeks ago.

'Get some clothes on,' I say. 'I'll bring everything in from the car.'

He tugs his pajama shirt over his head. He's got an infestation, now, of shiny white spots, two

103

on his forehead, three on his chest, and whole innumerable constellations across his shoulders and back, where the dermatologist had to dig out bits of cancer like mortar shrapnel from his skin.

Too much time in the sun when he was young, Frank told her. Too much exposure.

★   ★   ★

By the time I carry in the last sack, he's sitting at the kitchen table, fully-dressed and pulling on his socks and shoes.

'You going someplace?' I say.

'Thought I might take her outside for a bit. Show her the lay of the land.' He smoothes his hair against his head. His neck looks long and thin, and his clothes are too big, and wrinkled as if he'd slept in them all this time. He sways a little when he stands, has to press his fingertips to the table.

'Are you sure you're up to it?' I say.

He gives me a look of warning, and I don't say any more. Instead I set the potatoes to boil for some potato salad. That's his favorite. Usually I only make it for the holidays because it takes so long, between the potatoes and the eggs and the vegetables and the dressing, all the boiling and peeling and chopping, but I've got more reason to celebrate now than I ever do at Christmas.

He holds on to the counter while he lowers her food and water bowls to the floor. Seeing him bent down that far, it's all I can do to keep myself from hurrying over to grab his elbow. His hands spill half the water from the bowl as he lowers it, but I wait until she's gobbled up all her kibble without stopping to chew and he's pulled all the tennis balls off the feet of his walker — 'You ought to be glad I finally found a use for these old things,' he says, grinning, as he sits with the walker laid across his lap and tugs each ball free — and taken her out in the back yard before I clean it up.

I watch them through the open window over the sink. Frank hurls a tennis ball, and Daisy scuffles after it quick as she can, not by running so much as by folding and unfolding her stubby body in a way that launches her forward. Enough of the grass has fallen and died now that she can get around the yard a little easier, doesn't have to wear a path through the wilderness. The ball bounces off the wall of the shed, and she gets it in her mouth and shakes her head back and forth like there's a squirrel body attached to it and she's got to snap the neck joining them.

I stick a fork into the biggest potato of the bunch, bumping slow against the side of the pot. The tines slide smooth through the skin and flesh into the center, without that slight sandpaper friction you can feel when they're not quite done. I dump them into the strainer to cool for a bit. I will not peel a hot potato.

I lean forward, press my face to the screen for some fresh air. It's a nice night out, just barely a little coy implication of a chill in the air. The wires of the mesh blur, and spread, and pass from my vision. When you get close enough to something, when you hold it right up to your eyes, you can see right through it. Frank throws the ball for her for nearly two hours while darkness spreads outward from the woods, where night always seems to originate. The tennis ball tears a bright green streak through it. After a little bit, I can't even see Daisy chase after the thing. The night swallows her.

'Fancy,' Frank calls. He shakes his head. 'Willy — Snuffy — ' He looks to me through the screen, his face pained.

'Daisy,' I shout.

It doesn't matter, though. I can already hear the thump and whisper of her thick paws as they break the grass and scatter wet leaves. She gallops out of the darkness and into the half-circle of light from the bulb on the back patio, and offers up the tennis ball between her teeth. That's how it's always been with him and the dogs: No matter how far they've run or what name he calls them by, they always come back to him.

'Supper's about ready,' I say. It's seven-thirty. Usually he'd be real grumpy about having to wait this late to eat, but he lumbers in as I'm pulling the pork tenderloin out of the oven and doesn't seem to notice or care. He holds the door open and gestures like a fine gentleman for Daisy to precede him through it, which she does, broken tail wagging and jowls still bulging around the tennis ball. He scrapes his muddy heels on the mat and takes a long time to untie his shoes and set them on a piece of newspaper I lay over the tile, then he drags a chair to the door, sits heavily, and wipes her belly and paws with a dish towel. 'Drop it,' he says, pointing to the floor. She looks back over her shoulder, whimpering a little, and when he reaches for the ball, she scampers backwards and starts shaking it again with an enthusiasm so vigorous it slings strands of her saliva up and around to lash the top of her muzzle, iridescent like the paths of snails.

He makes her sit, and points to the ground about five times, telling her to drop it, before he finally reaches into her mouth with his own fingers, and still she won't let it go, starts growling and pulling her lips back to show her big ivory teeth, and he thinks it's funny. He thinks it's downright adorable. Starts patting her on the head and scratching under her chin while he works the ball gently out of her jaws and slips it into his pocket. Then he heads straight for the cabinet to start setting the table, opens it right up and reaches for a stack of china.

'Wash your hands,' I say. 'Unless you want dog slobber all over your turnip greens.'

'Dog slobber's good for you,' he says. 'It's got antibacterial qualities. 'And there was a certain beggar named Lazarus, which was laid at his gate, full of sores, and desiring to be fed with the crumbs which fell from the rich man's table: moreover the dogs came and licked his sores.''

'I used to watch Fancy eat her own waste in the backyard,' I say. 'Do you think her slobber had antibacterial qualities?'

He washes his hands, then goes back to the cabinet and stands there a long time, staring at the dishes. When he finally stacks our plates in an empty corner of the counter, the top one is our nice china, with a country house etched in blue on the cold white background. The bottom is bright yellow plastic.

'You can give me one of those, too,' I say. I try to hand the china back to him, but he starts laying the cutlery on the table: silver in my spot, blue plastic in his. He puts a sippy cup where his glass should go. I pour tea into it, and he snaps the lid into place. Takes him a minute to get it lined up right.

'Smells good,' he says as I scoop the turnip greens.

'Well. I thought we ought to celebrate.'

He sets the vinegar, in its faceted bottle with a glass stopper like something a rich lady would keep her perfume in, on the table, and we settle down to eat. My back hurts from standing so long over the stove. Daisy sits next to his chair, her glistening black nose right on the edge of the table, nostrils dilating so wide you can see the pink inside them. She puts one paw on his leg and stares at him imperiously. He brushes her away.

'You go on.' I shoo her from the table. She trots toward the hall but stops in the doorway to look balefully over her shoulder. 'I don't intend to raise a beggar,' I say, and she goes on down the hall. The animals always did like him better. They could smell something on me, I think, that they didn't trust.

Frank stabs at his greens three or four times with the blunt blue tines of his fork before he manages to skewer a bite. He washes it down with a swill of tea sucked through its tiny plastic spout and gets a funny look on his face, smacks his lips together real quick, as if there's a strange taste on them he can't quite place.

'You don't have to use those,' I say.

'I don't mind.'

'You should eat off a regular plate.'

'A plate's a plate,' he says. 'It don't matter.'

'I can take them back. I've still got the receipt.'

He cuts off a sliver of tenderloin, chews it slow and ruminant with a look on his face like he's listening intently to something far away coming closer through the trees. He does the same thing with his potato salad, chews one bite and listens close, still trying to track the snap and rustle, but this bite confirms what the last one did: there was nothing there after all. Just the wind shuffling leaves across the dirt, the creak of branches settling under their own heavy weight. Just the dog bringing back her tennis ball.

He swallows and sets his fork down.

'Don't you like it?' I say. He should like it. I know what he likes by now, and I don't cook meals he doesn't like.

'It's fine,' he says.

'The potato salad'll be better tomorrow. I started it too late, it didn't have long enough to sit.'

'It's real good.' He folds his hands in his lap.

'If you're doing this to make a point, you've made it. I don't care how you eat. You can buy a whole new set of fine china and eat off that if you want. I don't care.'

'You're still mad about that?' he says.

'It looks like you are.'

'I ain't mad anymore. I ain't thought about that in weeks. I just ain't hungry.'

I don't believe that for a second. He's doing this to be spiteful, I know he is.

'You shouldn't starve yourself just because you're embarrassed for me to watch you eat,' I say. 'I don't care if your hands shake.'

'I just ain't hungry.'

'You are too hungry. You haven't eaten a full meal in weeks and you've just been outside moving around for two hours. You have to be hungry.'

'I'll build back up to it,' he says. 'My stomach's probably shrunk from being out of commission so long.'

'It hasn't been out of commission. You haven't been using it.'

He shrugs.

'There's a difference.'

He wipes the corner of his mouth and waits politely for me to finish my meal. I don't like how good-natured he's acting. It's not like him.

'The tenderloin's perfectly good,' I say. 'There's not a thing wrong with it.'

'Tenderloin?' he says, as if he's never heard the word before in his life. 'Loins that are tender? That don't sound like something we ought to be eating.' He chuckles.

'Stop rambling and eat your dinner.'

He sighs. 'It's just that nothing you cook has any taste anymore.'

'What?'

'You ought to put some salt in it or something.'

'I can't put any more salt in,' I say, and I have

110

to speak real slow to keep my voice under control, 'because you have high blood pressure. If I put any more salt in, it'll kill you.'

'Well, you'd better do something,' he says, 'and quick.' And chuckles, chuckles as if that's the funniest thing he's ever heard. He gapes at the clock in surprise. 'Good Lord,' he says, 'it's eight o'clock already,' and he takes himself to the living room and turns on a rerun of *Win, Lose, or Paw*. On the screen, three women are faking heart attacks to see whose dog can dial nine-one-one fastest on an oversized foam keypad.

'How the time does fly,' he says to himself, or to Daisy, as he settles in his chair. I go back to the kitchen and saw off another bite of tenderloin already turning cold. The knife clinks against the plate. Between them threads of muscle snap and fray.

The electronic dog's howl they use as a buzzer when your time's up sets Daisy to wailing. She's got a harsh howl, real deep and shrill at the same time, sounds like some endless existential sorrow erupting up out of the earth itself, just using her as its rusty trumpet. She goes on for so long, and Frank doesn't do a thing to hush her up, issues not one word of rebuke, that I walk into the living room to make sure he's okay. And there she is, sitting in the very middle of the room, howling up at the ceiling some awful loss she's trying to sing herself free of, while he watches her and grins.

'I believe we might go on *Win, Lose, or Paw* ourselves,' Frank yells over her. He bends down close. 'What do you think? A hundred thousand

111

dollars'll buy you a whole lot of biscuits.'

She pauses for a second and looks at him, considering this proposition. Then she throws her head back and starts howling again.

'Make her hush up,' I say.

'She's fine,' Frank says. 'She's acclimating herself.'

'How is howling at the ceiling acclimating herself?'

'She's feeling the place out. By the sound of it.'

'She's not a bat,' I say. 'I got her because she was the only quiet one in the place.'

'Looks like she fooled you.'

'The neighbors might hear.'

'Daisy.' He snaps his fingers. 'Hush.' She quiets down and trots over, rubs her head against his dangling hand. The threat of the neighbors never fails.

'I wish she'd been around to dial nine-one-one when you were lying out there in the yard,' I say. 'Maybe they could have got you to the hospital before you lost your mind.' He starts chuckling again. 'I don't know what you think is so funny. Nobody's told a single joke this entire evening.'

He raises his eyebrows, like a recalcitrant teenage boy who doesn't understand why his teacher's so upset by his poor behavior, and stares at the television. Three men are gobbling handfuls of their cat's wet food to see who can eat the most without throwing up.

At least he's out of the bed. That's something. At least he's moving around.

You learn to ask for less and less.

112

10

The day of his mama's funeral was the only time I ever saw her. He found her one night when he got home from my shop, slumped over the kitchen table. We'd been together four years by then. He was going to graduate from college in the spring.

'She's dead,' he said over the phone, in a calm, consoling voice, as though he was afraid of the carnage this devastating news might wreak on my fragile constitution.

'Who's dead?'

'Mama.'

'Oh,' I said.

'They think it was a heart attack.' His voice wobbled a little. 'She was peeling potatoes. Had the knife still in her hand and all the parings heaped up in her lap. I thought the house was on fire when I first got there. From the smell of it. The water she was going to boil them in had evaporated away. The bottom of the pot was all crusty and burnt.'

'Who peels potatoes before they boil them?' I said. 'All the flavor cooks right out.'

The silence on his end took the form of a strange, mechanical clicking over the line.

'Are you all right?'

'No,' he said. 'I don't believe I am.'

'I'm sorry,' I said.

I tried my best to mean it.

He was so busy making the arrangements, and greeting his oversized family, and writing a florid, sentimental obituary about what a fine Christian woman and loving but firm mother she was that I didn't see him for the next two days, which was really for the best — the less sorrow I had to feign, the better — but he snuck me into the church the morning of her funeral, a couple hours before the service, told the preacher he needed some time alone with her. I didn't want to go — I hate funerals — but he sounded desperate.

'You ought to meet her,' he said early that morning, over the phone again. I was leaned against the wall of my kitchenette, half asleep, the phone wedged between my shoulder and face. 'At least once.'

I met him at the heavy double doors of the church, wearing his gray suit and tie and far too much menthol cologne. He never wore cologne, it smelled medicinal on him. We hugged and quickly let each other go, stood quietly for a minute on the pulpy boards of the porch. It was a clear, cool morning at the end of September. A cold front had rumbled through in the night, left its rain behind in wide, deep puddles that reflected the first autumn sky of the year, the kind of blue so startling children demand a reason. They reflected the trees that rose out of them, too, as if those trees had no roots but reached with their branches as deep into a sky at our feet as they did into the one above our heads, as if you could take one step and fall forever upwards. The world was a bright, strange

114

place, I thought, where none of us belonged.

The church looked from the outside like a glorified shanty, with white paint peeling in curls from clapboard walls that a wind of no great strength could have blown over, but inside, the dark wood floorboards were oiled and polished till they shone, as if the flood had swept beneath the doors of the church and gathered into pools: as if our feet would step through them, crashing down to the murky bottom beneath, and darken the cuffs of our pants.

She was tall and sturdy, like him, barely fit into her coffin. It looked like the thing was trying to squeeze her out. The hands folded on her chest were big, with thick, blunt fingers like a man's, and she had a man's stern, set face but a head of lustrous gray curls so delicate and well-coiffed they looked out of place on the rest of her. She must have tended them real carefully; they had that sort of graceful, natural curve achieved only by painstaking daily labor. It was downright pitiful, though, the job they'd done on her. They'd caked her in makeup, painted her lips and cheekbones with color more vivid than I've ever seen on anybody living, and still her face sagged on both sides toward the brocade pillow, looked like wax melting. I could've done a better job myself.

'Looks just like she's asleep,' Frank said, his voice wavering, uncertain. He squeezed my hand, quick and furtive, and let it go. 'Don't she?'

It's all one big waste of time, embalming. A good professional mount will last you a thousand times longer than pumping somebody's veins full of formaldehyde and painting them over with makeup will. Formaldehyde might keep them for a while, but you've still got to put them in the ground sooner or later, and soon as water gets into that coffin — and it will, no matter how hard you try to keep it out, no matter how many nesting Russian dolls of caskets and vaults you wrap around somebody, water always finds its way in — it washes the chemicals right out and the body starts to decompose so vehement and rapid and anaerobic you'd think it was making up for the late start. You ought to just skip all the moaning and crying, get them in the ground a little quicker, and save yourself the trouble.

And not once in my life have I seen an embalmed corpse that looked as if the person was sleeping. I don't know why everybody insists on saving that.

'She does,' I said. 'She really does. She looks just right.'

He leaned down and kissed her forehead. I wanted to squeeze his hand; I wanted to wrap my arms around him and hold him up. Instead we stood there for a long while, our arms hanging heavy at our sides, and I waited for something to happen, for some moment of recognition where I would see the two of them there, see the parts of her that were in him, and understand why he loved her so terribly, when even I might love her for a moment. The light undulated with clouds crossing a window; the floor rippled under our feet. Then he went home, to ride back over with his family, and I sat in my car and waited for the service to begin. It was the last one I ever went to. I didn't sign the condolence book, and I sat in the back pew, with three or four empty ones between me and the aggrieved, so I wouldn't have to speak to anyone. Her family had come up from Kinston, and they filled most of the place, but I could see Frank in the front row, between two women who looked unsettlingly like her, his blond head bent low but still stuck up above everyone else's. He was hunched forward, with his elbows on his knees, like he was about to be sick.

The preacher, a bald man with a goatee and a shiny, bulbous forehead, all of which left me with the impression that he would murder children if given much of a chance, availed himself of this opportunity to remind us that the Resurrection promised us in Scripture — I've always hated how they call it that, as if it's the only thing that's ever been written, or even the best — was not one of the spirit alone but truly one of the body, and urged us not to forget, or, worse, deliberately ignore this fact: that the true believer, he who has faith in the sacrifice and resurrection of Our Lord Jesus Christ and the salvation therein must also have faith that on the Day of Judgment — you could hear the breathy emphasis of the capital letters in his speech — when He returns to this troubled world, the body of this Fanchon Kirkman Clifton, and here he pointed down from his pulpit to her, with her man-hands folded atop her bosom and pink chalk smeared across her cheeks, this body, he said, pointing, this very body now laid out before us shall rise

117

whole at one uttered word of command from Our Lord. The earth covering her hallowed grave shall rend, and the lid of her coffin swing wide, and this body before us rise and meet her soul in the skies above, to be whole again for all eternity, never to be torn asunder.

A few women nodded and murmured their approval. Frank was still bent over, head hung, perfectly still. I was bored out of my mind.

And those of you who would see Fanchon again, he said, those of you who would see Fanchon again must believe this, as she did, must believe that this wracked, lifeless husk you see before you shall be made again pure and vibrant, if ye shall sit beside it at the throne of the Lord. Let there be no grief in your hearts at this parting; let there be only faith, and fear of thine own unworthiness, that such parting may be but temporary. For bodies, he said, bodies are nothing but seeds tilled into the earth, out of which, after their long germination, they shall uncurl their shoots, and bend toward the sun, and blossom.

★　★　★

He's working on getting his arm down the sleeve of his jacket. He goes out to the cemetery every Easter and Thanksgiving so he can clean up the family graves, rake away the dry leaves scattered over them and scrub the streaks of black and green grime from the face of each stone and dig the pollen from their names, where it gathers yellow in the bottoms of the letters. I don't usually go along, but now, after I've gotten up at six in the morning, in those last moments before dawn when everything in the dim, jumbled room looks made of rain and cloud, to roast the turkey and bake the green-pea casserole — he likes green peas better than green beans, so what kind of casserole do I make? — and get the gravy thickening on the stove, get the cranberry sauce and deviled eggs congealing in the fridge and the pumpkin pie cooling on the counter, and he's listened to a bite of each one and set his fork politely down, after I've cleaned up the whole mess by myself, which takes nearly two hours, and gotten his grave-scrubbing brush and bucket and rag from the closet, and run water into the rag so he doesn't have to go all the way down to the spigot by the caretaker's shed, and rummaged the artificial flowers out of their drawer in the hallway and finally managed to hobble myself into the living room, half-crippled with the ache in my back, he can't quite manage to get his own arm into his own sleeve. He's got one on, but he can't twist himself around enough to shove his arm into the other, even when I hold it out for him.

'Here.' I tug the sleeve off his arm and hold the jacket spread wide open and upside down in front of him. He walks forward, both arms held stiff straight out, and slides them into the sleeves.

'You've got it on the front of me,' he says. 'And it's upside down.'

'Lift your arms,' I say.

He raises them wriggling over his head. I tug

the hem until the jacket falls into place around him.

'Well, I'll be,' he says. 'Just like magic.'

Daisy follows us out the door and waits patiently while he gets himself situated in the car. He has a lot of trouble with it, has to grab the open door with one hand and the doorframe with the other and slowly lower his rear end to the passenger seat — I do all the driving now, which I thought he'd resent, but he doesn't seem to mind — and those last six inches he drops through so hard the seat sounds like it's giving way beneath him. Some spring reverberates loudly in panic and hurt. Then he pulls his legs in, one at a time, grabbing each knee with both hands to help it bend. The glue between the ceiling and its fabric has come undone in several places, so the gray cloth hangs down in sagging bubbles. It brushes the top of my head, but it falls down over his eyes so he's got to lean forward to get out from under it if he wants to see much.

Daisy hops onto his lap, lands so heavy she knocks him back in the seat. She's gotten a whole lot fatter in just the few weeks she's been here. He gives her a treat for waking up in the morning and a treat for going to bed at night, a treat when we leave the house and a treat for still being there when we come back, a treat for eating all her dinner or a treat for her self-restraint if she's so full of them she can't bear to look at her bowl. And you know you've given a dog that fat far too much food if she doesn't want to eat any more of it. I can't even open the cabinet her biscuits are in to get a can of beans without her stumping in there from the living room looking desperate and starved. She knows that cabinet from all the others, by the particular sound of its opening, or by the sound's particular point of origin. I don't have the heart to tell him to stop, though. The only way he knows to treat a dog is to spoil it.

She clambers over into the backseat and rides perched there on the very edge, pitched precariously forward so she can rest her chin on Frank's shoulder and look over it out the windshield. She loves riding in the car, scampers back and forth between her spot at his shoulder and the back passenger window, gunky and smudged with nose prints. Her hot breath pulsates clouded on the glass. Frank rolls it down so she can sniff the crisp, dusty smell of dead leaves. They're a month past their peak by now, most of them flared out and smoldering, or just embers crumbling to ash and falling to the ground every time the wind tries to stoke them. She stretches her head out far as she can, squinting against the buffeting air. She never falls down, even when I hit the brakes, has the best balance of any dog I ever saw. Bears down on Frank's shoulder with her chin to steady herself every time we turn, and uses that broken tail for support, presses it flat across the seat with the tip of it up the seat's back, like a bracket. Being fat helps, too. It's hard for any force to sling around such a great mass.

Frank shifts in his seat, spreads his legs wide, trying to get comfortable.

'We ought to think about getting ourselves a new car,' I say.

'This one runs just fine,' he says, which is the exact same thing he said about his old truck, even after it started coughing black smoke every time he started it. Thank God they started picking up the trash, or he'd still be driving that thing to the dump, burning oil and breathing in the fumes.

'I feel like I'm closed up in a coffin in here.' I bat away the loose lining over my head. 'And you nearly fall down every time you get in. We need something that sits higher up.'

'It is hard on my hips,' he concedes. 'And my knees.' They're folded up almost to his armpits.

'What we need is one of those big sport things. An all-terrain vehicle.'

'All-terrain vehicle,' he says. 'I like the sound of that.'

'The Schiller dealership's having an after-Thanksgiving sale. Maybe I'll go by tomorrow.'

'Schiller?' He raises his eyebrows so high he's lucky they don't fly off his forehead. 'You think I'm going to buy a German car?'

'Every single consumer report that comes out says they're the best. And it would save us a fortune in gas money. They're very efficient.'

'I ain't forgot what they did,' he says. 'They were efficient at that, too.'

'The war's been over for nearly sixty years. The men you fought are too old to have a thing to do with building these cars.'

'I'm not too old to build cars,' he mutters. 'I could build cars if I very well pleased.'

'They're our ally now. Our friend.'

'Maybe they're your ally. You never bashed one of their heads in with a rock.'

'And I'm sure they've all been chomping at the bit for their chance to take revenge on Frank Clifton. I'm sure they're waiting in the factory right now with bated breath for the order to plant a bomb in your new sedan.'

He crosses his arms and looks at me like I'm a traitor.

I shouldn't have said anything. I don't know why I even tried. It's only American-made cars for us: he hates the Japanese almost as much as he hates the Germans.

'You bashed one of their heads in with a rock?' I say.

He shrugs. 'That ain't the worst I did.'

The graveyard's the biggest one in the city, and one of the oldest, right smack in the middle of downtown in the shadows of the tall, shiny office buildings and the banks with their big digital clocks always flashing above the doors so nobody forgets the time, pressed against a busy four-lane road that runs all the way from the sagging, gutted factories on this end of town to the rolling cow pastures on the other, and landscaped such that the ground of the graveyard sits a full six feet higher than the road, with an old stone retaining wall that curves and bulges just a sidewalk's width from the curb to hold back the dirt. The graves run right down to it, and some of the tombstones, the oldest ones with their inscriptions so worn away and streaked with grime that the names of the dead have been completely erased, lean over it toward the street, tilting and crowded against each other like crooked teeth and pushing their dirt against the wall, bowing it out so far that a crack runs clear down it and rends the moss that's grown on the stone.

'Would you look at that?' I say. 'That wall's going to give right out. Spill dirt and tombstones all into the street. Or through somebody's windshield.'

'Shoddy craftsmanship,' Frank says, shaking his head.

We turn into the cemetery and drive slow along the narrow road that winds through it. It's wide and vast, all rolling hills and tombstones lined up one after the other, so much that the openness and repetition of it starts you to feeling it's one hill, even one row of graves replicated over and over until the road bounds its multiplication. Someday soon they'll run out of space — from the looks of that wall, they already have — but by then, I guess, the residents of the oldest plots will have fallen completely apart. They'll pull those rotten teeth from the earth and throw new people in the sockets as if the old ones had never been anything but soil. That's what I'd do, anyway.

On the radio they've already got Christmas carols playing, some new pop starlet embellishing 'Have Yourself a Merry Little Christmas' with so many trills and runs and arpeggios you can't even pick out the soft, sad melody they're supposed to be emerging from.

'You'd think they could let us get through

Thanksgiving Day before they started pushing Christmas carols on us,' I say.

'I like Christmas carols,' Franks says. 'Might cheer things up around here.'

'You think things need cheering up?'

'I think you need cheering up.'

'I'm full of cheer,' I say.

He hums along with the radio that slow, mournful current the singer's trying to make us forget, moving steadily and softly forward into that someday soon when we all will be together: if the fates allow.

★   ★   ★

The cars of the funeral procession wound across town, from church to graveyard. I rolled my windows down to enjoy the afternoon. I could have gone home then, I figured I'd fulfilled my faithful duty, but I soldiered on and stood at the edge of the mourners and did my best to look somber. Under the tent there were three large stones, above his daddy and brother and sister, and beside his daddy the open grave, and beside that two more plots, one for Frank and one for his wife, waiting for the shovel to break them open. His mama bought them all when Harvey and Iris died. Graves were going fast back then, and the proprietor said those particular spaces were hot commodities, in high demand. Had to sell her mother's heirloom jewelry to get them all while they lasted.

The hearse backed up to the pit so fast and close, its tires pressing runny mud from the dirt like juice from pulp, I thought it might fall right in. The funeral director opened the back doors and jostled the casket halfway out. It was a nice, dark mahogany, lacquered smooth. Frank leaned over it, his face tight, as if against real, physical pain. I wanted to ache for him, to hurt for him. I wanted to feel what he felt, and I arranged my face into all the proper forms, the lowered brow and clenched jaw of grief, but I couldn't find those things in me, no matter how hard I tried. Inside my chest, something folded itself shut, like a bird drawing its wings in close, about to take flight.

He placed his hand on the coffin lid. Inside the wood, dark, shining fingers reached up and pressed their palm to his.

Along with five other pallbearers — they'd tried to convince him to let someone else do it, but he insisted — he carried the casket over the grave by a fine silken rope tied to one of the handles, then lowered it into the earth. All the others did it carefully, as they'd obviously been coached, hand over hand, but Frank let the cord slide through his clenched fist. The sun was bright, and the air was cool and crisp, the clouds set impossibly high in the sky, and the light ran in a gold liquid line along the coffin's edge as it descended, and as the pallbearers bowed their heads, muttered a prayer, and let the tasseled ends of their ropes go, I felt gravity open wide, felt it loosen and flatten the knotted curve of space so that it stretched out in one vast expanse, and any move you made would carry you through it in the straight line of inertia, effortlessly and endlessly forward and up and out in the direction you meant to go.

How easy it seemed it would be then to live unfettered, and open to the world, and in it. I hadn't even known that was something I wanted.

As the bereaved began to disperse, I hurried to my car before somebody could greet me. From inside it, through the bird droppings my windshield wipers had smeared across the glass, I watched Frank shake the hands of his comforters, smile and take their condolences and tell them how good it was to see them, how much it would have meant to his mother. I'd never seen him with other people before. The chief of police was there in full regalia, out of respect for Frank's daddy. Frank talked to him a long time, listening thoughtfully and nodding and standing up unnaturally tall and straight, and at the end the chief of police held him out at arm's length and squeezed his shoulders as if to fortify him somehow.

He told jokes, and laughed, and gently ribbed the children, and appeared to genuinely enjoy himself, and when most of the family and friends had either gone home, or driven back to his house for the luncheon the Women's Auxiliary was busy spreading over every available surface, or walked off through the cemetery to pay respects to their own dead while they were in the respect-paying mood, three young men, strong and broad-shouldered like Frank, in suits they must have had since they were teenage boys, with constricted arms and wrists jutting past their cuffs, ambled over to him. Some part of him seemed to open when he saw them, to throw his chest wide. He looked younger all of a sudden. He looked happy. One clapped him on the back, and another, with a headful of curly red hair, tossed his arm across Frank's shoulders and left it there, hand dangling loose, with absolute ease and familiarity. They closed around him the way brothers would, with a brother's combination of tenderness and bravado, and herded him toward a car. He glanced at me over his shoulder, with a muddled expression I couldn't understand, and let them sweep him away.

★ ★ ★

Daisy jumps out the window. It happens so fast I don't know what it is she saw — I don't even see her do it — but all of a sudden, with a wild scrabbling commotion, she's not looking over Frank's shoulder anymore but landing on the road behind us in my rear-view mirror, so hard it splays her legs out from under her and smashes her belly on the asphalt. I hit the brakes. Tentatively she gets back to her feet, but she stays where she is, quaking in shock and bewilderment, and looking around like she, too, has no idea what happened or how she got there.

'Is she all right?' Frank says, panicked, trying to twist around in his seat.

'Open your door,' I say. He does, and I put the car in reverse and roll it backwards.

'Careful,' he snaps. 'Don't run over her.'

'I'm not going to run over her.'

She's still standing in that same spot when she slides into view through his open door, legs shaking, looking as stunned and ashamed as a dog can when it's already forgot what it did to be ashamed of. Frank pats his lap. She hesitates before she leaps onto it. He turns her on her back and examines her belly, brushes the dirt and bits of broken acorn from its thin fur and dabs the scraped skin with the sleeve of his jacket. Her belly's pink and spotted like a cow's. Gives off a warm, mulled smell. He takes each of her legs and guides it through a wide range of movement, watching for twitches of pain. Daisy looks like she's receiving a therapeutic massage, closes her eyes and lets her head rest on the pillow of his knee, tongue lolling out of her mouth.

'She's so fat she probably didn't even feel the impact,' I say. 'I'm sure it couldn't make it all the way through to her bones.'

'Quiet,' he says. 'She can hear you.'

'I just wish you'd feed yourself half as much as you feed her.'

He pats her full belly. 'Tight as a tick,' he says with evident satisfaction.

She climbs up on him, her front paws on his shoulders, and sticks her head over his shoulder, back out the window. I hit the button to raise it. She keeps her nose extended through the shrinking crack until the very last moment, pulls it in right before it gets caught. He holds one paw to his nose and breathes deeply.

'I do love the smell of dogs' paws,' he says.

'You're going to get sick from their germs, pressing them up against your mucous membranes like that.'

'Smells like the earth,' he says.

'I'd appreciate it if you'd keep those thoughts to yourself from now on.'

We've got maybe forty-five minutes of light left. They've planted some trees alongside the drive since the last time we were here, little bare saplings. The hood of the car slips under the long shadows of their skinny, naked branches and pries them up from the road, one after the other, each one scraping a little easier than the last across the metal. The moon hangs barely visible in the sky, a faint projection of something more real.

All his family is along one edge of the cemetery, near the back, by some old twisting oaks whose roots heave stones out of the earth now and then. I pull halfway off the drive onto the grass beside his parents. I don't think we're on top of them. Frank grabs the top edge of his open door with one hand and the doorframe with the other and tries four times before he succeeds in slow-heaving himself out of his seat. Daisy promptly marches over and makes a rainbow on a stranger's grave, then kicks up the grass covering them to mask her scent.

I set the flowers and cleaning bucket on the hood of the car and wait leaned against it. Frank's plot is laid out in front of us, looking like any other stretch of lawn. He wants a real military funeral, the bugler bugling 'Taps' up its rusty, somber peak of mourning. I suspect it's just so there'll be somebody at the thing besides me, the honor guard to fire their rifle salute that I alone or no one will hear. When they fold the flag back from his coffin and into its triangle, I don't expect they'll lay it across my waiting arms and thank me for his service. They'll send it off to some next of kin he never met, who won't know until they receive it that he's dead, or that he ever lived.

Even when he's gone, and left me the house and all his money, the story to anyone who asks is that we were very dear friends.

I always thought I'd be the one to die first. I used to worry about it, didn't want him having to see yet another body, but I suppose I don't need to fret about that anymore. Most likely the postman will spy my rotting corpse through a part in the curtains when he can't jam any more bills and advertisements into the mailbox. By then, Daisy may have begun eating me. And I'm sure nobody will be at my funeral. I always said I wanted to be cremated, make some space in this world for something else, but the truth is they can shoot me from a cannon at the county fair if they like. I won't be around to care one way or the other.

Or maybe we'll finally get lucky and go together. Tragic accidents are happening all the time.

Frank leans beside me and stares at his daddy's marker, his eyes just a little squinted like there's something in it he's trying to see but can't quite make out yet. I know now he can't get down on his hands and knees and scrub the markers clean, but he could at least brush the bird droppings from their tops. He could at least wipe the leaf dust from his parents' names.

I pull the flowers out of their plastic bag and fluff them a little. I bought them on closeout sale last spring. They practically had to pay me to take them. They're real pretty, though, blue hydrangea heads with some deep orange daisies between them, and some green and white sprays of baby's breath here and there, even if they are a little smushed from being shoved in the drawer. And they smell funny, like damp old carpet. Everything you put in that drawer starts to smell like damp old carpet after a while.

'Will you hurry up?' I say. 'I didn't come all the way out here because I thought it would be nice to spend my Thanksgiving in a graveyard. Get to work.'

Daisy turns her solemn, sorrowful face to me in silent rebuke. Frank crosses his arms on his chest and looks troubled. His shoulders, without moving an inch, seem to buckle under some great weight, the way they do when he's mad about something but wants me to have to draw it out of him.

'What's wrong?' I say.

He gives me an exasperated stare. How is it, this stare asks, that he's managed to live his entire adult life with such an oblivious fool?

'You'd better go on and say it. Before you sulk away the little bit of daylight we've got left.'

Daisy sits slumped against his mama's stone and starts licking her privates. Makes a real loud, wet clicking sound. Frank and I stand here

132

listening to her for about five minutes, until I can't take it anymore and go and shoo her away, knock the droppings off the stones myself with a twig, wipe their faces with the damp rag, collect the faded roses from the urns, the edges of their petals frayed, and replace them with the hydrangeas, which still look crumpled no matter how much I fluff them, lean lopsided over one edge of the urn like they're about to fall out.

The wind picks up, blows his jacket open and his shirt against him. It molds itself to his jutting ribs. They keep showing clearer and clearer under the skin, like fossils being slowly excavated, the years of dust and dirt that cover them carefully brushed away, a little at a time.

'This ain't a graveyard,' he says.

'It sure looks like one to me.'

'A graveyard,' he says, with the kind of voice you'd use to explain the most basic facts to a class of exceptionally dull school-children, 'is a yard full of graves. The yard is part of a church. It's a churchyard. The yard, of a church, full of graves. That's a graveyard. *This* is a cemetery. A cemetery stands alone. It don't belong to nobody but the dead.'

'You're a regular poet,' I say.

'And I didn't even know it.' He chuckles, and just as quick as it rumbled in, his bad mood disintegrates.

I throw the rag and the old flowers in the bucket and the bucket onto the backseat. It's getting dark, and it's getting cold. My fingers are stiffening. 'Well? Is there anything you want to do? Or can we go home now?'

He makes a face like he's thinking about it real hard, that sort of face nobody ever makes when they're actually thinking hard about something. Then he slowly walks forward, with both hands shoved in his pockets and shaking wild, so it looks like there's a squirrel squirming around in each one. He stands over the graves for a long time, looking down on them, and then he rests one hand on his daddy's marker, his fingers spread wide, and bows his head as if in prayer.

'A tombstone,' he says, 'is the stone that goes on top of your tomb. Holds it shut in case you decide to try climbing out.' He pats the top of it, walks back to the car, and lowers himself in. Daisy follows him closely.

I get myself into the car, turn it on, buckle my seatbelt. Frank leans back in his seat and presses the loose fabric against the ceiling. It sticks there for a second, and he watches his handprint disappear, slow, like it had been pressed into wet sand that fills itself from underneath. The fabric falls loose again.

'What's gotten into you?' I say.

Daisy, curled on his lap, looks up at me in warning without lifting her head.

'Nothing's gotten into me,' he says. 'Besides your turkey.'

'Not nearly enough of it, that's for sure. You're probably delirious from hunger.'

'Delirious?'

'You're not yourself.'

'Don't know who else I could be.'

'Stop joking around. I wish you could be serious for two minutes. Just two minutes. Long enough to act a little solemn at your own parents' graves.'

'It's Thanksgiving,' he says. 'I'm just giving thanks.'

'Thanks for what?'

He makes his thinking face for a long time, then shrugs.

'That's what I thought,' I say. 'And you're going to be giving thanks from the ground beside them pretty soon if you don't start eating something.'

He frowns and leans away from me in his seat, looks out the window at his silhouette pressed flat to the glass, trying to get inside: just his empty shape, no detail or features, nothing within it but dark trees and tombstones. He could lean into it like Narcissus, until he drowned in himself, and never see his face.

I turn the car around, tall grass rustling against its undercarriage. Its headlights scrape the trees' scarred bark, slide bright across the smooth face of a stone. Soon as they sweep away, on down the road, the darkness rushes back in to fill the places they've pushed it out of. This world never will let an empty space exist in peace. Every gap's got to be filled, every hill and valley leveled out. As we turn out of the cemetery and head home, the vast, dark space between here and there funneled through our high beams and beneath our wheels, the bulging, broken wall struggles to hold itself up against the pressure, and all the while gravity's trying to tear it down, and all the while the dirt and bodies behind it strain to break through.

He showed up that afternoon while the sun was still shining, still in his funeral clothes but with his shirt untucked and wrinkled and the jacket left who knows where, looking ragged and red-eyed and exhausted, like he hadn't slept for days, just as I was pulling a deer's cape over the fleshing beam. He leaned in the doorway a long time, then sank into a rickety wooden chair and leaned it back on two legs, his crossed ankles and muddy shoes propped on my work table, and watched in silence as I drew the fleshing knife, a long, barely-curved blade with a wooden handle on each end, light and swift across the hide, skimming away pink flesh in thin, delicate curls from the bluish-gray skin beneath. My whole body moved in rhythm with the blade, back and shoulders rolling as if rowing a boat, and when I'd cleared one strip, I turned the hide on the beam, pulled it tight like stubbled skin over a jaw, so the razor has a flat surface to scrape clean, and started on the next. You've got to get all the meat and fat and flesh off, every little bit, so there's nothing left but skin when you put it in the pickle, just the thinnest, outermost surface. Everything underneath, the real substance, the heft of a thing, you've got to let go, and use your memory to recreate it as best you can, just a little streamlined, and a little smaller, so you can fit the skin back over it without too much trouble.

'Who were those boys?' I said.

'Just some pals from school. We used to play football together.'

'Where'd you go?'

'Downtown. Got a bite to eat. They said I needed a break from old ladies fawning all over me.' His words smelled like juniper and bile.

'Were you drinking?'

He considered this a moment.

'I may have had some gin,' he said.

'How much?'

'Can't remember.' His words sounded loose, slipped from his mouth before his lips had time to shape their edges. 'I do know that I've thrown up twice.'

'Jesus Christ,' I said. He gave me a disapproving look. 'You didn't go to the luncheon?'

He shook his head. Sweat was beaded all along his hairline.

'The women of the church will be scandalized.'

'So will my aunts. But I don't care. I don't. I don't care.' He sounded surprised by this.

With a smaller knife, I pared peelings from the deer's face: the thin edge of his lip, the smooth insides of his cheeks. 'You have to be careful,' I said. 'If you shave too much away, the whiskers all fall out.'

Frank nodded.

'You acted like you were real close,' I said. 'With those boys.'

'We were.'

'You never talk about them.'

'I don't hardly see them anymore.'

137

'Why not?'

He shrugged. I held the face up to the sun, setting in one of the tiny, tempered windows high in the cinderblock wall. It burned pink through each eyelid, red inside the tiny, empty blood vessels visible in the skin like fossils in mud, the ridged spines of extinct animals. Not even bones: just the feathery imprints they left in the sand.

'Well,' I said. 'It was nice of them to come.'

'I want us to move someplace,' he said.

'What?'

'I want us to move someplace.'

I draped the hide across its beam and sat on the edge of the table facing him. His tattoos showed dark through the thin white sleeves of his shirt, like twigs and leaves under the surface of a frozen pond. The fresh-leather smell of his shoes mingled with the damp sourness of the sweat inside them, and the cuff of one pant leg was caught halfway up his calf. I twisted the hairs on his shin together, let them go, and watched them unwind. They held their shape in a loose peak.

'Not too far,' he said. 'Just — outside town someplace.'

'You're drunk.'

He gave me an exasperated, self-righteous look. I opened the fingers of his right hand. White, blistering welts had risen from the pink rope burn across his palm.

'Wouldn't that be nice?' he said. 'Our own little place out in the country?'

'What about your house? You love that house.'

'There's too many people around,' he said in

disgust, swinging his hand as if to knock them away. 'Too many families.'

'You like people,' I said. 'You like families.'

'But you don't.'

'It's not that I — Let's talk about it later. When you're in your right mind.'

'They could put us in jail for this, you know.' He said it real casual, like it was just an interesting little bit of trivia he'd learned.

'Is that what the chief of police was telling you?'

He laughed wearily, sadly. 'The chief of police was telling me what a fine, upstanding young man I'd turned out to be. How proud my mama and daddy were up in heaven.' He shook his head. 'They could lock us away for sixty years. It's a crime. We're criminals.'

'We're not criminals.'

He raised his eyebrows to indicate he wished he could be as blissfully ignorant of the laws of our state as I was.

I twisted a whole mountain chain of hair down his shin; I smoothed the whole chain flat.

'Didn't you think that preacher was a little low-class?' I said. 'Using your mama's death as an opportunity to spout his own dogma?'

'She would've liked it.' He laughed, and leaned back in his chair, and stared up at the nubbly popcorn plaster of the ceiling. He ran his hands down his face, as if trying to wake himself.

'I wanted to tell her,' he said. 'About you. I did. I know you think I — '

'It doesn't matter.'

'It does. It does matter. I wanted her to know

me. I wanted her to know I was happy. That she'd done all right. But I couldn't — I never — '

'You were home in time for dinner,' I said. 'Every night. Just like you promised her.'

He sat forward quickly, the chair's front legs clacking loudly on the tile. He pressed his face to my stomach and sobbed great, heavy sobs that wracked his chest and shook his shoulders until I thought they would shake him apart; he wrapped his arms around my waist and clutched me so tight it hurt. I brushed the hair from his temple, and I kissed his forehead. His tears soaked hot through my shirt.

I think I loved him then most of all: drunk and crying in those quiet, empty hours, while the evening light grew heavy, filled with copper, and sank to the floor.

★ ★ ★

And when we're gone, nobody will remember any of it. Nobody will see our photos and marvel that we, too, were young once; nobody will wonder about the things we never told them. It will be as if none of it ever happened. I wish, sometimes, I do wish that I could have believed that old preacher, that the Judgment Day would come, and the righteous would rejoice and the guilty would suffer, and Gabriel would toot his horn and all the bodies of the dead would rise from their thousand years' slumber, clean and naked and pure as Adam in the garden, fingers not even sullied from clawing open their coffin lids, and those who'd been dead so long that even their coffins and vaults had crumbled would find their hair pulled in threads from the trees whose roots they had nourished, unraveling their bark, that corpses would burrow their way up from the earth like cicadas and swarm to meet their souls in the air, that the bodies of the dead would clot the sky until the sun was sealed over with their flesh and left the world in darkness.

But I've lived too long to believe foolishness like that, and I've seen too many living things disappear from this world to believe that anything, anything at all will survive of me. No, the best I can hope for is that some child, ten or twenty years from now, will see a dusty deer raising its head in a shadowed corner of his grandfather's house and think, for one moment, that it's living.

I turn on the Christmas carols, as loud as I can bear.

11

We drove for weeks that fall along the narrow country roads outside town, looking for houses we'd seen in realty pamphlets, sometimes long after dark when the trees stretched into an endless blur alongside the car, out of which I could pull one trunk at a time if I picked it at a certain point precisely halfway between the window and the unfolding darkness at the furthest edge of the headlights, sifted it up and out so it held itself within the borders of its bark, and turned my head with it as it slid past and fell away behind us. But as soon as I let my concentration drift or my eyes go fuzzy, even for a moment, it melted irretrievable back into the long smear of bark and leaf. The FOR SALE sign at the end of the dirt driveway flickered white between them, and when we slowed the car, when we stopped with the headlights turned on high and shining up the drive, the commingled trunks and muddled branches separated themselves into individual hickories and oaks, dogwoods and pines, so many that you couldn't see the house any more than when they were all smudged together. The driveway curved off behind them and disappeared.

We inquired about and visited the house separately, days apart from each other. It had been a hunting retreat for some crazy timber baron who may or may not have hanged himself in the woods. We never could get a clear answer on that one, but Frank bought it, and the land surrounding it, with a GI Bill loan and the money he got from selling his mama's house to an old philosophy professor and his nice young wife.

We both thought it was a little too small, and that the rooms inside it didn't quite fit together, as if they'd all been stolen from other homes, other lives. But it was a good forty-five minutes from town and a good mile from the next house, and we thought we'd make it bigger, fix it up, redecorate it so the rooms all looked the same, tear down the wood paneling and paint everything light, make it all wide and open. I drew the plans on drafting paper so thin it seemed the letters and numbers, no matter how light you sketched them, would fall right through. I loved the straight lines, the precision of the angles. We were going to knock out the whole back wall of the house, so the hallway floor, instead of running into the bathroom, would unroll across the backyard, with the bath and a guest bedroom on one side and a dining room on the other, attached to the kitchen with no door between them, just a big open archway where the window looks over the sink, and at the end of the hall, stretching along the back of the house, a screened-in porch where we would sit every night after dinner, looking out on the yard.

And the most important thing was those trees, anyway. Later, when the Missile Crisis was on and everybody was scrambling around digging bomb shelters in their backyards and stockpiling canned goods in their reinforced basements and determining the best place to crouch in order to shield themselves, terrified that the end of the world would fall from the sky while we slept and with a single squeal and a flash of light wipe us clean from the earth, leave it smooth and gleaming as ice, or else fall in irradiated snow over everything, Frank and I weren't scared. We thought the shadows of the trees would shade us from the obliterating brightness; their leaves and boughs, we thought, would cradle the fallout high over our heads.

* * *

Soon as we'd settled in, over his Christmas recess, he walked through the woods to look for trees that had fallen, whose roots had lost their grip on the slippery soil, and dead limbs with big, spongy silver scales and soft bark that crumbled away from the wood underneath when you ran your hands over them. The trunks he sawed into segments, the limbs he piled atop them in the wheelbarrow, precarious and high, though somehow, impossibly, their branches managed to tangle and hold on to one another, so not a twig fell loose though the whole pile shifted and swayed. He split them in an old rotten stump that stood thigh-high in the yard. Insects were forever carrying out its insides, trickled shining down the wrinkles of its bark until what was left of it rose in craggy spires, black and gray and crumbling as ash, around a desiccated pit just deep enough to jam a log into upright and to catch the halves as their strands separated along the maul. He did it for hours sometimes, for entire winter afternoons, split log after log and stacked them against the house, covered over with a tarp in case the wind blew rain under the eaves, until the dry skin on his knuckles cracked and bled, and my fingers couldn't tell which parts of his shoulders were muscle and which were bone.

He never did have the patience to let them cure long enough, tried to burn them when they hadn't been split but a month earlier, so it took longer to evaporate out enough moisture that they'd catch than they actually burned. In the evenings that first winter, when the walls were still bare, he sat on the floor in front of the cast-iron wood stove, studying and drinking coffee while he stuffed logs onto a bed of burning newspaper that turned black as the words it unwound as it shriveled, the letters spilling out of themselves, soaking the pages. They didn't deliver that far out, of course, and we wouldn't have let them if they did. I picked up the evening edition in town before I came home every night.

He drank his coffee the most laborious way I'd ever seen, poured a splash from his cup into the saucer, then held the saucer to his lips and blew carefully to cool it. The coffee rippled, lapped up just to the porcelain edge but never spilled over, and then he tipped the saucer and slurped the coffee right off, jumping every time a loud crack rang in the stove as a pocket of water vapor heated and burst free, splitting the grain that had

145

been closed around it, wrenching open the tree's rings. It seemed like such a waste: all that work, all those years of rain and sun and slow growth, and it all amounted to a couple hours of light and warmth. The heat never even made it out of the den — we still had to swaddle ourselves up just to walk to the bathroom, and pile blankets and quilts heavy as six feet of dirt atop us in the bed — but he sat there for hours feeding it, didn't seem to mind at all, perfectly content to prod page after page into the fire until it could latch onto the logs, while everything that had happened the day before, and the day before that, and the day before that, dissolved into the white-noise hiss of water leaving wood.

★ ★ ★

That spring he graduated, and instead of applying for the police force, or for any job at all that might justify four years of college education and a degree in American History purchased for him by the American Taxpayer, he got a job in the denim plant, unloading seventy-five-pound spools of thread from the truck that brought them over from the spinners and carrying them to the dyeing racks, where he heaved each one onto its spindle. It was only temporary, he said. Just until he could find something better. Big, burly men ten years younger than him, football champions and weightlifters just out of high school, routinely had heart attacks on the mill floor even in winter, it was so stuffy and hot in there, and in summer they were always fainting

146

like society women overcome at the utterance of a profanity. But Frank, after he'd picked them up and set them down in a chair with a paper cup of water from the cooler, just kept on going back and forth between the dock and the racks, the rolls clutched to his chest and his shirt slung ever wetter and heavier from his shoulders, slapping against his sides. Never even rolled up his sleeves. His cuffs clasped his wrists like manacles.

We were real careful. We never went anywhere together, not to the store or out to eat or on vacation, not after that first time. I got all my mail at the shop, and had it listed as my place of residence until I retired, and Frank kept correspondence with his aunts only through a post office box, told them he was doing fine, just fine, and conveniently forgot to respond when they invited him down for a visit, or said how much they'd love to come up and see the new homestead. I learned to distinguish the grumble of his truck on the gravel, the particular speed and pitch of it, from all others, from insurance salesmen and hunters wanting to inquire about deer on the property and other strangers who knocked on our door rarely but still far too often for comfort, so I could huddle in the hallway and pretend not to be home. And in the mill men wore out quickly, came and went and were too winded the short while they lasted to make conversation, and Frank kept to himself, read his pulp novels while he ate his lunch, and not a one of them ever knew. No one had ever known with him. Even in the army, even in the showers, surrounded by all those men in various stages of filthiness and nudity, with aching muscles and grass stains on their knees and the puddle over the clogged drain turning milky with soap as it widened toward their feet, nobody ever knew. Not the slightest inkling. He always prided himself on that.

The secret, he said, was that you had to look a little. Not looking was the most suspicious of all. It meant you cared. So you learned to move your eyes over their bodies without really seeing them, he said, to look just long enough and then away: the way you do to look at the sun, real quick, before it can burn a green hole in everything you'd see after.

I was never quite as adept at it. There was some softness in me that betrayed itself in ways so subtle even Frank couldn't tell me exactly what they were. My own customers always looked at me a little askance, even as they brought me their pheasant and their fox, as if there must be something wrong with me to want to render this service they themselves wanted rendered, as if I, too, might secretly be dead as the animals on the wall, and just made up to appear otherwise.

★　★　★

In the years that followed, the stories started appearing in the local paper, sporadic at first, then more and more frequent as we passed the middle of the decade, of men being arrested, sometimes in parks, in seedy bars, in public restrooms, sometimes behind the closed doors of homes, behind hotel curtains. Their names and addresses, their places of work and photographs, were printed alongside the stories. At best, they were fired from their jobs, evicted from their homes, and abandoned by their friends and families. At worst, they were sentenced to prison, or sent to the sanitarium, where they might have electrodes taped all over their bodies, clustered like sores on their privates, to deliver a painful Pavlovian shock every time the image of a naked man was projected on the cinderblock wall, or die from hypothermia in a dark basement after having buckets of ice water thrown on them as part of an experimental and exciting new therapy, or simply be strapped to a table and castrated.

In the psychiatric literature, in the diagnostic manuals, they described the pathological disturbance of *the homosexual*, in Congress they railed against *degenerates, deviants, pederasts, subversives, sodomites, sexual psychopaths*, in the *New York Times* it was *perverts*, it was *unnatural relations*, but for the papers down here, even that was too specific, too close to describing some actual thing. When those men were arrested, it was for *crimes against nature*, as though they'd been caught kicking up a public flower bed. That's how truly unspeakable it was: we didn't have the words.

Now, of course, they're walking around as if it's perfectly normal, now they're 'proud,' now they're marching and chanting and streaming the bright rainbow flag of no nation I've ever

149

heard of, spontaneously strutting out of the waves of California beaches like Venus from the foam of her castrated father's blood in the surf, gazing at their own nakedness in mother-of-pearl hand mirrors while angels and nymphs flutter around trying to get some clothes on them, now they're romping through the streets and cavorting half-naked in leather harnesses, or in milky sequined dresses glittering like nebulae, groping and fondling each other like a bunch of frenzied Bacchae in the midst of tearing Orpheus limb from limb. It's no wonder they're all dying from social disease, acting like that.

Homosexual. That one's still the worst of all. Sounds like another species, a big-skulled, low-browed ancestor of decent men, dragging its knuckles through the dust of evolution.

★ ★ ★

At the end of each summer, he walked the perimeter of the yard, his hands on his hips, and scanned scowling for places where the world tried to squeeze itself through in innocuous glimmers among the leaves, shifting and dimming for no apparent reason, like stars will. To those spots he carried pine saplings from the back of his pickup truck, their root balls wrapped in burlap, got down on his knees, and planted them in the cracks, packing the dirt tight around their slender trunks to hold them firm in just the right spot, where they swelled, slowly spreading their needles, and sealed us off like a splinter the skin's grown over.

12

We're outside, bundled up in our jackets, filling the bird feeders while Daisy paces the fence for deer. Frank reaches up, maneuvers the feeder off the crook in the gutter, and holds it out while I work the top off and pour nyjer thistle, tiny and black like splinters of old, rotten wood, out of an iced tea pitcher and into the long tube, trying to keep the stream lined up with the opening as it wobbles in his hands. Dust drifts through the mesh. It's real fine, so the slivers don't fall out, and it doesn't have any perches, so only the finches and the other little birds are light enough to cling to it and reach their long, thin beaks inside. He stretches his arms overhead to hang the feeder back on its crook, and his rumpled pants fall halfway down his behind before they find some hook of bone to grab on to and keep them from pooling around his ankles. He hauls them up by the belt and holds them around his waist, the way teenage boys on the television who are trying to look tough do.

And I've added more salt. I've added more butter to our rolls and more dip to our barbecue, but it doesn't make a bit of difference. Once in a while he'll snack on some toast, or a bowl of cottage cheese, but every meal I put in front of him of any substance goes entirely untouched. I might as well deposit his Social Security check

151

directly in the trash, the way we throw food away in this house.

'That fashion statement you're making came from prison, you know,' I say. He keeps missing the hook. 'It signifies that you're a rapist.'

'If you were a rapist,' he says, 'you wouldn't be out to signify it to everybody. Then they'd know to watch out.'

'You need a new belt. Or some new pants. Before you moon the whole neighborhood.'

Finally he manages to latch the feeder on the crook. Above it, the sky's pulled tight, its blue strained thin and pale, so thin it barely holds itself around the earth, with scratched into it some faint cirrus clouds, like the ripples in skin stretched beyond its natural inclination.

'My belt's fine,' he says.

'At least let me put a couple new holes in it,' I say. 'Come on.'

He sits down by the back door and takes off his shoes. I make him leave them there on the newspaper all the time now, rain or shine, after he tracked Daisy's mess all over the floor. The house is filthy enough as it is without having feces smeared over everything. He hasn't cleaned in months. Bathtub porcelain's dingy and clouded, and there's enough dust and dog hair gathered in the corners and drifting along the edges of the rooms in tumbleweed bolls to knit a throw with. All the side tables and bookshelves and picture frames have grown a thin coating of dust, and the deer are so covered in it their glossy noses have dulled to matte. I don't think I'll ever get it all out of their fur.

I take some scissors to the living room and turn on the noon news. They're doing their 'Intimate Debbie' segment, which consists of several people with alarmingly tenuous connections to her divulging 'shocking new details about her private life.' A worker at the battered women's shelter says Debbie and Larry spent two weeks there at the start of the year, when he was just a couple months old — despite the fact that, by Debbie's own admission, his daddy hightailed it out of town as soon as he found out she was pregnant and she hadn't been able to get a date since — that she'd never seen a mother more devoted to her son, and that Debbie cheered up the other battered women by doing a song-and-dance routine from back in her pageant days.

Frank shuffles in. The soles of his blue, swollen feet are edged with grime, look like he's stomped in a fireplace. 'Hand it over,' I say. Reluctantly, he undoes his belt and gives it to me. 'Pull your waistband out.' He does, and he could fit Daisy, glutton that she is, in the empty space between it and his belly. She sits a few feet away and watches him with her head hung just ever so slightly downward now, not as bad as it was in the shelter but still so she has to look up at him in what seems to be a combination of terrible shame and disapproval. When he glances at her, she turns her nose up and her face away from him, real haughty. She doesn't want him to know she was watching.

'If you don't start eating something,' I say, 'you're going to end up right back in the hospital, getting fed through a tube. Like a baby.'

'They don't feed babies through tubes.' He chuckles a high, airy chuckle I've never before heard from his throat.

'They do when they're too stupid to eat the food that's offered them.'

'I thought I was supposed to watch my diet,' he says. 'Lose weight. Open up my arteries.'

'You are,' I say. 'But you're not supposed to starve yourself.'

'Oh, I'm fine.'

Daisy turns her stare right back to him, looking even more serious and shamed than before. She can't go very long without looking at him.

'You may not have noticed this,' I say, 'but you only say things are fine when they are in extremely dire condition.'

He holds up his britches with one hand while he lowers himself into the chair. The whole thing, creaking, tilts a little to the left. I wanted to get us both the new kind I saw advertised on television late one night, with a button you hit makes the whole seat lift up and push out to help you stand, but he won't agree to that until this one collapses right out from under him. Why he's got to be such a cheapskate I don't know. We've got plenty of money and nobody to leave it to when we go, but he insists on walking around here like a pauper.

Daisy shoves her head between his knees and strains her nose toward his crotch. She's barely tall enough to do it, rests her chin right on the chair. He squeezes her skull between his legs while he spreads her big ears flat across his thighs and massages them. Calls it 'making pancakes' for how her ears spread out. Her broken tail swishes back and forth the whole time, and when he stops, she shakes her head so her jowls fly out and make a wet slapping noise against her teeth, their undersides flashing pink, and jams it right back in. She can stand there like that for hours.

I pull his belt over one point of the open scissors. The black's worn off from the tan underneath, and the leather's brittle, permanently warped into the shape it's held over the pin and under the buckle. If we're lucky, the strain of getting a new hole punched in it will go ahead and rip it apart. I dig the point of the scissors into the strap, twisting as I go. The leather bends around it until a pimple raises on the far side, where the skin crackles and turns pale as the blade strains to push through. I flip the belt over and poke the scissors into it from the other side, push the pimple back in.

'What do you want to eat?' I say. 'There's got to be something that sounds good to you. Just tell me what you want and I'll fix it.'

He starts absentmindedly digging clods of dirt out of his stolen vacuum and placing them into a trash bag, both of which have been sitting beside his chair for weeks, half-full. The very next morning after Daisy charmed him out of bed, the first thing he did was drag that thing back up from the curb. If I was smart, I would have waited a few more days for the trash truck to come before I went and got her.

On the TV, a fat woman with a tight-coiled perm and big, watery eyes stands in front of her trailer while two children cry on the stoop and a chained-up spaniel lunges at the cameraman, choking itself half to oblivion, and says her son saw Debbie on what she imagines could have been the very night of the murder, when Little Larry was still bobbing face-down on the sudsy surface of his bathwater, that she was wearing a real short red dress down at Buck's Bar, drinking tequila and dancing up against multiple strangers.

'They say her daddy abused her,' the woman says, real low, drawing the word *abused* out long and sagging under the weight of its own implication. She tugs her floral blouse down over her belly and asks when people in this world got so mean.

Daisy starts whimpering and squealing and running frantic around the house, snuffling at the floorboards and vents and window frames. All week she's been doing it, clawed half the paint off the windowsills trying to get through them. Bucks are in the woods, ready to spar. She can tell it by the smell of the rut, of aggression and unbearable desire and newly hardened antlers scraping their velvet across the trees, ready to lock.

The point of the scissors breaks through the leather. I twist the strap further down the blade to widen the hole.

'All I can taste is sweets,' Frank says, holding what appears to be the final fistful of dust and hair midway between the vacuum and the trash bag. It's threaded with a piece of silver foil from a stick of chewing gum.

'What?'

'I said, all I can taste is sweets.'

'Why didn't you tell me that before?'

'It just now occurred to me.'

'All you can taste is sweets?'

'Everything else tastes like metal.' He carefully places the clod into the trash bag.

'Fine. Wonderful. I'll make you some sweets. What kind of sweets do you want?'

'I don't know,' he says. 'I believe I'd like some sort of cake. But I can't put my finger on exactly what.'

'You want some pound cake?'

'Maybe.'

'You love pound cake.'

'I do,' he says, but he doesn't sound too sure about it.

'What about red velvet?'

'Maybe.'

I hand him his belt. He pushes up from the chair. His arms shake trying to lift him.

'That would be a whole lot easier,' I say, 'if all you had to do was push a button.'

He pretends not to hear me. His shaking fingers have a hard time threading the belt through its loops, keep missing them right at the last second, and it's hard for him to twist around enough to get it through the back ones. He stands there a long time putting it on, real careful, and still he misses a loop, but I don't say anything. He turns around once, modeling it for me. His pants stay put around his waist, the extra fabric gathered up into bunting ruffles. Daisy scrabbles at the heat vent, trying to tear it out of the wall.

'How do I look?' Frank says.

'Downright respectable,' I say.

★   ★   ★

I spend all afternoon baking his three favorite cakes: pound, red velvet, and pineapple upside-down. Soon as one's in the oven, I start sifting the ingredients for the next. I wait until right before it's ready to bake before I mix the wet into the dry, though. You don't want your batter to sit there relaxing too long, everything in it getting too close and comfortable, or the cake comes out all rubbery. He does like his pound cake a little fallen, though, how dense and moist it gets, so I open the oven door and slam it shut halfway through.

While the pineapple upside-down's in the oven and I'm spreading cream-cheese icing across the red velvet cake, a goldfinch pauses on the bird feeder, tiny toes reaching through the wire. It's a male, though the summer brightness is faded from his feathers, turned him dingy and gray for the winter, like winter's light. He reaches inside with his beak, carefully draws a black splinter through the mesh, and streaks away. They mark their territory, the males, by singing as they fly along its boundaries, drawing the sound like twine from branch to branch. It stays there, thrumming in the air, long after it fades from our ears. The sound presses against their feathers when they try to fly across it.

So that's our supper for tonight, three kinds of cakes. It's a good thing neither of us is diabetic. Not diagnosed, at least. Those swollen feet of his make me suspicious. I lay a slice of each one on his plate, the red velvet with its icing, which melted a little and ran onto the platter because I didn't let the cake cool long enough before I spread it on, and the pineapple upside-down with a nice, perfect ring of pineapple and a mound of whipped cream on top, and the pound cake, plain and unassuming. It didn't fall as much as I'd have liked.

At first I don't even pick my fork up, I'm so busy watching him as he debates which one to try first, but then I go ahead and eat some myself so the pressure doesn't get to him. Daisy sits leaning against his chair, her legs splayed out. No modesty at all. He takes a bite of the pound cake, chews it with that same listening look on his face, and nods to himself. The red velvet makes a bigger impression — he raises his eyebrows in surprise and takes another big bite — but after that he gets bored and moves on to the pineapple upside-down. He takes three bites of that one, one right after the other, leaves whipped cream on the corner of his mouth. I don't like the taste of it much myself. The pineapple was canned in syrup instead of juice, makes the whole thing too sweet, but he seems to be enjoying it. The texture of it keeps his interest, the stringiness of the pineapple. I can tell from the concentration on his face while he chews, the way he pushes it around on his

159

tongue. Then he sets down his fork.

'Well?' I say.

'They're just fine.'

'Do they taste like metal?'

'Only just a little bit,' he says, real encouraging, as if to imply he's sure I'll be able to do better next time.

'I shouldn't have given you pound cake. It's more buttery than it is sweet. The pineapple's sweet, though. Too sweet for me. I thought that was what you wanted.'

'Just fine,' he says, as if continuing his thought uninterrupted, 'but it's something else I've got a hankering for. I wish I could put my finger on it.'

'What about chocolate rum? You like chocolate rum.'

'It could be chocolate rum.' He rests his chin on his fist like he's thinking about a matter of great philosophical difficulty.

'You've got whipped cream on your face.' He wipes it on the back of his hand and wipes his hand on his pants, while his napkin sits on the table, trapped underneath his fork. 'At least eat a little more. For my sake. I spent the whole afternoon on them.' He uses his fork to break open the upside-down cake and separate out the pieces of pineapple. 'I should have waited longer to ice the red velvet,' I say. It soaked up the melted icing, and now it's sopping as a used sponge, falling apart on the plate. Between his thumb and forefinger, Frank holds a piece of pineapple in the air between us and studies it. Daisy stares at it, transfixed. Saliva starts streaming uncontrollably from one corner of her

160

mouth. A few cake crumbs fall off the pineapple onto the table.

'Stop acting strange,' I say. 'What you need to do is figure out what kind of cake you want. What about birthday cake?'

He frowns and shakes his head. Daisy bumps the elbow of his pineapple-holding hand with her nose and stares at him gravely, as if trying to mesmerize him into giving her a bite. Her saliva forms an enormous bubble, like the kind frolicking children draw through the air with a soapy wand.

'If you give a bite of that cake to the dog,' I say, 'I will drive her back to the pound first thing in the morning.'

He drops the pineapple and leans back in his chair, holds his hands up like I've got a gun trained on him.

'Eat.'

Slowly, glumly, he hunches over his plate, skims some whipped cream onto his fork, and holds it in front of his face. I nod. Daisy looks back and forth between us, trying to appear patient and bored while the bubble hangs quivering from the corner of her mouth, and waits for the standoff to end.

★   ★   ★

I bake every cake I know, and some I don't: rum and earthquake and spice, angel and devil's food, German chocolate and lemon-blueberry and oatmeal-coconut, and when I run out of cakes, I start on cobblers: cranberry and blueberry and strawberry, peach and pumpkin and rhubarb, and when I run out of cobblers, I start on pies: pecan pie, apple pie, lemon meringue, key lime, banana cream. Daisy keeps me company, at least, while I cook, stands right behind my legs, wheezing with an addict's desperation and waiting to vacuum up any crumbs I might drop.

Each one Frank takes his obligatory single spoonful of, chews it and listens close, then sets his spoon and napkin down on the table and goes back to the den. I put the leftovers on the floor, and Daisy sets on them like a wild beast, gobbling up entire pies in two or three bites, and then I start on the cookies: blondies and brownies and chocolate-chunk delights, ginger molasses snaps and snickerdoodles and rosemary-rosewater-poppy-seed tea biscuits.

Those last ones he takes one look at and turns his head away from the decorative platter I've brought them on, artfully arranged with holly painted around the edge of the china. Won't even touch them.

'I said I wanted something sweet,' he grumbles. He always gets into a funk after the leaves have fallen.

It takes me a week. Then I trudge, with the little strength I have left, from the kitchen to the living room.

'Congratulations,' I say on my way down the hall. 'You win. I have officially run out of desserts. You're now free to starve to death.'

But when I get to the living room, it's empty. The bathroom's empty too, and so's the bedroom. 'Frank?' I yell. The front door's shut and locked, but I know they can't have gone out the back, so I open it up and step onto the porch. It's raining, big fat drops just barely not cold enough to be snow. Far away, through the bare trees, Daisy's paws scatter the leaves on the ground. I can see them rustle, the movement around her, more than I can see her. After a second that disappears, too. The leaves settle placid.

'Frank,' I yell, but there's no answer. I grab myself an umbrella and coast the car slow down the drive, and there, at the far edge of our woods, almost to the street, he's leaning against a hickory with his hands in his pockets, looking very intently out at the road, while the rain soaks him.

I roll down the window. 'Get in the car,' I yell, but he doesn't seem to hear. Daisy sits next to him, her tail swishing back and forth through the wet leaves, steady and swift, and looks over her shoulder at me, urging me to do something, anything, so she doesn't have to keep sitting out here in the rain.

'Frank,' I yell again, as I'm getting out of the car and opening up my umbrella, but it's not until I've made my way over to him and shaken him by the shoulders that he looks at me, and still that same expression, like he's watching something far away and indistinct slowly take shape as it moves closer, stays on his face. There's mud smeared across his cheek, and caught in the hairs on his forearm, and grass stains on his knees. Water runs down his

163

forehead, along his nose, and drips off it. He turns back to the road. I hoist the umbrella over our heads.

'What happened?' I say.

'I don't know.' He sounds distracted, dazed.

'Are you all right?'

'I don't know,' he says. 'How did I get here?'

'Did you fall?'

'I don't think so.'

'You fell. You must have fallen.'

'I wouldn't have been able to get back up if I'd fallen,' he says.

'How else would you have grass stains on your knees?'

He looks all around, as if for clues: at the last curdled leaves dashed from their branches, at the rain pounding loose the yard, gathering it into trembling pools that seem to seep upward out of the dirt instead of falling down on it.

He shakes his head. 'The cleanliest of waters,' he says, 'becomes tainted as soon as it touches our human refuse.'

'Is anything broken?'

He moves his hands up and down his arms, squeezing. 'I don't believe so.'

'How long have you been out here?'

'A while,' he says. 'I believe.'

Human refuse. He must have read that in a book someplace. Lord knows he didn't come up with it himself.

'Let's get in the car,' I say.

He shakes his head. 'One minute I was watching that program, then all of a sudden I was out here. I was doing something, though.

When I got here. I got here right in the middle of doing it. I just don't know what it was.'

'You must have fallen asleep,' I say. 'You must have been walking in your dreams.'

'Naw.'

'You must have been.'

'When have I ever done that? I sleep fine. You're the one who sleeps crazy.' I used to talk while I dreamed, he said. Sometimes I even sat up in the bed and carried on long conversations he couldn't understand without their other side — Not that one, I said, not that one, with increasing desperation, no, please, no — until he could hush me and pull me back down to the mattress and keep me there with the weight of his arm flung over my chest.

That's what he says, at least. I never remembered any of that myself.

'I didn't fall asleep,' he says. 'I was watching my program.'

'There's no other explanation. Unless you think there was some kind of supernatural force came and transported you out here and decided to smear grass and mud all over you. Unless you think there was some sort of happening.'

He doesn't answer. He's distracted again by whatever he's looking for, but there's nothing there to find: just the road, and the trees on the other side, and a river of red clay running out from the roots of an oak and into the street, washing in waves across it.

'What're you looking at?' I say.

He shivers, crosses his arms, and keeps on looking at it, until finally Daisy can't take it any longer and stands up with her muddy forepaws on his knee and nuzzles him. He pats her on the head. His hand's covered in fine scratches.

'Come on and get in the car. My arm's tired.' I shake the umbrella, and it flings drops of water in a circle all around us. Frank keeps staring across the street. 'You're going to get pneumonia,' I say. 'They could try me for manslaughter. Criminal neglect. You want me to spend the rest of my days in prison?'

He ponders carefully. 'Naw,' he says. He's shivering bad.

'Then get in the car.'

When we've got him in it, and Daisy seated on the floor with her head jammed between his thighs, I turn the heat all the way up. It blows thick and hot in our faces. Frank presses his palms to the vent. The rain pounds the roof of the car, sounds like machine-gun fire. Or at least how it sounds in the movies.

'We ought to take you to the doctor,' I say.

He points to the street sign across from us.

'Hillcrest Drive,' he says. 'That's where we live. On the crest of the hill.'

'Look around you. There's not a hill in sight. And there surely isn't a crest.'

'You know what that means, don't you?' He chuckles. 'It's all downhill from here.'

'There's no slope to this road whatsoever. It's just a name.'

'Somebody's lying, then,' he says. 'And I'll put my trust in the sign, thank you very much.'

'Why do you keep talking like that?'

'Talking like what?'

166

'Tearing words up. Acting like you don't know anything.' Like somebody who was just learning what words meant and still trying to figure out the boundaries they drew, testing the edges and seams of things.

'I'm just trying to explain it,' he says.

'All you're doing is rearranging the exact same terms. You're not defining them at all.'

'It all makes perfect sense,' he says, 'if you can just break it down into its components. Look at one piece at a time. Then it's all clear.'

'All I need clarification of is how you got out here in this condition.'

He shrugs and scratches the inside of Daisy's ear, right where it meets her head. She leans into his hand with all her weight but looks at me sidelong, warily, for the signal that it's safe to relax.

'Just break it apart,' Frank says. 'Look at one little bit at a time. It's easier that way.'

'Stop it. You make me feel like I'm losing my mind.'

'Maybe you are,' he says. 'You've been acting mighty strange.'

'Like nothing makes a bit of sense.'

'Maybe it doesn't.'

'But you just said that it does!' I shout. 'You just a minute ago said it makes perfect sense.'

'See?' he says. 'You never used to have outbursts like that.'

Another empty spot hovering over the street catches his attention, even though not a single thing has changed. I pull out of the driveway, through that very spot, flattening it as I turn the car around. I can't drive in reverse too well these days. Not the whole way back to the house, that's for sure. Hurts my neck to turn it around that long, and I don't trust the rearview mirror.

And as soon as we're facing the house, he looks all around, bewildered, and for the first time seems to fully comprehend where and who he is. He reaches one shaking hand out and runs it over my arm, as if to make sure I'm really here. Panic widens his eyes.

'Wendell,' he says. His voice is troubled, trembling. 'I — '

His mouth keeps moving, but he can't manage to get anything else out of it.

'I know.' I put my hand on top of his. 'I know. It's okay.'

I drive the car rattling over the gravel and park beside the porch. We sit here a long time, waiting for the rain to ease, watching it wash down the windshield. It warps the porch, blurs the trees beyond it into dark shapeless swaths. He keeps his hand on my arm.

'That rain sounds like machine guns going off,' I say.

Frank listens to it, carefully, as if it's a dessert he's chewing.

'Naw,' he says. 'Not really.'

★ ★ ★

The rain ends. The eaves drip into the raw silence it leaves behind; the waters seep into the dirt, the sky reflected within them breaking apart

168

around the blades of grass. Frank takes a warm shower, dresses himself, and sits in his recliner. I drape an afghan over his lap. He's still shivering. While he flips through the television channels, trying to find something decent to watch — they never play anything good once the holidays get near, just a bunch of sentimental nostalgia for a time that, as far as I can remember, never happened in the first place — I page through the newspaper in the one measly circle of yellow light from the lamp between our chairs. The house feels shut up and huddled close. I can feel it drawing tight around me. Can't hardly turn the page, I'm so tired.

Daisy sleeps with her back pressed against his feet, so she'll feel it if he moves, her paws twitching like they do when he tickles the fur between their pads. She whimpers, and her jaws work, desperate to feel the weight of dream rabbits.

In the Lifestyles section, there's a recipe for a maraschino cherry pie. I raise myself up out of the chair. The living room floor groans as I step onto it, and Frank looks down in surprise, as if it were a living thing, a person so quiet he hadn't realized it was there. Daisy blinks and looks blearily up. With my thumbnail I pick the crust of sleep from the corner of her eye. She's got the biggest, most sorrowful-looking tear ducts I've ever seen on a dog, and the haws raised up pink over her eyeballs make her look drunk. She sighs deeply, breathing out the heavy weight of the world, and settles back to sleep.

'Now, floorboards,' Frank says, 'are the boards — '

I head to the kitchen, rummage through the cabinets, and open up a dusty can. The cherries and syrup inside are red as bright blood from a deer's cut throat. I turn on the oven.

13

He'd got hired on at the mill at the best possible time, when the textile bubble was still big as it could be without popping, swollen with the entire country's demand for every bolt of fabric it had been denied during the war. It was only a few years before there was too much production and too much competition, and the factory cut everybody's wages, then fired a quarter of the workers; then, when things started to pick back up again due to renewed clamor for quality denim, instead of hiring anybody back, they implemented a little something they called the 'stretch out,' which required everyone who remained to increase his or her output by fifty percent. A woman who had tended fifty looms now paced behind seventy-five; Frank had to almost run from the loading dock to the dyeing racks to keep them full. Two men died of heatstroke that winter, there on the shop floor, and another about drowned when his sleeve got caught under the spool and pinned to the rack in his rush, dragged him across the floor and through the air and dropped him into the vat of indigo, shimmering and dark, so blue it was black.

It got so bad, some of the workers tried to organize themselves a union. Frank never had as much trouble keeping to himself than he did those months. Every day, somebody was tracking him down to talk while he smoked on the loading dock during their recently-reduced break, or bothering him in the bathroom while he tried to relieve himself, which he had trouble doing if there was another person anywhere nearby, much less leaning over the stall to talk about how his kids' growth had been stunted because he didn't make enough to feed them, or about how he didn't want a bunch of race-traitor pinkos coming in to take his wages and send them home to Mother Russia. Regardless of who was talking to him, or what they said, he nodded, and tried to make his face look real sympathetic, but said as little as he possibly could and never agreed to come to a meeting, not to the union hall or the Chamber of Commerce.

Against all odds, and to the credit of how terrible conditions in the mill were, the union actually managed to win the election, by three votes: four-hundred seventy-five to four-hundred seventy-two. When they made the announcement, a brawl broke out on the shop floor. Frank voted against it. It was supposed to be a secret, but you had to put your name on the ballot, so the Labor Board could verify your eligibility as an employee in good standing. The last thing he wanted was his name associated with anything that might bring him under the slightest scrutiny or threaten the sanctity of the Southern woman, which was, apparently, very much at stake.

Not that any of it mattered in the end. The union and the mill management only made it through four days of negotiations before everything fell apart. The management filed a formal complaint questioning the union's legitimacy for some obscure and arcane technical reason, and the union called for a strike. The strike lasted approximately forty-five minutes.

★ ★ ★

It was in the middle of all this that I got home one evening and found him hunched forward in his reading chair, a hideous high-backed thing he'd found on the side of the road one afternoon in the rich part of town, where he had no business driving anyway, upholstered in toile de Jouy, which he thought looked refined but whose pattern of pilgrims in buckle shoes fancy-stepping behind their hounds struck me as ghastly and deranged. Usually he took a shower and changed into short sleeves first thing after work, so the animals on his arm could stretch and breathe, but he was still in his uniform, the straps of his overalls shrugged from his shoulders, draped over the arms of his chair. He was shivering and staring into the empty fireplace, his hair and shoulders wet. I perched on the edge of my chair, across from his, and waited for him to look up.

★ ★ ★

His aunt Sally had been there when he came back from work that afternoon, wrapped in an oversized man's peacoat and rocking in one of the chairs on the porch, despite the cold, the gray sky low and sagging with leaden snow.

When he saw her, he imagined for the briefest of moments, before thought bridged sight to reason, that it was his mother there, or his mother's ghost.

She was his favorite aunt, his mother's youngest sister, the wild one her siblings shook their heads and clucked about. She was twenty years old and living with his parents when he was born — she'd got herself into some trouble with a married man and had to leave their home down east for a bit while everyone recovered from the scandal — and she carried him around on her hip so much those first few years, half the people in town thought he was her son. By the time he was old enough to really know her, she'd calmed down a bit and got married herself, settled into a lighter-hearted version of her sisters. She still came to stay with his family from time to time when he was a teenager, for a good while after his daddy died, and whenever she and her husband got into particularly bad fights. He liked to drink, and she liked to throw things, and every six months or so they'd have to spend a few weeks apart in order to decide that they couldn't live without each other. He'd died, too, while Frank was overseas. Liver stopped working. The women in her family, Sally said, had a tragic attraction to men who weren't long for the world.

Frank was slow to unbuckle his seatbelt, to pick his metal lunch pail up from the floorboard, trying to give his heart time to steady.

'There you are,' she said, when he finally got out of the car.

'Here I am,' he said.

She hurried down the steps to hug him before he was halfway to the porch. 'It's about time. I've been waiting out here in the cold for half an hour. Like a pauper. And that's not counting the forty-five minutes I spent driving around in circles trying to find this godforsaken place. Hasn't anyone out here ever heard of a street sign?' She held him at arm's length, her hands clamped to his waist, to assure herself he hadn't been starving.

'What are you doing here?' he said.

'What does it look like I'm doing? I'm visiting my favorite nephew. I went up to see Bruce at school for the weekend and thought I'd drop by and see you on my way back.'

'How did you — ' He was afraid to finish the question, for the risk of sounding suspicious.

'The post office,' she said. 'I had to call them up — long-distance, might I add — and ask them where my own nephew lives. Since you always forget to respond to that particular part of my letters, somehow. It's a real mystery. And then do you know what they told me? They told me they'd been instructed not to give out your address. 'To anybody whatsoever.' Special instructions, they said, as if the FBI were involved. As if I were nosing around for state secrets. I had to call them umpteen times, talk them up one side and down the other before I finally wore them down. A couple times I had to weep. It was a real debacle, the whole thing.'

He shook his head and laughed, despite

175

himself. 'You should have let me know you were coming.'

'I didn't want to give you any warning.'

On the other side of the door, the dog whimpered at the sound of their voices. Her tail thumped the floor.

'Well?' Sally said. 'I'm on the verge of losing my fingers to frostbite.' She held them up. Her hands were covered in big costume rings, one with a cut-glass amethyst that took up her entire knuckle, her fingertips red.

Inside, of course, there was a coat on the hook, too small to be his, right beside the door. There were two towels on the rack in the bathroom, one still a little damp from the shower I'd taken that morning, two toothbrushes in a glass upon the sink, the bristles of one frayed from what Frank insisted was the entirely unnecessary force with which I brushed my teeth.

'The house is a mess,' he said.

'I've just come from a boy's college dormitory. I'm sure your filth pales in comparison.' She waited for him to open the door. The dog's nails clicked as she paced back and forth behind it. 'Fine. You want to make an old lady sit out in the cold, I'll sit out in the cold.' And she did, there on the porch step. She was, he told me, rather spry for her age. Frank lowered himself beside her.

'How's Bruce?' he said, as lightly and casually as he could. 'School treating him right?'

'He nearly failed his first semester. Went skiing instead of to class half the time. He wants to be an 'oceanographer,' whatever that is. As if we don't already know where all the oceans are. It sounds like an excuse to spend all day at the beach to me. The one place he could think of that would be more conducive to frittering all his time away than a ski town.'

'And Alice?'

'Oh, she's fine. A bit overwhelmed, I think. The new baby's thirteen weeks now. A little girl. I'm just praying she doesn't turn into the spoiled little tyrant her brother is.'

'He can't be that bad.'

'You haven't met him,' she said, laughing.

It wasn't meant as a rebuke, but it stung him as though it were. He hadn't met any of this next generation of cousins. The boy was nearly five now. Frank watched the afternoon dissolving into dusk, gray emerging from every little crack between the trees and grass and gravel. Any time now, my car might rattle up the driveway.

'You look more like your daddy every year,' she said. 'When you were little, everyone said you took after your mother. Or me. But now it's faded off of you somehow. And there he was, right underneath. The whole time.' She shook her head sadly.

He pulled his knees up, wrapped his arms around them.

'Frank,' she said. 'What happened?'

'What do you mean?'

'You know what I mean. We hardly ever hear from you. Nobody's seen you since your mama's funeral. My children, I could understand if they decided never to speak to me again. But not you.'

'I write you,' Frank said.

'A couple sentences every few months. That tell me slightly more than nothing.'

'I've been busy. Whipping this place into livable shape was an endeavor unto itself.'

'And how long ago was that? Seven years now?'

'Work keeps me occupied,' he said.

'Did we do something? To drive you away? I know we should have stayed longer after your mama died, I shouldn't have left you alone. It was just — '

'No. No, it's nothing like that. You didn't do anything.'

'Then what is it?'

'Nothing,' he said. 'Honestly. Everything's fine. Great.'

'Your mother would be worried sick if she knew you were out here all alone, in the middle of nowhere. You know that? And she'd be furious at me for letting it go on this long.'

'I like the quiet.'

'Quiet's one thing. This is something else. You should come down, stay with us for a little bit. It'd do you good. Do us good, too.'

'That's sweet of you,' he said.

'Tell me that after you've met the little tyrant.'

Frank picked at the step. It was old and warped, full of deep fissures that ran the length of the wood, so many of them it was unclear what substance, what force held the rest together.

'I thought you'd have one or two of them yourself by now,' Sally said. 'Why haven't you ever — ?' She nodded to the empty spot on his ring finger.

Our standard answer to this question, which complete strangers inexplicably often felt empowered to ask, was that we were widowed. Saying you'd never married, at thirty-seven, raised all kinds of suspicions, meant there was something deep-down, dangerously wrong in you, festered and spoiled or else withered and desiccated, but saying you were a widower never failed to keep a person from prying further, afraid they'd hit some weak spot and have to endure the resulting effusion.

'I just ain't found the right one,' he said.

Sally groaned. 'Oh, Frank. There is no right one. Especially not at your age. You waited too long, the right ones all got snatched up fifteen years ago. Just pick one that's decent enough and hold on. That's all anyone does, really. Some people just make a better show of it than others.' She crossed her arms and shivered theatrically. Frank shrugged out of his coat, draped it over her shoulders. 'Your mama and daddy weren't perfect, either. They used to fight like the dickens. Your mother could cuss like you wouldn't believe.'

'She used to wash my mouth out with soap,' Frank said, in mock indignation, 'if I said *darn* too emphatically for her liking.'

'That's because she didn't want you ending up like her. Parents never do.' She put her hand on his, the metal bands of her rings cold against his skin. 'I miss them too, you know. Both of them. And I know losing them when you're young is

179

hard. But you don't have to give up on the whole world.'

'I haven't — that ain't it.'

'Then what is it? A person doesn't cut off all ties with his family and move into a shack in the woods for no reason.'

'It ain't a shack. It's a nice place. I've worked hard on it.'

'How would I know?' she said. 'This place, this job — ' She licked her thumb and brushed a blue smudge from his cheek. 'Do you know how many of the people in that mill would have killed for the chances you got? To go to college? You could be anything, do anything you want. This life you're living, it isn't yours.'

'It is,' he said.

'You're still young enough. It's not too late.'

'I'm happy.'

'I've known you since you were a little boy,' she said. 'I've known you since before you can remember. You think I don't know what your face looks like when you're happy?'

He searched the trees for the flash of my headlights.

'What is it?' she said. 'What are you trying to keep so secret?'

'Nothing.'

'I'm not a fool, Frank. You couldn't act more suspicious if you tried. You won't even let me in your own house, for heaven's sake. And it's freezing out and getting dark. Are you in some sort of trouble?'

He shook his head.

'You're not mixed up with those communists

180

trying to take over the mill, are you?'

'Of course not.'

'Then what? What is it?' He was quiet. After a minute, she sighed. 'I had lots of time before you got here to prowl around, you know. Peer through your curtains. It certainly doesn't look like you're all alone in there. Unless the two chairs by the fireplace are both for you. Unless you've taken up baking in your spare time.'

The thickening dark, mercifully, made it hard to see the look on her face, which meant it must be hard to see the look on his.

'It's getting late,' Frank said. 'You ought to be going. Before you catch cold.'

'Is she married? Divorced? What's so bad that you can't — '

'You should go. And you shouldn't come back.'

'You don't mean that.'

He tried to make his voice cold and hard. 'If I ever wanted to see you,' he said, 'don't you think I would have made it a little easier to find me?'

She waited a moment, watching him. Then she grabbed the banister and hauled herself up. Frank stared at his lap.

'Don't tell anyone where I am,' he said. 'Don't even tell them you saw me.'

'Frank — '

'Please. Can you do that for me?'

She set his jacket over his shoulders, kissed him on the cheek. 'I didn't mean to upset you. I just — I was nearby, and I knew my sister would want me to. She always worried about you. Said you took the world too hard. I never believed her.'

He didn't watch her go. The gravel crunched under her shoes. The car door groaned as it opened.

'You were always my favorite, you know,' she said. 'When my children were growing up, I used to wish and wish they would be more like you.'

He covered his face with his hands. She closed the door softly and drove away. Frank sat on the step long after the jacket had slipped from his shoulders. The snow began to fall, in fat, wet flakes that sank quick and heavy from the clouds. They melted as soon as they touched the ground.

★   ★   ★

'I guess I'd better close up that PO box,' he said.

I got up from my chair and balanced on the arm of his. 'You don't have to do that.'

'I do. It's safer this way.'

'Not really. She already knows where we are.'

How nice it must have been, I thought, for someone to track you down. How much they must love you.

'Do you think she'll tell anyone?' I said. I leaned against his shoulder, ran my fingers through his damp hair.

'No. I don't think so.'

'Then you shouldn't close it. There's no reason to. She cares about you. And it's good to have some link to the outside world. You shouldn't cut that off.'

'I'm not sure you're the one who should be lecturing me on the importance of family.'

'Fine.' I stood. 'Do whatever you want.'

'I'm sorry.' He grabbed my hand and pulled me back to him. 'I'm sorry. I don't want to fight with you. Seeing her, talking to her, it's just — it's too hard.' He had to whisper to keep his voice from breaking. 'It's too hard.'

He looked up at me, his eyes wide and gutted. 'I know,' I said.

★　★　★

For a couple weeks after that, he threw up his breakfast before work every morning. He tried to be quiet about it, but I heard him through the walls while I packed his lunch in the gray dawn, the gag and rush, the wet cough as he tried to breathe in the moments afterward. When he came out of the bathroom and I asked if he was okay, he said, 'Of course,' as if he didn't know what I was talking about, and kissed me goodbye, his breath sickeningly sweet with toothpaste.

On the morning of the strike, he stood in the dirt parking lot with the rest of the scabs, hundreds of other men in the same uniform, the same overalls and gray long-sleeved shirt, indistinguishable from one another but for their size, their relative degrees of exhaustion and stoop, the sun's pastel light radiating from behind the red brick walls as if generated from the engines churning inside the building itself, and watched as the police and state troopers rushed in and tore the picketers from the gates they blocked, dragged them in handcuffs to the waiting paddy wagons. A few of the men beside him threw rocks at the strikers who dodged the policemen's clubs. A German shepherd closed its jaw on a woman's calf and dragged her to the ground. It was over before the sun rose from the smokestack, some industrial byproduct, some molten waste, before the steam whistle blew to summon the workers inside, nothing left but a few sprays of blood turning dark in red dirt among the remains of the old mill town, the company houses and school and playground, the company police station and hospital and general store, built so the workers would never be beyond management's purview and razed when it was no longer profitable, to free up the extra land and capital when the owners decided to expand. The rubble of their cinderblock foundations still studded the earth, still thudded dully under Frank's tires every morning, every afternoon. He stepped over them on his way through the gates.

Inside, the machines hummed and clanged. He lifted each spool from the truck and cradled it to his chest like an injured comrade, he hurried across the concrete floor, he gave it into the waiting metal arms. The rack lifted, the spool spun, the rope unwound. The rack lowered it into the pool of indigo and held it under until it turned blue.

14

I'm putting up the Christmas tree. It's a tabletop artificial one I bought from the dollar store, no taller than my tibia is long, with 'fiber-optic' lights, whatever that means, built into it so the tips of the plastic pine needles themselves change from red to blue to purple to yellow in waves of color, each one washing away the one before it. Frank watches them with a bright, blank look on his face, as if he's being hypnotized, while Daisy sits by his chair and obsessively licks his elbow with such insistence his whole arm moves back and forth to the rhythm of her lapping. I've got the opening arguments of the Debbie Drowner trial on the TV for a little festive accompaniment. It's about time. Took them a month just for the jury selection. Apparently knowing that she's guilty counts as being prejudiced, which means they had to find twelve shut-ins with very tenuous connections to reality to charge with the task of determining whether she was in her right mind at the time of the the murder — a description to which the defense objects, demanding that the event in question, though it is not, in fact, in question at all, henceforth be referred to as 'the incident.'

Debbie sits real prim and proper at the defense table, wearing a blue prairie-girl dress and a frilly white bonnet over her fried blond hair. She's found God in jail, the news anchors say, and God's told her to dress up like a pioneer woman. In a tiny box in one corner of the screen, set inside the bigger courtroom feed, they've got a panel of religion professors approximately the size of ants debating whether she's become Amish, or Mennonite, or one of those fundamentalist Mormons that live in desert compounds and think men ought to have as many wives as they please. Her own defense team is the one that asked the judge to let the proceedings be televised. I suppose that's one thing I ought to thank her for.

I wrap the pre-lit branches with our old strands of big bulbs, the enamel color on most of which has begun to crack, so it looks when you plug them in as if bolts of lightning were branching through them. On some, the color's flaked off so bright white shines through in big patches, and a few are completely bare now, look like the bulbs you'd screw into any tiny lamp. The branches sag under the weight.

'You want to help me hang the ornaments?' I say. We've got a box of miniature ornaments for the miniature branches, tiny reindeer and snowmen and glass balls. Frank shakes his head. They're so small he probably couldn't pick them up without breaking them, anyway, much less thread the little hooks through their little holes.

Not guilty by way of temporary insanity, that's what they're going for, so the prosecutor's pacing back and forth — he's a real infirm-looking fellow, tall and sickly but with 'kind eyes,' the newspeople keep insisting, as if they'd personally cast him to generate as much sympathy as possible — talking about how long she drove around with that poor little boy in the trunk of her car, how he rotted so long in his trash bag that when they moved him, the skin of his fingers slipped off his tiny hand, like a glove two sizes too big.

And it is shameful, how long he was out there, but his skin sliding off doesn't have a thing to do with it. That can happen in just a day in the hot summer like it was, especially shut up in a plastic bag like that. A whole lot of animals I had to turn away at the dawn of the plastic trash bag; they'd moldered in there so long and so bad that when I lifted the carcass, its hair fell out in handfuls, and the skin on its legs came undone and piled up about the hooves. Once your cells stop working, their membranes bulge and rupture, and the fluids burst forth and sweep through you and get between your skin and muscle, the way boiling water loosens the peel from a peach when you slice a cross in its bottom and drop it in the pot. Close a corpse up in plastic, so all the heat and wet and noxious gases are trapped in with it, and it spoils quicker than ever.

'Fruitcake,' Frank says.

'You sound like a fruitcake,' I say, picking up a thimble-sized porcelain basset hound dressed in a Santa outfit. I got it for Daisy, for her first Christmas with us. I write her name and the year on the bottom of it in permanent marker, which is no easy feat; I almost spill over the edge and sully the white fur trim of her coat. I shake the old tupperware container full of hooks until one

187

falls loose from the tangle.

'That's what I've been hungering for,' he says. 'Fruitcake.'

'You want fruitcake? To *eat*?'

'I surely do.'

'You don't even like fruitcake. If you liked fruitcake, I would have made it already.'

'It's a cake,' he says, 'made up of fruit.'

The wet clicking of Daisy's tongue resounds from the cavern of her mouth. Frank's whole body sways with the force of it, while her tail sweeps back and forth across the floor, gathering the dust and dirt and her own shed hair into a barrier ridge on either side of her.

'You want fruitcake,' I say.

'Yes, sir. I certainly do.'

'How much do you think you could eat?'

'The entire thing,' he says. 'I believe I could eat an entire fruitcake right now.'

I pop the ornament back into its plastic tray, grab his shoes off the mat, and drop them in his lap. I switched the deadbolts on all the doors while he was asleep, so you have to have a key to turn them even from the inside, and I've got the only one. If there was a fire while I was gone, they'd burn up, him and Daisy both. It's a different, probably irrational calculation each time, the equation of risk: subtracting how long they'd be here alone, how long he'd have to leave the stove on or trip and fall and leak his brains out, from the relative dangers of wherever I need to go, the heaviness of the traffic he could wander into, factoring in the intensity of his palsy at that particular hour, how likely it seems

188

that his fingers could grasp the tiny post by the window to unlock the car door. The easiest, cleanest solution, of course — just coming in the store with me — he continually refuses.

He manages to wriggle his foot into one shoe, but his fingers can't pinch right to hold the laces. He keeps dropping them, and focusing every bit of attention he's got to pick them up, and not being able to keep them between his fingers. Debbie prays and prays, her head bowed as far as it can bow, her hands clasped to her whispering lips. Finally he has to fold his laces into bunny ears and try to wrap one clumsily around the other, like a child who hasn't learned how to tie them right. Puts me in too sour a mood to watch. I go to the bathroom and wash the flakes of colored enamel off my hands, blot the sweat from my forehead with a piece of toilet paper.

He wanders into the hallway and stares silent and grim down it at me, like a ghost. His shoelaces trail loose from their eyes.

'I'll shuffle,' he says, when he sees me glaring. 'So I won't trip.'

$$\star \quad \star \quad \star$$

'Don't move,' I tell him when we're in the parking lot. 'Stay right here.' I parked as far from the door as I can walk, to reduce our chances of being seen. Daisy scrambles over the console and into his lap. 'And you make sure he doesn't get into any trouble while I'm gone.' She pauses, accepts her charge placidly and skeptically and

189

with her usual tinge of sorrow, and resumes her licking. I lock the car doors.

I always go to the store late on Sunday mornings, so the good people of town are in church and out of my way. Now it's swarming with them. Soon as I step in, there's two women who've parked their shopping carts in front of the corral, chatting away and completely oblivious to the fact that anybody else who might also like to use a shopping cart must now try to squeeze past them to reach one. I grab a basket and take it right to the seasonal aisle, glittering with candy in red and green foil, the shelves hung with tinsel and holly and racks of cheap stockings embroidered in sweatshop factories where the workers kill themselves because it's the only way to get a day off, and there, at the far end of the aisle, is a bin piled high with fruitcakes, perfectly uniform beige blocks studded with bits of bright red and green and yellow that used to be fruit. I don't know what you'd rightly call them now. I've never liked fruitcake myself. It's too sweet and too dense. A slice of cake shouldn't have the same consistency as a slice of cheese.

I buy half a dozen of them, and the oily teenage boy at the register, as he transfers them from the conveyor belt to the plastic bags, looks at me warily, confirmed in his suspicion that only the decrepit could eat such a thing. Usually I try to pick the register with the handsomest bag boy, even if that line's a little longer, but there wasn't much to choose from today. This one's got stringy hair and rosacea. The handsomest ones must be on vacation.

'Are these good?' he asks, real stilted, nervously shifting his weight from one foot to the other while I count the dollars and nickels and pennies out of my pockets, as if it's somehow inappropriate for silence to exist between two people while one of them is busy trying to provide the other with exact change.

'No,' I say.

'Oh,' he says. 'Okay, yeah. Great.'

I hurry back to the car. Frank's asleep, his head tilted back over the headrest at such a drastic angle I'm surprised his neck hasn't snapped, and Daisy's still licking his elbow. She may have worn the skin off by now. The slam of my door jolts him awake. He blinks once, twice, and looks around the car and the parking lot as if it's taking form from the inchoate primordial mass as we speak. It's the third blink before recognition wipes the glassiness from his eyes and memory starts to assume the very loosest of shapes inside them.

'Here,' I say, handing him a fruitcake.

He holds it in both palms for a second, testing its heft. Daisy runs her nose snuffling and wet along the clear plastic. Then, slowly, with a deftness I thought had long since drained away from his fingers, he tears open the end of the wrapper and peels it back into a neat cuff. Glorified plastic wrap, that's all it is, just a hair thicker than the kind you buy on a roll to stretch across your leftovers. He bites into the fruitcake like it's a fried turkey leg, tears out a big hunk and chews it slow, mindful, working hard on the tough fruit bits and the nuts, and then there it is, that same old listening look.

I knew it. I don't know why I wasted the gas.

He smacks his lips together real quick. 'That was good,' he says. 'Got a right good taste to it.' Even he seems surprised. He takes another bite, and another, and by the fourth he's not listening at all.

'I told you I wanted a cake,' he says. 'And you tried to feed me cookies.' He shakes his head with great sorrow.

'Fruitcake isn't even real cake,' I say. 'They ought to call it a fruit brick. A fruit log.' He nods, smiling, and tears off another fleshy bite. I shouldn't be encouraging that kind of word play. 'What made you think of it in the first place?' It's not the sort of thing they show commercials for.

'They kept talking on that trial about whether or not she's nuts,' he says, pumping his eyebrows jauntily on the word *nuts*. He pushes the final bite out of the plastic and into his mouth.

'I am absolutely sure no one in that courtroom used the term *nuts*,' I say.

He folds the wrapper, real neat, and slips it into his shirt pocket so just the corner peeks out, as if it were a fine silk handkerchief. Daisy surreptitiously sniffs his elbow and starts to licking.

'You got any more?' he says.

'Glory, glory,' I say. 'Hallelujah.'

★ ★ ★

On the way home, I pull over to the Burger Bonanza. I like a little treat after I've gone out in

192

the world. A little reward.

'This calls for celebration,' I declare. 'You want a hot fudge sundae?'

He shrugs.

'Hot fudge sundaes all around. I don't even care if you eat it.'

There's train tracks cut through the road right in front of the driveway, stick out so high they nearly tear the undercarriage out of the car, and then the line for the drive-through's wrapped halfway around the building. I park by the big metal dumpster in the corner, so it obscures the general view of our car, and head inside, where I get to wait in line behind eight disease-riddled members of the general public, with their stringy hair and red-ringed nostrils and tired eyes. Looks like a refuge for the homeless in here. The woman directly in front of me is wearing nothing but extra-large sweatpants, the drawstring waistband of which she has managed to pull all the way up over her bosom, then tied the string behind her neck to hold it up as if it were a bathing suit. The man behind me cradles his arm against his ribs. Something's trying to poke out through his skin.

As a man herds his children out the door, Frank drifts through like a piece of trash the wind blows skittering across the floor, this way and that. Finally he gets blown against the aquarium, full of plastic seaweed and rocks and without a single living thing swimming in its unnaturally electric-blue water, and stares into it while the last woman in line eyes him suspiciously to make sure he doesn't try to sneak into her spot. And then, right as I'm about to order, he shuffles up and stands right here, right here beside me, for anyone in the world to see.

The girl at the register smiles at him. She's real homely, heavyset, with puffy cheeks the skin of which is stretched tight and shiny, and blond hair almost the exact same sickly color as her skin falling loose out of its ponytail. Her name tag says Lorraine. I've never seen a girl her age with that name. Didn't think anybody liked it anymore.

I tell her we want two hot fudge sundaes, an order of french fries for Daisy, and two sodas. 'Light on the ice,' I say. Otherwise they cram the cup with as many cubes as it'll take, and you're lucky if they manage to squeeze any soda at all into the crannies.

'Lorraine, Lorraine,' Frank says in his singsong voice as I'm handing her our money. She smiles at him. 'The rain in Spain falls mainly on the plain. The wide crane swings its old ball and chain. I feel her pain: such a shame she's so darn plain. Lorraine, Lorraine.'

Her smile doesn't waver while tears boil up into her eyes. She stares down at the register and slowly counts out my change, then hurries away to the soda fountain to fill our cups. Frank laughs that high, airy laugh I hate so much.

'Where've I heard that before?' he says.

'Nowhere. You made it up.'

She pulls the lever on the ice cream machine, and it lets loose long twisted strands of soft serve she catches in a plastic cup, tilting it around in a circle so the ice cream piles up into a big swirl.

When she turns it off, she pulls the cup away real slow and gentle, draws the last strand of ice cream out into a delicate, pointed peak. It flops over.

'I've heard it somewhere before,' he says. 'I believe it was a popular song.'

'You made it up,' I say. 'Just to be cruel.'

I can feel the line of the infirm piling up behind me, the clammy, aching pressure of them. Somebody coughs a wet, hacking cough. Lorraine comes back with our sundaes and our sodas wedged into a cardboard tray. She's smiling as big as she can, so it pushes her cheeks upward and they squeeze her eyes almost shut, closing off the flow of tears. She's trying hard, she's trying her best, not to let them fall. She hands me a small paper bag, its bottom shiny and damp from french-fry grease. I squash it in between the cups.

'He can't help it,' I say, patting her hand. 'He's gone mad.'

'Oh,' she says. 'Oh, my gosh. I'm so sorry.'

'Well. He had himself a good life.'

She smiles. Young people like to hear old people say they've lived a good life. It makes them feel better. Makes them think you can go on living it, even after it's over.

'Have a nice day,' she says. Her voice is coiled up tight.

'You, too,' I say.

We're halfway to the door when Frank suddenly cuts around the napkin and ketchup station, makes a beeline through the tables and out the side door to the children's pen, a big playground of red plastic and foam, with a big tube of a slide that dumps them into a huge pit of plastic balls enclosed in black netting. Makes them look like a bunch of animals in a cage.

Next to the plastic rack of little round cubbyholes into which their children's dirty shoes have been stuffed, a gaggle of mothers bundled in puffy, shiny jackets hug themselves tight against the cold and watch in alarm as Frank lurches past them, toward the foam steps that lead into the ball pit. The children shriek and howl for no apparent reason. Frank rests his knees against the sagging top step and leans against a foam-wrapped post while he starts digging through the balls. Out in the middle of them, a little girl throws one so hard at a boy's head it bounces off and hits the net. They cackle maniacally and start rolling around like beached whales.

'Get your hands out of there,' I hiss, grabbing his elbow. 'There's germs swarming all over this place.' Even with all the diseases they've gotten rid of, completely eradicated from the world, there's a whole lot more to catch than there used to be. Everything's more communicable.

I try to tug him away. He tightens his grip on the post and reaches deeper into the balls, nearly up to his shoulder.

'A little germs are good for you,' he says, pulling up a miniature race car. He tosses it over his shoulder. 'Keeps your immune system working.' He then graciously explains to me what the phrase *immune system* means.

'What are you looking for?' I whisper.

He pulls up the bare stick of a lollipop, green and scarred with teeth marks, hair stuck all over it, tosses it aside, and keeps digging. A dark-haired boy comes rushing through the enclosed slide, his arms thrown up over his head like he's on the rickety roller coaster of some county fair, breathing a whispered shriek as he does it, the cries of all the joyful, fearful riders condensed. The slide throws him facedown in the balls with a muffled thud. He lies there completely still. He may be dead.

Frank pulls from the jumble a pink plastic Easter egg, holds it up to the light as if attempting to determine its authenticity. The little boy — he's maybe three or four, with pointed features clustered too close in the center of his face — watches as Frank works a fingernail into the seam around its equator, pries it open, and stares at the emptiness inside. The boy crawls through the plastic quicksand toward us. His mother stares with undisguised nervousness, either because we're two old men on a children's playground together, or because one of us has fruitcake glaze smeared shiny to one side of his mouth, and sidles over with feigned friendliness.

'Hi there,' she says. Frank doesn't seem to notice. 'Are you — '

'There's nothing in here,' he says to the boy. 'Ain't there supposed to be candy in here? What happened to the candy?'

'I think those are just for play,' the mother says. 'For the children.'

'I'm sorry,' I say. 'He doesn't mean any harm.' I reach for his arm, but he snatches it away, turns his shoulder to block me.

He wipes one half of the egg on his britches, polishing it. The boy stands a few feet away, up to his knees in balls, and watches Frank with fascination.

'When I was your age,' Frank says, 'my brother Harvey used to hide these all around the yard for me to find on Easter morn. As yon sun rose in the east.'

'Is he — ?' she says. I nod, very fervently, to accept whatever diagnostic excuse she's willing to give us.

'Each one had a different treasure inside. There was a bullet pulled from the mortal wound of a Confederate soldier, and a murdered strumpet's ear sent through the mail by her murderer to taunt the police, and a ring taken by a grave robber from the finger of his own mama's corpse, right out the coffin. The rest of her he sold to the medical school for vivisection.'

'That's ridiculous,' I say. 'Absolutely ridiculous.'

'He tapped a hole in the shell with a nail,' Frank says to the boy, who watches him, rapt, 'let the yolk and the white drain out into a bowl for Mama to scramble for Easter breakfast, and then he'd slip the treasure inside and papier-mâché over it. Tucked them into the knotholes of the dogwoods, behind loose bricks — '

'And just how did he manage to fit a bullet through a nail-hole?' I say. 'Or a ring?'

'And just how do they manage to fit those model ships through the neck of a bottle?' he says, real smug and satisfied. His breath's bad.

Smells like drowned mice.

'The masts are hinged,' I say. 'So they lie flat to the deck. Then it's slim enough to fit through the bottleneck, and when it's inside you raise the masts and unfold the sails. With little tweezers and hooks. That's how. Now come on. Our sundaes are melting.'

'He assembled them inside the egg,' Frank pronounces. 'With little tweezers and hooks.'

The woman looks at her son, gauging the distance between him and Frank.

'I thought Easter was better than Christmas,' Frank says.

'None of that ever happened,' I say. 'You just made it up. He just made that up,' I say.

. He leans forward and holds out to the boy in his shaking hand the two halves of the egg, smiling eerily, just exactly as if he were trying to lure him into a car to drive him off and chop him to bits, and the stupid child walks right over to him. A look of slowly-building panic pulls a smile tight as a wire across the mother's face, deep into the wrinkles of her cheeks.

'Leave that child alone,' I say. 'You look like a pervert.' I hook one finger through his belt loop and try to tug him away, but he hunches right down close to the boy's face, with a fanatic's bright eyes and breathless certainty.

'He melted that ring down and poured it through the hole in a river of gold, reached in with the tweezers as it cooled and bent it back in the shape of itself. It was still warm when I crushed the eggshell. Burned a pink circle in my palm.'

He grabs the boy's wrist and pokes his clammy hand. His mother hurries forward, and the boy recoils, wriggles his arm and tries to shake loose, but Frank's got ahold of him good.

'Enough,' I say. 'That's enough.' I shift the tray against my chest, hold it there with one arm while I try to pull him off — I'm afraid if I tug too hard he'll fall backwards — but he drops the egg so he can clutch the foam post, digs his fingers into it.

'Come on,' Frank says, and starts trying to drag the boy out of the pit. 'It's time to go home.'

'All right,' the mother says. The smile pulls tighter across her face, deeper in, and she pats Frank's hand as a pretense for prying his fingers up. 'All right, now, that's enough.'

'Don't talk to him like that,' I say. 'He's not an imbecile.'

'You can have a hot fudge sundae when we get there,' he says. 'A hot fudge sundae and a soda.'

The boy wrenches his arm free so hard it tugs Frank forward and me with him, soda spilling over my arm and all down my shirt, and he has to throw one arm into the ball pit to catch himself, the other still clutching the post, ends up sagged over the foam steps. The boy clambers past him and runs to the shoe cubbies, sobbing. His mother chases after him while the other two women hurry over, kneel beside Frank on the steps, and throw their arms out in a barricade so their children can scramble safely out of the pit without getting their ankles grabbed. They hurry away to the cubbies, exchanging knowing,

200

sympathetic pursings of the lips and shakings of the head.

'He's just confused,' I shout at them. 'That's all.' I help get his feet under him again, then, fast as we can go, before the authorities show up, I drag him to the car, where Daisy is sitting perfectly upright and attentive in the driver's seat, as if she's ready to man the wheel, and so excited to see him her whole rear end sways with her wagging tail. I shoo her away and sit down, only to discover that the entire back of my seat is sopping and cold from her licking it, and that her front teeth have left little pale crease marks all over the upholstery from her nibbling.

'Look at this,' I say. 'Do you see what she did?'

I pop her on the nose. She looks startled, absolutely dumbfounded, and slinks off to tuck herself into the floorboard behind Frank's seat, where she thinks I can't reach her. I shove the tray with our sundaes and sodas — what's left of them, at least — onto his lap and turn the key in the ignition so hard the engine coughs.

'You want me to drive?' Frank says. 'I'm not sure you're in the best frame of mind.'

I laugh one sharp, humorless laugh, so he knows what an utterly ridiculous idea that is, and back out of the parking spot as fast as I can. Somebody honks at me. I honk right back.

The afternoon sun burns cold in my eyes. I pull on my sunglasses, the big wraparound-visor kind — they really block the light — and then, right as I'm about to pull out of the driveway, there's a clanging and a flashing of red lights, and two white arms lower and cross in front of the road to hold us back as a freight train chugs past. They don't carry passengers through this town at all anymore. Nothing but heaps of coal and wood chips, and mountains of gravel trailing dust through the air sure as the smokestack's plume. Frank leans forward to watch it, swatting the tent-top fabric away from his face. In my rearview mirror, one of the mothers shakes her arms at a beleaguered man with a thick mustache and plastic french fries spread in a fan atop his hat. She points to our car. I lock the doors.

'I've never been so ashamed in my life,' I say. 'Never.'

'You look like a spaceman in those glasses,' Frank says. 'Like you've just landed.' He reaches up and feels along the edge of the ceiling.

'What were you thinking? Were you actually trying to snatch that child?'

Next to his window, the fabric's frayed enough for him to work his fingers behind it. He rips the cloth along the edge.

'Stop that,' I say.

The woman stares at us, arms crossed. It wasn't even her child he tried to take.

He tears the fabric from the ceiling all along his side, and then around its entire perimeter, unbuckles himself and twists around and reaches over the seat, over Daisy, over me, ripping and gathering the loose material in his hands until he's torn it completely free. The corkboard ceiling behind it is orange and cracked, rotting with moisture from some hidden leak. He throws the fabric onto the floorboard.

'There,' he says. 'Now we can see clear.'

Wood chips blow off the tops of the train's piles and eddy away in the breeze. A few land on the windshield. I turn on the wipers and they scrape across the dry glass, sweep the shavings to one side. Frank digs into the ceiling and pulls a chunk out of it. It crumbles away in his fingers, grinds into dust, and the place it leaves in the ceiling looks like a crater on the surface of the orange moon. Its residue glitters iridescent on his fingers, probably with little shards of plexiglas. The caboose streams past us. Another bell clangs up a racket and more lights flash as the white arms open themselves wide to the bright blue sky. The woman finally goes inside.

'And what sort of 'fast food' restaurant,' I say, 'situates itself such that its only entrance and exit is blocked for minutes at a time?'

Frank watches the rail cars go, the caboose slowly shrinking into a black circle, the circle closing in on itself into a dot, the dot closing in on itself into nothing.

'Look at the train,' he says, 'long and black. Running on down the railroad track. One of these days when you turn your back, I'll jump on that train and I won't come back.'

He opens his mouth in astonished, genuine delight at his own cleverness, eyebrows raised in anticipation of my acclaim. Saliva stretches in a thick, whitish strand between his tongue and the roof of his mouth. I take a sip of soda and hold a smashed bundle of french fries out to Daisy. She snaps them up so fast she nearly takes my fingertips off.

'You can't just rhyme *back* with *back*,' I say.

He thinks seriously about this criticism for a long moment, a frown digging troubled lines about his mouth, before he nods, as if conceding a point in a very civil debate. He leans back in his seat and paws the ceiling. It crumbles into a yellow fog. The particles sting my nostrils, gather heavy in the bottoms of my lungs. The dust settles over our skin.

★   ★   ★

I shove so many fruitcakes into his stocking that on Christmas morning, when we shuffle into the den, the yarn loop's ripped and the whole thing's fallen from its nail on the wall. Mine still hangs there, tattered and sagging like his heart in his chest. When he sees the fruitcakes spilled across the floor, he looks so happy you'd think he was a little boy who'd just got his first bicycle. He heads straight for them, and I have to grab his arm before he can try to bend over and grab one. Even Daisy knows they're not real food: she hasn't touched them, and she'll eat anything.

I herd Frank to his chair and give Daisy her Christmas bone, one of those cow femurs you get with the gristle still on and the marrow still inside, which she will only be getting at Christmas due to the greasy smears and slick spots they leave on the floor. She walks around the dark house with the bone in her mouth for five minutes, whimpering some awful terror while she desperately tries to find a spot to hide it. She sets it behind the trash can, then pulls it out and nudges it under the couch, then pulls it out and drops it end first into Frank's shoe, so it sticks out like his bony leg, then pulls it out, puts it in the corner, and frantically nudges her bed over it with her nose.

I set Frank's stocking in his lap and turn on the Christmas tree. Its colors wash across his face, each one dissolving beneath the next as it sweeps across. It moves too fast, the way they've got it programmed, like a carousel wheeling out of control. Makes you dizzy if you look at it too long. He pulls the first brick of fruitcake out and raises his eyebrows in surprise.

'This is just what I've been hungering for,' he says, as if he hadn't eaten a fruitcake in years. He digs into his stocking, deeper and deeper, surprised each time he pulls one out, as if every minute the world made itself anew. He pulls the final fruitcake from the sock's toe, places it atop the heap in his lap, and shakes his head in bewilderment and gratitude.

'This is what I've been hungering for all along,' he says. 'I just couldn't put my finger on it.'

Daisy unearths her bone and starts to gnaw, the muscles atop her head flexing on either side of the bony crest that runs down the center of her skull. Frank tears open a wrapper. It ought to make me happy, how positively thrilled he looks in the bright, shifting light washing green across his face, washing yellow. It ought to make me happy just to see him eat. Instead I watch him peel the wrapper back, smudged and greasy, and I think of the skin slipping down a deer's leg, I think of that boy's hand pulling free of his fingertips, of how quick the thing that used to be you separates into flesh and muscle, like the waters dividing from the waters, into sea and sky.

15

He started to work on the yard with such attention and fervor, you'd have thought he believed it indicative of some greater moral uprightness. Every Sunday afternoon, after we'd eaten our brunch, he changed from pajamas to work clothes while I washed the dishes, then dragged one of the kitchen chairs into the square of sunlight that fell through the open door and sat there, soaking in its warmth, while he pulled on his grass-stained mowing shoes. They smelled the whole place up like sweat and gasoline so bad I knew it even from the kitchen any time he pulled them from the rag he kept them wrapped in at the back of the closet. He mowed the yard slowly, tenderly almost, like he was scared to hurt it, first the front, then the back, pushing the mower along the perimeter in constricting, concentric squares, each one overlapping the last precisely halfway so that every spot was cut twice and cut even, the freshly-mown strips bright and suffused with green against the duller patch they circumscribed, the mower turning more quickly with each tightening pass until, at the very center, it seemed to spin in place. When he was finished, he crawled along the flowerbeds and the house's brick foundation and meticulously clipped the lawn's edges with a pair of shears.

And any patch of grass that started to look thin, any stretch of dirt that started to show bald beneath it, he sowed with seed and nursed back to fullness, though there was one spot that he never could get to grow a thing, no matter how hard he tried. It's still there, just a long swath of dusty dirt along the back fence, interrupted here and there by roots that break up through the ground and plunge back into it like cotton-mouths arrested in the midst of slipping back beneath the river's surface. He went out there with a burlap sack sagging from one hand, scattered seed over it, and worked the seed into the loose dirt with his rake, made us drive ten miles down the road in the very middle of the night, climbed the barbed-wire fence into some farmer's cow pasture, and stole their dry old patties from the field, holding each one up to the moonlight to examine it for sprouting weeds before he dropped it into an old paper bag, and hurling the ones he didn't like over his shoulder while I waited in the getaway car with the engine running like a common criminal. He crumbled the manure, scattered it over the seed, and watered it with his thumb stuck in the nozzle of the hose so the water spread in a fan he moved slowly across the earth, darkening it as though a cloud were passing overhead. The air was sharp with the smell of it, that fresh metallic tang particular to water from a hose that doesn't smell like water at all, but like lawnmower blades and wet grass stuck to bare shins. He covered it in straw, roped the whole patch off so the dog wouldn't wet it, ordered me with a lieutenant's crisp firmness not to set foot across that line, as if he suspected I might be sneaking home from work every day to take secret walks up and down the fence for hours, rubbing the earth bare, and set the sprinklers to water it every morning until winter hardened the dirt against the drops, and by the next spring, a few sprigs of grass had pushed up through what was left of the straw, promptly shriveled, and died. Most of the straw didn't even decay, just lay there atop the dirt the way it had the day he set it down, only a little dingier, bleached gray. When he pulled it away, in the spots where rain had stamped it into the ground, it left behind its imprint like slender ribs in plaster.

He spent an entire afternoon planting with hand and trowel individual clumps of grass he'd bought from some hayseed shyster on the side of the road, and after one good rain washed them all away, left them piled against the fence posts as though it had been a hurricane flood, he spent a month's wages on a motorized aerator he pushed like a tiny steamroller across the packed dirt, cutting plugs the size of my thumb he left scattered all over, and laid down those patches of sod that come like squares of carpet with grass for pile, this particular strain of which the woman at the nursery swore could thrive upon the snow-spread peaks of the highest sierra, and doused them with chemicals to make them grow, wearing his gas mask from the war, spraying the chemicals from a long silver wand attached to a tank he carried in the other hand, stopping every minute or so to pump a handle and pressurize the chamber, and for a few weeks that grass rushed up lustrous and plush from the soil, so glossy green it made the rest of the yard look pitiful in comparison, but by May it had turned yellow, and by June it had dried into scrub, and he wriggled on his belly halfway under the twine — even then he didn't want to set foot on that plot, was afraid his full funneled weight would compact the soil and crush any little fragile life it had left inside it — the string pushed upward by and digging into his back, and ran his hands over the dead grass as though feeling for seams in the earth, for patches that might unhinge.

It was a Saturday morning, early, warm and wet and gleaming as if it was just created, somebody's bright new idea before doubt's had time to dull it. The slanted sun fell in long, heavy blades between the limbs of the maple stretching over the fence. He worked his fingers into the ground and pried up a square. It opened like a door into the earth.

'What're you doing?' I said. What I wanted to ask was why he bothered. But after so long, you start to say things you don't mean, or even believe. You start to ask only the questions whose answers you already know.

He sat all the way up, his back pushing on the twine until the twine heaved its stake out of the ground and fell away at his feet, and held the square out to me as he lifted it free. It fell apart in his hands, the sod crumbling away from withered blades and roots that had never taken hold.

'I ought to go to that store and get my money back,' he said. 'That sod they're peddling ain't worth two cents.'

'It's obviously not the sod that's the problem,' I said.

'I don't care what it is, but I sure ain't going to let a whole load of it sit here useless in dirt that could be growing something.' He flung his handfuls over the fence, toward the trees. They burst into clouds and rained hissing down among the roots. 'Even that truck can grow grass,' he said, pointing in accusation at it, parked in the shade beside the house. Its bed had so much dirt gathered along the edges and in its corners that weeds and even a few little trees sprouted in the piles of it, and a mucky black puddle against the cab that never evaporated. It smelled reptilian. 'I'll be damned if I can't get my own yard to do the same.'

He lifted the squares one by one, some of them falling apart like the first, others held loosely together by their webbed, stringy roots, sagging between his arms as he carried them to the fence and slung them over.

'You could help, you know,' he said. He knelt and pressed himself close to the spot he'd just uncovered, a bright blade sliding across his ribs. 'Instead of just standing there.' He clawed at the dirt with his bare hands, combed his fingers through the soil and ran the soil through his fingers, squinting at it, examining it for the cause of its uselessness.

'It's just one little patch,' I said. 'The whole rest of the yard looks fine.'

He stopped and stared at me, eyebrows reared in shock and dismay. That man could raise his eyebrows a hundred different ways. Took me a long time to learn them all, but I did. Every single one.

'You want me to just let it sit there like that?' he said. 'Like we're a couple reprobates?'

'What does it matter? No one's ever going to see it.'

He crawled on his hands and knees and ran his palms over the ground as if searching frantically for something he'd lost, brushing dirt away from dirt with a soft, whispering scrape to see what was hidden underneath, only to discover that there was no secret, that there was no answer: that the subterranean was exactly the same as the surface, as far down as you could reach.

'I will,' he said.

★ ★ ★

It took months of luring and praise and dinner scraps, after he finally gave up, to convince the dog to do her business there. He'd had it roped off so long, and scolded her so bad each time she ducked under the twine to chase a rabbit across it, that even after he tore the rope down and pulled up the stakes, she refused to cross the old boundary. She'd follow him right up to it, but she wouldn't set a paw in the dirt, and when he cooed her name, she turned away as if she just couldn't bear to hear it, the string imprinted in the air the way, if bound too tightly round a bird's body to hold its wings in place while it dries, it leaves deep, permanent creases in the feathers.

★ ★ ★

He planted his vegetable garden that next spring, started from seedlings in soup cans I saved for him with holes we hammered in their bottoms for drainage, where the sprouts slowly unfurled under plastic wrap, breathing a thin coating of mist onto its underside as their tender stems struggled with every bit of sunlight condensed to heave up and shrug off clods of dirt no bigger than a bit of fluff you'd pick from an eyelash. He placed the garden so it blocked the dead patch entirely from view, tilled the whole thing with a spade, turning the earth one narrow shovel's-width at a time, until the plot was wide and deep as if he'd dug out the foundation for another house. He went out of his way, I think, to make every single thing he could as difficult as possible. I thought he was going to have a heart attack before he was done, going out there after a full day at the mill, where they still had yet to install the new air-conditioning system, though they had bricked the windows over to keep the cool air of the future trapped inside, every night for a week and all day long that Saturday, digging long, narrow trenches six inches deep into the earth, and filling each one with the dirt he'd dug up from the trench beside it. All day I listened to the grunt, the muffled strike as the ground split apart, the whispered hiss as he slung soil from the shovel. The surface of the earth was dry and cracked from the sun, but what was just underneath, in the cuts he tore open and overturned, was dark and damp.

213

He didn't come inside until six o'clock, sweat dripping in big beads from his nose, limped slow and stiff toward the bathroom, wincing a little with every step.

'Are you all right?' I said, leaning in the bathroom door.

He unlatched the straps of his overalls and peeled his shirt away. It was soaked, made a reluctant sucking noise as it let his chest go. He grunted and dropped it on the floor, didn't even walk the three steps to put it in the hamper.

'Back's just a little sore,' he said.

It took him the better part of five minutes to slowly lower himself onto the lip of the tub to turn on the water, and I could almost feel the tight muscles in his thighs seize as he bent to untie his shoes. He was breathing heavy and shallow, the birds' wings clasped so tight around his chest he couldn't open it enough to get the air in.

'Why don't you just buy a tractor?' I said.

'I don't want a tractor. I like doing it the old way. Like my daddy did.'

'The old way was hooking your horse up to your plow.'

'You want to buy a horse and plow?' he said.

'If the old way had been how you do it, the human race would have gone extinct from starvation by now. Or exhaustion.'

He managed to pull his shoes off, and lifted himself just enough to shove his overalls and underwear down his legs. He smelled like mulch, like wood wet and rotting. I used to love that smell, the real smell of him only I knew.

'This is how my daddy did it,' he said.

'Then your daddy was not as smart a man as you've led me to believe.'

He scowled, and I left him sitting on the edge of the tub, staring warily at the rising water as if it were an obstacle to surmount. When I came back an hour later, Fancy was curled up on his undershirt, which she'd nudged into a nest, and Frank was hunched forward in the tub with his elbows on his knees, his head hung down and his eyes closed and his shoulders drawn practically all the way up to his ears, like mountains driven from the earth by centuries of underground plates scraping slowly and painfully across each other, and therefore not inclined to sink back down any time soon. He was too big for that tub anyway, had to fold his legs up so they were barely in the water.

'Dinner's ready,' I said.

He opened his eyes and sat forward a little, water rushing off him. Shadows creased his belly. He'd put on a good twenty pounds in the last few years, and though he carried it well, the animals on his arm had swollen, the buck too distended to hunt, his chest fatted with pride, the whale buoyed up toward shore by its own bloated belly. He cupped water in his hands and poured it slowly over his head, flattening his hair, darkening its blond. It was starting to thin on top. The streams ran branching down his neck and into the bathwater. With him hunched out of it like that, it didn't fill half the tub.

'Dinner's ready.'

'I'm too sore to move,' he said to the rippling

215

water. He didn't seem to be able to lift his head.

'Don't be a baby.'

'Who're you calling a baby?'

'I don't see anybody else in this room.'

'I would storm out of this house right now,' he said, 'if it didn't necessitate moving.'

'And who'd feed you? You'd starve to death.'

'I'm in terrible pain,' he said, suppressing a grin, 'and you see fit to joke.' Probably he was exaggerating the whole thing. He did like being the recipient of some tender ministrations once in a while.

I rolled up my pants and sat on the lip of the tub, in the corner where it met the wall, slid my legs in on either side of his back — the water was already turning cold — and pressed my fingertips into the hollow between his shoulder and collarbone. He grunted, his shoulders forcing themselves even higher: the darkness between the stars widened, the empty sky spread apart. The muscle was hard and static at first, like clay when you peel away the plastic, so brittle you pull on a corner and it breaks clean off, but gradually it began to spread against the warmth of my hand, into malleability. I kneaded it the way, when I was mounting that mountain lion for the museum, I shaped the muscles of the clay model one by one, in wet, shining layers that turned dull as they dried, and worked the hollow into the muscle of its hindquarters, pushing down toward the wooden bone, feeling the cool clay smear and condense under my thumb until it took a shape I believed was true.

'You're working yourself too hard,' I said.

'We've got to eat, don't we?'

'That's what the store's for.'

Languidly he tapped the surface of the water with his fingertips, watching the seaweed on his forearm sway underneath it.

'You work all day. All week. You shouldn't come home and work more.'

'I like being good and worn out when I lay down at night.'

'I don't see how there's anything left of you to wear out.'

'I come from working stock,' he said. 'We're bred for labor. Like oxen.'

'Oxen die quick.'

Water slapped against the sides of the tub.

'You're exhausted.' I said. 'I can tell.'

'The best cure for exhaustion is work,' he offered hopefully. 'It's invigorating. It's bracing.'

'You're an awful liar.'

Without even turning his head, he raised his eyebrows in skepticism. The best lies, we'd learned, don't ask you to say a word. They practically tell themselves.

'You have to rest,' I said.

He stared at his palms. Dirt was etched into every wrinkle, and blisters bubbled across the tops of them, just underneath his fingers, where the shovel had rubbed the skin loose.

'I don't believe I know how,' he said.

I dipped a washcloth in the warm water, wrung it out, and laid it carefully across the back of his neck like a strip of burlap, dipped in plaster and pulled between my fingers to squeeze away the extra liquid, that I pressed into the

217

mold of that mountain lion, working it into every groove of engorged vein, over every bulge of a muscle's hollow, smoothing away the bubbles. If there's any air, any empty space at all between the layers, the weight of the skin flattens the contours. That kind of mount you can only afford to do for a museum. It's long work, slow and full of waiting, shaping your way from the outside in, laying just a couple layers of burlap and mesh at a time so they don't sit there soggy too long and rot. Some days you go to lay down the next one and can't tell that the last three are even there, and with each one, the details of the surface become less and less distinct, and you wonder if that shell will ever be strong enough to hold up the hide. And then you lay down the next layer anyway.

When I was a younger man, I dreamed of all sorts of fantastic mounts in lush museum dioramas, of Komodo dragons locked in combat on burning coastal sands, of lions tugging a zebra down by one hind leg into snapped savanna grasses that flattened themselves to a single dimension as they crossed onto the painted backdrop and stretched away to some periwinkle horizon, but I must have mounted twenty buck for every one of any other animal, wound from wood-wool and twine into clumsy approximations of themselves, rote variations of the same three poses distinguished only by the angle of the head. In the fall, when the cold air and dark afternoons dried up their soft antlers like the leaves, turned them bloodless and brittle, there were so many of them some days that I had to pile sacks of salt and alum on top of all my freezer-lockers, each one big as four seafaring trunks, just to hold the lids shut against them, and stay there long into the night, peeling their skins away until my hands were chapped and sore, and come home to a dark house, to Frank already fast asleep.

'Anyway,' he said, 'it's done now. The rest is easy.'

In the mornings, before work, he watered the garden by hand, out of a can shaped like a swan, from whose beak the drops dribbled sputtering onto the leaves, walking back and forth to the spigot every few plants to refill its bladder. He ate his supper each night quick and silent so he could get out there as soon as possible, patrolled for weeds and, later, for fruit, anxiously pacing the rows. The ripe he tugged free and tossed into a sack hung from his wrist, the split or rotten he threw to the ground in disgust, as if they were a personal affront. From the back door, from the window above the sink, I watched his pale, bent back dwindle and disappear into the dark.

They did taste fine, though, those tomatoes. Flavor practically burned your tongue. I never tasted a tomato with as much flavor as those, that first summer, full of his ache and sweat.

The washcloth, as it dried, stiffened and took on the shape of his spine, cupping his vertebrae. I still long sometimes for the feel of plaster, thick and cold like mud, like life in your hands. In my memory, everything he touches, everything that brushes against him, reminds me of something else, something that never seemed to matter at

219

the time, when it was really there.

After a while, when the water was so cold we both had chill bumps, he gathered the courage to very slowly sit straight up, then very slowly lean back against my leg. The water rose around us, surged up to soak the cuffs of my pants and draw them heavily down. I leaned over him, cupped it in my hands, and pulled it over his stomach and chest, the way the moon pulls waves across the shore.

He ruminated on the big knuckles jutting from his clenched fist. The birds on his chest folded and unfolded their wings, flying always toward his heart and always getting nowhere, while his shoulders, still standing rigid guard against the pain long after it had vanished, finally surrendered. He breathed deep and rested his head on my thigh. I wished that we were young again, that we didn't know a thing about each other, when just the brush of my lips to those birds' trembling bodies was enough to drive them to the sky.

I kissed his closed eyes. They felt smooth and hard, like pebbles under their thin, soft lids. We all ought to have gone blind by now, with so little to protect them.

16

And here's what he's reduced me to at last: I am cleaning the house myself. At least I'm trying to. By the time I've given the books on the shelves and the remotes on the coffee table my best imitation of a good dusting, I'm already exhausted, and that's before I drag his stolen vacuum out of the closet and down the hall. Thing's so heavy you'd think the dust chamber was filled with concrete. Daisy crams herself under the coffee table when she hears it coming. The table's down so low she has to lay on her belly and drag herself by her forelegs to get under it, hunkers there like she's waiting for the sky to start tumbling round her.

Frank's no help at all, of course. Just sits there watching the TV while I stand here bent over, all the blood rushing into my head, and make a fool of myself trying to figure out how to pull the extension hose off the side of the vacuum so I can clean the animals. The hose itself comes loose if I pull on its accordion plastic, but the nozzle on the end's snapped into the side of the vacuum and won't yank out. I try pushing it down, I try jerking it up, I try tugging on the hose until the plastic's stretched pale, I try slapping the side of the vacuum in rage and considering that I should go ahead and give up now and settle for the satisfaction of having tried, and then I see there's a tiny button up against where the hose nozzle tucks into the vacuum, so small it's almost not there. I press it down, and the whole thing pops free. It's no wonder the neighbors threw it away, with little mechanisms like that you can't hardly see to use. If we'd paid for the thing, I'd write a letter of complaint. I may do so anyway.

I stomp the big gray button beside one of the wheels. Headlights pop up and flash on from the front of it, and Daisy jumps up, startled, knocks her head on the underside of the table and nearly overturns the whole thing, glasses and remote control and all. She stares at the vacuum, wild-eyed, tilting her head to one side, then the other, as if she's just on the verge of sudden and complete understanding.

The vacuum shudders as it hums higher and higher, to such a high pitch that the hum breaks open into a roaring, insistent emptiness, and a ball of dust six inches away gives up its grip on the baseboard, slides across the floor, and disappears into the hose. The room smells of hot dust and vinyl.

'It actually works,' I yell.

Daisy creeps along the wall, holding herself low to the ground, staring at the vacuum. She has to pass us to get down the hall to safety, oily hackles raised, and she pants the closer she gets, her huge tongue hung out one side of her mouth and lapped with lines of saliva like the edges of foam successive waves, each one weaker than the last, leave on sand. It looks like she's smiling. That's the problem with dogs: they look like they've never been happier, when really all they're trying to do is cool themselves down enough to keep from dying in the heat.

She scrabbles so hard and fast to get past us, her nails slip on the hardwood, and she falls down before clawing her way back to her feet and launching herself down the hall. I screw the round dust brush onto the end of the hose and ruffle it through the raccoon's fur. All the animals gather dust, but he's the worst. That thick, mangy undercoat really hangs on to it good. I make my way around the living room and down the hall, running the brush over the birds, their wings bending stiffly, and the deer reaching out of the wall overhead until the blood runs out of my fingers and they start to tingle. I'm digging it into a buck's ear — a lot of dust builds up cupped inside them — when all of a sudden the vacuum makes a choking sound and a high-pitched, fluttering gasp. I stomp the button to turn it off. The room feels like a brittle veneer without the noise, sucked hollow and dry. I pull down the brush, and there, caught in the end of the tube, is a balled-up fruitcake wrapper.

He carries fruitcake with him all the time now, shoved into his bulging pockets or clutched in his greasy fingers, nibbles it all day like it's the rations of war and he never knows when he'll get another bite. I went to every grocery store in town after Christmas and bought up all they had on closeout clearance sale. Took me five entire hours over two days, had to go in and talk to the managers and have the bag boys load whole unsold boxes of them into my trunk, but I wasn't about to pass up those prices. Plus I liked watching the bag boys work, how the veins swelled on one's forearms as he heaved the boxes to his chest, how the hem of another's shirt rose when he bent over to set them in the trunk, bared the soft blond hair at the base of his spine and the shadow of a hollow that funneled down and disappeared under his low-slung belt. Luckily the good-looking ones were all back from vacation. Made the whole ordeal much more pleasant.

I came home with five hundred logs of it, and it didn't cost me but two-hundred and fifty dollars. That kind of stockpile ought to last us at least half the year, and the way they keep shoving the holidays on us faster and faster, the new ones'll be on the shelves by the time these run out. I bring them in an armful at a time and leave the rest stacked up in the trunk. There's not enough room for them in the pantry. I'm just glad it's got all those preservatives in it. I don't know what we'd do otherwise.

'Frank,' I yell. 'Why is there a fruitcake wrapper in this deer's ear?'

Daisy glances at me from the bathroom, where she's got both paws on the toilet rim. She sniffs the water and ponders whether it's worth the drinking, the short whiskers on the end of her muzzle barely brushing its surface. Her breath wrinkles it.

'Get out of there,' I say.

She gives me a look of grave disapproval and lands heavily on all fours. In a big wicker basket beside the commode, we've got rolls of toilet paper stacked in a pyramid, and there, inside the cardboard tube of a roll halfway down, is another wrapper. She sniffs my hand as I pull it free, her nose so cold and damp it's a kind of relief. I scratch the spot behind her shoulder that makes her hind leg thump the floor and the corner of her mouth pull back. She leans against my shin, so heavy she about bowls me over. Her breath smells like cigar smoke.

'Come on,' I say, and she leads me through the hall, into the living room. Frank's at the front door, furiously jostling it, trying to yank it open. He stops for a moment to regroup, plants both feet on the floor, spread as wide apart as he can get them, grabs the doorknob in both hands, and prepares to heave back with all his might and weight, almost positively ensuring he will fall and crack his bones across the dusty floor.

'What are you doing?' I say.

For a moment he stands absolutely still, as if I've caught him at something illicit. Slowly he lets go of the doorknob and drops his hands to his side.

'We're late,' he says. 'I knew just as soon as you started you were going to make us late.'

'Late for what?'

'For supper,' he says, as if this fact couldn't be more obvious. 'We're supposed to be there at eight.'

'It's just after six.'

'I knew you'd make us late. I said so.'

'You did no such thing. And I already had supper.'

'Why'd you do that? You know how Mama

225

gets when you don't eat enough.'

'Mama?'

He takes a long, scrutinizing, and apparently unsatisfying gander at me. 'You could look a little more presentable. Put you on some decent clothes at least. She already thinks you're a heathen.'

'Your mama's been dead fiftysome years,' I say.

He gapes in scandalized outrage. 'What a awful thing to say. My mother adores you.' He pounds on the door, as if there's somebody on the other side waiting to unlock it. 'Help me get this thing open,' he says. 'It's become stuck.' He pretends to study the gap between the door and its frame, runs his shaking fingers along it as if he's not quite sure, can't quite see, how one fits into the other. 'Might need to sand it down a little. You painted the paint on too thick.'

He starts pressing on the door at various points to test its resolve. 'Now help me get out, will you? She's waiting.' He pounds the door as hard as he can, so hard the paint crackles under his fist. 'She's waiting,' he says. 'She's waiting on us.'

'I'll tell you what,' I say, pulling his elbow. 'Why don't you just sit down, and I'll see if I can get the door fixed. How about that?'

'I'll call her.' He starts for the hallway. 'I'll call her and tell her we're running late. So she's not worried.' He stops short, staring in alarm at the vacuum, at the swirl of dust and hair in its clear plastic lung. Daisy waits nearby, willing him in vain but with unflappable focus toward the kitchen, toward the treat cabinet.

'What?' I say.

'I just got this thing working,' he grumbles, outraged, and stomps over to the vacuum. He pops the dust chamber free. 'I just got this thing cleaned out, and you've gone and clogged it up again.'

He reaches inside, pulls out a handful of dust and dirt, and hurls it to the floor. It bursts outward across the boards, into dark, feathery streaks. Daisy watches, nervous, and paws his shin. I hurry toward him. He gathers up and hurls down to earth another dark cloud, breaking it open across the wide wood plane, then another, then another. I grab his hand before he can reach in for the next, but the cylinder's nearly empty. He jams it back onto the vacuum but can't get it lined up quite right to snap in place, leaves it hanging half on for just a second before it crashes to the floor. Daisy pounces on it, wraps her stubby legs around it as best she can, and starts chewing its plastic edge in her back teeth, the good tearing ones.

'I just got that thing clean,' he grumbles, shaking his head. His fingers are coated in a fine layer of pale gray silt. 'Just now got it clean.'

'Sit down. You shouldn't be wandering around like this.'

He starts to cross the room to his chair, then thinks better of it and shuffles his agonizingly long way around its perimeter, slippers whispering across the floor and one hand stretched out to the wall in unbroken contact, his fingertips smudging streaks of dirt and dust across it that

227

fade the further he goes, all the way to the television, where he rests slumped for a few breaths before launching himself into the slow, headlong plunge across the last six feet of empty space to his chair. He leans forward a little more with each step, and it's only by luck that he makes it there before the speed and angle of his stoop topple him over, and when he does make it there he has to clutch the backrest, hug it with both arms as if he's out on the high ledge of some building and it's his last desperate purchase against vertigo and the wind, while it rocks groaning under his impact.

He lowers himself onto his knees in the seat, then turns, digging one shoulder into the backrest for support, throws his arms wide to grab the arms of the chair, and slides down onto his behind. He leans all the way back, footrest up, to make it appear he's just been resting all day long, just watching a little Sunday football like any regular fellow. The treads of his slippers are worn smooth.

I don't know how he can even see the television from that angle. It's got to hurt his neck.

The six o'clock news is on. I stomp in front of it and drop the wrappers in his lap. Daisy stares up at them in wild-eyed surprise, mesmerized by the way they slowly unfold, crackling like his knees when he stood up too fast. One of her jowls catches under her bottom teeth so it looks like she's snarling.

'Now,' I say. 'Why are you hiding fruitcake wrappers?'

'Hiding?' He makes the indignant face guilty people make to express just how sincerely they can't believe you'd ever suspect them of committing such a heinous crime. 'I ain't hiding them.'

'Then what are you doing? Saving them up in case their market value skyrockets?'

'I ain't saving them,' he says.

'Then who is?'

He's trying hard not to smile, but I can see it there, incipient on his lips. I don't even want to know. He pulls Daisy's free jowl, thick and soft, upward so it matches the other one, then higher, over her gums. The bright pink muscle of her tongue rests between her teeth, stringy blood vessels running along its side. He pokes the edge of it, where it spills over the jagged mountain of her molar, and she sits there and lets him, staring at the wrappers the whole time.

'Don't try to blame the dog,' I say. 'I'm not that stupid.'

'They've got to go somewhere,' he says.

'They've got to go in the trash can.'

'Nope. Now, you see, a trash can — '

'I know what a trash can is. What I want to know is why those things aren't in it.'

He sits back, raising one finger, to deliver a lecture on the proper place of the fruitcake wrapper in the home of modern man. One of them rustles in his lap, and Daisy snaps her head back in alarm, like it nipped her. She thinks everything's alive, scrambles cowering away with her tail between her legs any time, wagging, it thumps against the leg of the table and rattles the glasses on the table's top. Her jowl comes unpinned.

He leans forward and kisses her muzzle, the soft, iridescent fur right under her nose where her lips meet. She snuffles, shakes her head, and sneezes.

'Oh my goodness,' he says, and does it again. She suffers this with a look of weary forbearance. He loves it when she sneezes.

'She was about to eat one in the bathroom,' I say. 'She could get a clog of plastic in her intestines. A blockage. They'd have to cut her open to pull it out. You know how much that costs?'

'She licks their insides clean, but she don't try to eat them. Just enough to get the taste. She can't get enough fruitcake.'

'You've been feeding the dog fruitcake?'

'You think I could eat three of them all by myself?' he says. 'In one day?'

'You can't feed dogs fruitcake. She's probably going to get pancreatitis.'

'A log or two, now that's one thing. But three?'

'Now I'm going to have to follow her around in the cold to check her stool every time she goes out. Just how I want to spend my days.'

'Ain't given her any problems, far as I can see.'

'Rivers of blood,' I say. 'I bet it's just rivers of blood.'

'Yes, sir. She's just fine.'

'She's fat. Look at her. I bet she's gained ten pounds in the last month.'

'She comes over and nudges my arm if I forget to give it to her. Knows when it's time and everything.'

'And when is that?'

'Any time you ain't looking.' He grins. His incisor's a crumbling crag beside an empty, blasted pit in his gum. 'She's a smart girl,' he says, and scratches her under the chin. 'Who's my smart girl?'

'You need to wear your partial.'

'I'm pretty partial to you,' he says.

'I used to be partial to you. Back when you were — '

Something's burning. Daisy smells it first, starts waving her snout all around in the air, desperate to fit it into the scent's invisible groove, and I catch it right after that, the sharp tang and clouded smolder, like the time I set a piece of tupperware on a hot burner, melted it into a puddle.

'You smell that?' I say, stalking around the room. 'What is that?' I bend over to sniff the lukewarm air blowing into my face from the vent, stale and odorless. Daisy stays where she is, head tilted back. A thin, high-pitched keen wheezes in her throat.

Something crackles by Frank's chair. He sees me turn toward the noise, and glee brightens his face, sends his mouth gaping wide in dumb anticipation.

'What?' I say.

There's another crackle, and a sound like a thick bubble popping. It's coming from the lamp beside him. I hurry over to it. Frank turns his face upward, waiting for some response. I look inside the lampshade from above for the half a second before the bulb's brightness burns a black hole into the very spot it burned brightest, the way the biggest, most luminous stars collapse into themselves and pull in everything around them, even the light itself, and there, wrapped around the lit bulb, slipped over it in a sheath, is a fruitcake wrapper, melting in the incandescent heat. Its wrinkles flatten, its flat expanses bubble, and then it, too, is pulled into darkness. I squeeze my eyes shut, reach under the shade, and turn the light off.

'Are you out of your mind?' I say.

When I look straight at him, the black hole takes up half his face. It fades to green as its burnt edges constrict, drawing it shut. Slowly his chin and his eyebrows emerge from it, raised in something like expectation. I lift the lampshade off and throw it on the couch. The wrapper's already cooling, hardening into a new, stream-lined shape that mimics the bulb's curve, all its wrinkles smoothed away or else forced upward into little bubbles that burst and vanish, the words of its ingredient list, all those unpro-nounceable chemicals smeared into one uniform pink blur.

I unscrew the warm bulb, so tight in its socket I nearly shatter the thing, I have to grip it so hard to make it turn. The edge of the wrapper's gathered into a frilled collar at the bottom of the bulb. I work my fingernails under it, try to peel it from the glass, but it's melted on there near inseparable, and all they manage to do is tear off the brittle edge and scrape faint lines through the rest of the plastic.

'You could have killed us,' I say. 'You know

that? We're lucky you didn't catch the house on fire. Burn the whole thing down and the two of us in it.'

He looks surprised, and somewhat disappointed, as if it had never occurred to him that wrapping a thin piece of plastic around a burning bulb might be a fire hazard.

'I guess it serves me right,' I say, 'for letting you out of my sight.'

'There you go.' He nods real encouraging, the way you would to a sensitive and untalented child. 'You're starting to get the hang of it.'

I claw plastic from the glass in measly, crinkled shreds. And as I'm doing this, as I am standing right over him, he palms one of the wrappers from his lap and slides it into the crease between the arm and the cushion of his chair.

'I can see you,' I say. 'I'm right here.'

Slowly, real slowly, believing apparently that my vision registers only the quickest, most jolting of movements, he returns his hand to his thigh.

'Get up,' I say. 'Put your teeth in. You ought to at least look like yourself.'

'I'm busy,' he says, huddling down in his chair. I throw the bulb on the couch, grab him around the arm with both hands, his armpit closing hot and damp on my fingers, and try to haul him up, but he crosses his arms and sinks further into the recliner, as if he's growing heavier by the moment, the upholstery closing round to clasp him tight.

'Fine.' I march to the bathroom, bring him back the glass with his teeth in it and a new light bulb from the hutch in the hallway. 'You've made me walk back and forth through this house so many times today, I'm probably going to get shin splints.' I screw the bulb in its socket and switch the lamp back on, and he turns his face away from the light as if it hurts him, like some creature of the underground or night. I hold the glass right in front of his face. The solution the dentist gave him is clear and so thick the plastic jaws hang suspended in it.

'Put them in,' I say. 'Now. I'm not going to stand around here all day and watch you looking like some toothless idiot.'

He leans to one side, trying to catch a glimpse of the TV, but I block him, and then he leans back to the other side, and I have to block that one too before he finally huffs and shoves his big fingers into the tiny glass so hard the solution spills out on his lap. He recoils and glares at me, as if this is somehow all my fault.

'You're just lucky I held on to the glass,' I say.

He picks out the top jaw, a little more carefully this time, holds it between thumb and forefinger. His hand shakes as he moves it into his mouth, and he spends a long time rooting around in there, shoving the partial to one side, then another, then further back. You've got to get it lined up just exactly parallel to the actual jaw and then push it just exactly straight on, without tilting it at all to one side or the other, so that the teeth you've got left can slide through the holes in the plastic gums, and the plastic gums can latch around the bases of the teeth you've got left. Saliva leaks over his bottom lip and drips

234

onto the fruitcake in his shirt pocket. His hand moves furiously back and forth inside his mouth. Then he rips it out and hurls the partial across the room. It hits the raccoon in the side, knocking a cloud of dust up from his fur, and clatters to the ground. Daisy runs over and starts licking it.

'It doesn't fit anymore,' Frank says. 'It's broken.'

I walk calmly to the umbrella can and take out my mechanical arm, but Daisy scampers away before I can get close, her tail between her legs and his teeth between hers. I stalk her across the room and finally get her cornered between the vacuum and the wall.

'Drop it,' I say.

She turns her face away, growling.

'You see this? You've turned this dog into a monster.'

I reach for her mouth with my pincers, squeezing the trigger so they clamp shut with a loud clack, and she drops his teeth right into one of the mounds of dirt and dust and drags herself under the coffee table, hind legs splayed. I pick the dentures up, soil and grime and dog hair all stuck to them by saliva. It hardly makes a difference. He hasn't brushed them in weeks, just soaks them every night, when he even remembers to take them out. There's little bits of food stuck between the molars. I dunk them in the solution and swirl them around.

'Open wide,' I say, pulling the jaw out and holding it over the glass to catch the drips. Reluctantly he opens his mouth, a wide pink maw littered with just a few teeth leaning this way and that, most of them capped in metal. 'Put your chair back,' I say. He yanks the wooden lever, raising the footrest, and reclines. I set the glass on the table, next to the styrofoam cup from Burger Bonanza he's been saving for weeks — a *styrofoam cup*, the sole purpose of which is to be thrown away — despite the fact that I won't let him drink anything out of it, its rim crenellated where he's chewed away crescents of styrofoam all the way around, and lean over him from behind, push down on his chin with one hand and reach inside his mouth with the other. It's warm in there, and my knuckles brush the slimy insides of his cheeks, broken here and there by rough patches where he's bit himself and the skin's healing over.

I tap the partial onto his gums, but it gets stuck halfway, lodged tight, and I have to rock it back and forth to wrench it off. He tries to say something, but I push the dentures back down. His tongue shoves my hand, tilts it just a degree to one side so the partial grates across his teeth and won't slide the rest of the way. He squirms under me and tries to groan something. Daisy starts howling her long, strident howl.

'Hold still,' I say. 'The problem is you're moving around too much.'

I jostle the dentures back and forth, try to scrape them down his teeth a little at a time, angling them one way, then the other. He starts bellowing like a cow, then runs out of air and starts wheezing, grabs my wrist and tries to wrench it away, but I keep it right where it is, pull the partial off and shove it on again, a little harder this time, so hard my fingers slip off and jab his pulpy, wet palate. He bites my hand. Feels like a blunt door slamming shut on my knuckles. I yank them from his mouth, and soon as my fingers are clear, he snaps his jaw shut, hard, with the sound of plastic cracking. The gears in his chair ring loudly as he throws the lever to lower the footrest. He hunches forward and coughs long, wet coughs, struggling to pull breath in between them.

'You bit me,' I say.

'I couldn't breathe,' he wheezes.

'You're not supposed to force it on. You probably broke it.'

'I couldn't breathe.'

'You've got a nose, don't you?' I shake my hand. Each bleeding knuckle feels like a heavy, pounding heart. Blood washes down my fingers.

'Keep your hands out of my mouth from now on,' he says. His eyes are watering.

'Smile,' I say.

He pulls his lips wide, so wide he looks ghoulish, but all his teeth are in place. The top ones, at least. He starts coughing again.

'Run up to the store and get me a fruitcake,' he wheezes, waving me toward the door, as if that's going to clear his airway.

I snatch the half-eaten block from his shirt pocket and drop it in his lap.

On the TV, the weatherman says we might get some warmer weather this time next week, the first faint currents of spring. They're always saying something like that, finding some glimmer in the distant future to keep us all going a little longer. By the time it gets here, the forecast's changed.

In other news, a lady reporter's pleasant voice informs us, an elderly woman in town was raped and beaten half to death in her own home at three o'clock this afternoon. The man who did it followed her from the grocery store, then lounged around in her living room when he was done and ordered a pizza while she bled out on the bedroom carpet and quietly dragged herself across it to get to the phone. Had to wait for him to stop naming all the toppings he wanted before she could call the police, and they didn't get there much sooner than the pizza boy.

'You ought to be glad of it,' I say. 'Your mama. You ought to be glad she died. If she'd lived, if any one of them had lived, any one at all, you'd have ended up married to some nice girl. Just to make them happy. You know that?'

I pinch the knuckle of my index finger shut. The skin's loose, bunches together and turns red, and when I let it go it's slow to flatten, slow to remember its shape. The seam of blood barely holds it together. I daub it on my britches, careful not to tear the clots, gather the trash from his lap, and stand over him with my mechanical arm while he peels the wrapper back from the fruitcake, slow and exhausted, slumped in his chair. As soon as it's loose, I snatch it from his hand with my pincers.

'If you don't start putting these in the trash can where they belong,' I say, waving it in his face, 'I'm going to stop buying you fruitcake.' He forgets that it's all stocked in the trunk.

'Yessum,' he says.

I pinch his leg with the mechanical arm. He sits statue-still, the fruitcake in his lap, statue-still except for his jaw and his hands on the armrests, always working, always clenching and letting go. The old woman on the television sobs.

You can spend a whole life trying to withdraw from this world, sealing yourself off from it as tight as possible, and still it does its best to sneak in. Still it follows you home.

'Pancakes?' Frank says.

Daisy shoves her head between his knees.

17

We both worked just as long as we could. I kept the shop open for years after everybody else had switched to prefab styrofoam forms you shaved down to the size you wanted and started sending the skins off to somebody else to tan, after the trash started creeping closer in strip clubs and pawn shops and tattoo parlors that only the train tracks restrained from spilling onto my side of the street and I had to put bars over the windows and the doors to keep the hoodlums from breaking in and stealing my chemicals, even after the bureaucrats of the Fish and Wildlife Service started stopping by with their tomes of forms to fill out for each carcass to ensure I wasn't mounting any endangered animals.

'If it's lying dead in my shop,' I told their agent, when he paid me a visit to discuss my lack of thorough documentation, 'I believe it's past the point of being endangered.'

And Frank, when his knees buckled one day as the spool dropped into his arms and drove him to the ground as if in supplication, as if in prayer, took the reassignment to dye-vat operator they offered him, pulled the lever to lower the ropes of denim into the vats and pulled the lever to raise the ropes dripping back out, over and over until they reached the commanded shade. By then, they were really trying to make things cheap, weren't even using real indigo anymore

240

but some synthetic sulfur compound, came home on him every day smelling like rotten eggs. Soon after that, they got rid of the entire loading-dock crew, had one man do with a forklift what they used to pay twenty to do by hand. We were just a little over fifty years old.

We left the house together one time — one single time — in all those years. One hot Sunday at the end of summer, I was drying the dishes after breakfast with a succession of dish towels, each one growing wetter and wetter until it was good for nothing but pushing water around on a pan, when he trudged in, sat down, and started brushing black polish out of a tin and into a thin, dull film across the toes of his dress shoes. He was wearing a clean white shirt and khaki trousers and had his hair combed slick back, looked like he'd dolled himself up for an important date. I stopped drying and watched him.

'I thought I'd go with you,' he said, buffing the toe of his shoe with a strip of muslin. He didn't look up. 'To the store.'

'Really?' I said.

'I don't want to stay cooped up all day. It's nice out.' Something about him, about the frantic, mechanical speed with which he drew the strip of fabric back and forth across the leather until the sun splashed bright across it, in the tight set of his shoulders, seemed restless and wild, like he was that night he showed up breathless and prowling in my shop, but he sounded real casual, as if all of this was absolutely normal. With a shoehorn, he tugged the stiff back of his shoe out and shoved his foot inside, yanked the laces so hard and tight I doubted he would ever be able to get the thing off.

I tried my best to adopt the same casual tone, so as not to break it. 'What about the yard?'

'I reckon it'll still be here when we get back.' He stood, brushing dust from the front of his trousers. 'You divide up the grocery list,' he said. 'I'll follow you over there in the truck.'

We each had our own cart, and we pretended not to know each other, that we just happened to be meandering at roughly the same pace down the aisles. The tile was a dingy orange linoleum, and there was a dark red stripe halfway up the white cinderblock wall, painted all the way around the store, bending in every corner. There was hardly anybody else there, and the creak of Frank's soles was loud and grating. He'd never had much occasion to break them in.

'Excuse me,' he said, as I was picking through a crate of peaches. 'Can you tell me which of these is ripe?' He nodded to a heap of cantaloupe. He liked them almost rotten, the rind so thin you could practically peel it away from the warm, wet meat. Anything else he said didn't have enough taste. I picked one from the top of the pile, scattering gnats, and he watched closely as I pressed it to my ear, its skin rough against my cheek, and rapped it with my knuckles, listening for the telltale resonance of the hollow. I started to put it in my cart before I remembered to hand it back to him.

'Thank you,' he said.

I nodded and went on my way, but he pushed his cart so slowly, gaping in dilemma and wonder at every endcap and sale, nervously rolling up and unrolling his list, that I had to wait for him to catch up, and pretend for a long time to read the ingredients on a jar of pickles while he agonized over which green beans to get. A young woman in a bright sleeveless dress and green eyeshadow, with hair that the night before, at least, had been swaddled shiny and high into a beehive, wandered into the aisle, her plastic basket dangling from one elbow and knocking against her bony hip. She smiled at him. Her lips were thin, her teeth large, and seeing him there, out in the open and so close to her, close enough that his elbow nearly brushed her waist as he finally made up his mind and reached for a can, stirred something in me. I couldn't stop staring at him, watching his fingers close around a smooth glass jar, his pressed collar dig into his thick neck, the skin above it flushed, the vein swollen.

'Excuse me,' he said, shuffling a step closer. She was right there, she heard him talking to me. The breath in my chest drew dense around my heart, holding it still. It strained to beat. 'Have you tried this crunchy peanut butter?'

'I don't believe I'd like the texture of it myself,' I said. 'I'd rather not bite down on something hard in my peanut butter. Makes me feel like I'm eating rocks.'

'Thank you,' he said, and shambled off. The girl wandered toward the cash registers. I wished she'd come back, tried to think of something I could say to make her stay, but she turned the corner. The aisle was full of heavy, Sunday morning quiet.

'Excuse me,' Frank said, just a minute later, ten feet down the very same aisle. 'Are strawberry conserves the same thing as strawberry preserves?'

'There's no one else here,' I said, laughing softly, and I brushed my knuckles against the knob of his wrist, exposed beyond the buttoned cuff of his shirt. He pulled it away and picked up another jar, ostentatiously lowering his brows in studious examination.

'And how do they differ from jam?' he said.

I pushed my cart to the meat case, left him there frowning at all the jams and preserves and conserves, and a minute later, when he pulled his cart beside mine and started scrutinizing some chicken breasts, he'd piled a jar of each one right on top of a loaf of bread. I tugged it out so it wouldn't get smashed even more, and the jars clinked loudly as they tumbled into the bottom of the cart. He bristled and looked anxiously all around.

'Relax.' I picked up a pound of ground beef. Its blood had spilled over the edge of its styrofoam tray and gathered in the creases of the plastic wrap underneath. It was real thin and watery, barely like blood at all. 'If anything's going to arouse suspicion, it's you acting like bombs are going off. Nobody here cares what we do. They don't even know us.'

'Speak for yourself.' He poked his thumb into several different spots on a chicken breast and watched the dimples rise and flatten again, as if that would reveal something about its freshness. 'And speak quieter. My family were respected members of this community.'

'Then go be respected in the cookie aisle and get me a box of vanilla wafers.'

He glanced at the scrap of paper in his hand. He'd rolled and unrolled it between his fingers so much it was soft and wrinkled, the words rubbed away.

'That's not on my list,' he said.

'I'm spending so much time answering your questions I haven't even looked at my list. So do me a favor and go get the vanilla wafers.'

He opened his mouth to say something. I pushed my cart toward the fish counter. The man behind it was too busy to notice us, entirely preoccupied with assiduously piling different combinations of salmon onto a scale to make sure the customer, a middle-aged woman with orthopedic shoes that dug into her fleshy ankles, didn't get a single ounce more than she wanted, but Frank stared at him a minute, looking sick, before he dropped the chicken breasts on top of the bread and hurried off. A wheel on his cart caught as he turned the corner, dragged screeching across the floor.

I found him in the freezer aisle fifteen minutes later. His cart was out in the middle of the floor with not one single thing more in it, and he'd slid open the glass door of the ice cream case and was hunched over it, clutching either side of the opening with his face and chest hung down close, letting the cold air buffet his cheeks. His

245

vertebrae pressed visibly against the underside of his shirt, just beneath the collar.

I parked my cart behind him and looked over his shoulder at the ever-growing variety of available ice creams. He didn't turn. The freezer shuddered and hummed.

'This was a bad idea,' he said, each word a cloud that bloomed and vanished.

'It wasn't mine.'

He nodded. The cold air billowed out in an endless, dissipating fog. I reached past him to tug out a bucket of Neapolitan ice cream.

'Preserves has chunks in it,' I said. 'Jam is smooth.'

'What about conserves?'

'Conserves are smooth but thicker. They dry the fruit out first.'

He nodded, pushed himself upright with what seemed an exhaustive effort, and put the jars of conserves and preserves in the freezer case.

'What're you doing?' I said. 'Put those back where they belong.'

He stared straight ahead for a moment, as if through the shelves of paper towels and cleaning solution and sacks of flour, all the way back to the empty spot where the jars had been. He took a deep breath and shut the freezer door. His fingers cut lines of clarity into the frost.

'Let's go,' he said.

'You haven't got half the things on your list.'

He gripped the handle of his cart tightly and let his head hang down between his shoulders. 'Please,' he whispered. 'Please, just be quiet.'

He pushed his cart toward the registers. I

waited a while before I followed, watching the cold cloud the glass once more. We paid for our groceries, and loaded our bags into our cars on opposite sides of the parking lot, and didn't look at each other again for a long, long time, even when we got home, and didn't leave the house together, or arrive together at the same destination, for another twenty years, until the day that tiny plaque in one of the arteries inside his heart finally ruptured, and the blood, clotting round to close it over, sealed the vessel so tightly not even the blood itself could break through.

18

I push my way up from the table and put my bowl in the sink: and there's Frank, out in front of his shed with the lawnmower, there's the red gas can in his hand and grease stains already all across the front of his pants. He tilts the gas can, but nothing comes out. He holds it there for a second, turned completely upside down, before he rights it to unstop the dingy yellow spout. He lost the plug years ago, just keeps a paper towel twisted up and jammed in there. He tugs it out, soaked and dripping, and tosses it to the ground.

I turn the doorknob. The deadbolt's locked, and my keys aren't in my pocket.

He bends down, one hand on his knee, to pour the gas, but even bent down he's still too high up. The gas streams from the spout in an iridescent brown ribbon that misses the tank completely, soaks the motor and the tires, and, as if he didn't just witness this, he goes and screws the cap right back on the tank and sets the can in the doorway of the shed. The screen closes with a loud crack.

I hurry to the living room. The front door stands wide open, my keys dangling from the deadbolt. I yank them free and head out the back.

I yell at him to stop, but either he doesn't hear me or he's pretending not to. I hurry across the yard as fast as I can, but I have to chop it up into tiny, mincing steps. A stride any bigger feels like somebody startling you out of the first moments of sleep, that feeling like you'll never stop falling.

Daisy stumps into the doorway of the shed from someplace inside it, a long bolt tucked like a bone between her back teeth, and watches the lawnmower warily, her head turned the opposite direction but her eyes trained sidelong and suspicious on it. Frank yanks the mower's chain so hard he sways backwards, barely manages to grab the handle in time to keep himself from falling over. The mower grumbles, coughs exhaust, but doesn't start. He yanks the chain again, harder this time, and the mower shudders to life with a dry, grating roar, and soon as it does Daisy's bursting out of the screen door, teeth bared and hackles raised. She shoves her way between the mower and Frank's legs, trying to protect him, and he doesn't even notice she's there, just pushes it rattling and smoking along the yard's edge, where it performs its ritual duty in vain and a cloud of red dust. 'Watch out,' I yell. Daisy scrambles out of the way and starts running circles around the both of them, barking so furious and shrill and high-pitched it's almost more irritating than the grind of the mower itself, which moves through the scrubby, dry grass, too low for the blades to brush, for about ten feet without leaving any visible trace of itself before it chokes, hacks, and stops. Frank tilts it up on the back wheels, so the blades are off the ground, and heaves the chain to turn them slowly, the way he did when the grass was wet and gathered into thick clumps that clogged them, so they could shrug the clippings off into ridges at his feet and start to spin again. Daisy paces back and forth, hackles still raised, watching it. A raspy growl rattles low in her throat.

'It's not clogged,' I say. Finally I'm close enough that he can't pretend not to hear, though he does pretend he's surprised to see me, and, apparently, a little irritated. He looks all around, through the bare trees, and leans down to push in the primer on the side of the motor.

'You ought not be out here,' he says. When he pulls his finger away, the yellow rubber button slowly fills back up and pops convex. 'Ain't no leaves on the trees.'

'What do you think you're doing?'

'What else would I be doing with a lawnmower?' Just a few months ago he would have said it like a defiant teenaged boy, daring me to forbid him. Now he says it like I'm an idiot for not recognizing the machine's intended use. 'I am *mowing* the *lawn.*'

'It's February,' I say. 'The grass is dead.'

He looks all around, breathing scraps of cloud into the sky. They scrape wet against the sides of his lungs. To the east, the first stars are faintly visible, each one dragging the next from the darkening sky by the invisible thread that's supposed to hold them together.

'So it is,' he says, 'so it is,' and yanks the chain. The mower starts again, a wild screech flittering now inside its roar.

'Turn that thing off,' I yell, but it drowns me out. Daisy sprints up to the mower, gets herself

250

between it and Frank's legs again, and snaps at the engine, nearly tears the spark plug loose. 'Turn it off,' I yell. I grab his arm, but he pulls it away. Daisy scuttles out from under his feet as he pushes the mower along the fence, onto the bald spot. One of the blades nicks a root, sends a splinter ricocheting inside the mower before it shoots out so hard it lodges like a bullet in the earth, but he just keeps on going, all the way to the corner, and there, now that she's got it trapped, Daisy dashes at it, barking, saliva flung down in strands from her teeth. Frank tilts the mower up on its back wheels to turn it. They catch on another root. 'Turn it off,' I yell. I grab his arm and try to pull it away from the handle. He tips the mower further back, yanking it this way and that, trying to jostle it free. Daisy lunges at it, snaps, and turns to run, terrified by the shuddering of the air. The handle slips out of his hands.

The sound is the worst sound I have ever heard. The engine's guttering grind, and the screeching blades, and Daisy's single, pained yelp, high and short, the kind she'd give if you stepped on her paw, nothing more, and underneath it all the wet, dull thud of blade lodging in flesh, of flesh tearing.

The mower pulls her further into it. She digs her claws in the dirt and looks over her shoulder, her mouth open like she's crying but with not a cry coming out. The mower makes the same wet, choking noise as if she was so much damp grass, and coughs exhaust as it gives up, her body lurching with each slowing turn of the blades.

Then everything's still.

Frank stares down in surprise.

'Fancy?' he says.

The front half of her sticks out from under the mower. She doesn't make any noise, doesn't even try to move, just lies there with her belly pooled on the ground and her forelegs flat to the earth, bracing herself against it. She looks up at me, panting, panting, like if she could just draw in enough air, just catch her breath for a minute, she'd be all right.

'Is she okay?' Frank says.

A thick edge of blood unrolls from under her belly, spreading across the dirt toward her elbows, then past them. She leans down and smells it, as if she doesn't already know what it is, and what it means.

'Get her a biscuit,' he says. 'That'll make her feel better.' But you can tell from the wavering of his voice that even he doesn't believe it.

'Go inside,' I say. 'Now.'

'I'll just get her a biscuit,' he says.

'Go inside and stay there.'

He shuffles back toward the house, stopping to look over his shoulder every few steps, as if some miracle might have happened in the meantime. I wait until he's inside, until his shadow disappears from the kitchen door, before I grab the handle of the mower. Daisy tenses against just that tiniest movement. I tilt it back and drag it off her, the blade sliding and scraping out of her, and still she doesn't make a sound, just raises her eyebrows as if in question. When I set the mower down beside her, her front paws scrabble in the dirt, trying to lift her, but she can't get up.

The tear, ripped open more by force than by the sharpness of the blades, goes almost all the way through her: her spine's severed, her intestines are ruptured and spilling out, one leg's cut clean through and the other's barely attached to the hip by a few strings of bone about ready to snap. There's little pieces of her all over the ground. She breathes shallow and fast, chest palpitating, ribs trembling like her lungs can't quite open enough to lift them out of the way. Her huge, pink tongue lolls out of her mouth, pooling on the dirt.

I pull my sweatshirt over my head and hold on to the mower with one hand. She looks away, far off into the woods like she's tracking rabbits, while I lift up her back half and slide the shirt underneath. I wrap it around her, tight as I can, to help hold everything together. She whimpers just a little as I lift her up.

'That's a good girl,' I say.

I hold her to my chest like a baby, her breastbone knocking against me with each panting breath, and she licks my neck while her blood soaks through the sweatshirt and onto my undershirt, a slick warmth that spreads down toward the hem. It gets heavier and heavier, sticks to my belly. Smells like metal and excrement.

She breathes in and out, in and out, each one a thin, whistling wheeze that brushes my neck fainter than the last.

'That's a good girl,' I say. 'That's a real good girl.'

She lays her head heavy on my shoulder. I pat it, run my finger and thumb along either side of the bony crest on its crown. I rub the inside of her ear. The skin's waxy and cool, but the air inside it's still warm. She leans nuzzling into my hand.

'It's all right. You're okay.'

I can't tell the exact moment when it happens. You'd think I'd know, by now, the difference between the living and the dead.

'That's a good girl,' I say.

I rub her ear a long time. When I pull my hand away, her head lolls against my shoulder. I kiss the corner of her mouth, where her soft bottom lip scoops lower than her jowls, and carry her back to the house. She gets heavier and heavier, until the bones in my arm strain to hold her up. Have to shift all her weight to one elbow to open the door, barely get it open without dropping her.

In the kitchen, over the trash can, I peel the sweatshirt away. Her loose leg falls heavily down, pulls her so wide open a coil of intestine flops out and slaps the inside of the trash can. The sweatshirt's stained a dark red, edged with yellowish-brown, crusted and stuck to her belly. It drapes down with one cuff brushing the garbage. I pick it from her fur and leave it heaped in the trash, drape her over the lip of the sink to drain, her front half pulled up to rest on the counter, paws extended like she's trying to drag herself out of the basin, and walk to the bedroom.

'She's dead,' I say.

Frank's sitting propped up in the bed, against the headboard, real stiff and upright and pushed into the pillows, his eyes wide and the light skittering across them like he's bearing witness to some cosmic unfolding on the other side of the window, the brightness and force of which drives him backwards into the cushions. He doesn't look at me. He seems emptied, somehow, doesn't even realize I'm here, right in front of him. Just keeps staring past me, muttering under his breath.

I shake him by the shoulders. 'She's dead.'

'You look like a maniac,' he says, grimacing at my shirtfront, soaked with blood and turning cold, the red stains splotching my forearm. 'Just escaped from the penitentiary.' He smells like gasoline.

'You killed her,' I say.

'Killed who?'

'Daisy. Your dog. Who loved you more than anything else in the entire world, for some reason that escapes me.'

He squints, scouring pale memory. 'That don't sound like something I would do,' he says.

'You drove over her with the lawnmower.'

'I believe I'd remember doing a thing like that.'

'It wasn't fifteen minutes ago,' I shout. 'There's pieces of her scattered all over the dirt.'

He chuckles. 'Well, maybe I can finally get some grass to grow out there now that it's got some good fertilizer in it.'

'What in God's name is wrong with you? You loved that dog.'

'Which is precisely,' he says, one finger raised, like one of the detectives in his novels caught in the rapturous throes of unraveling the case's solution, 'why I wouldn't have killed her.'

I shake my head, speechless; I slog back to the kitchen and slide the cutting board beneath her body; I pull taut the leg that's still attached, splinters of bone crackling, and with a meat cleaver pound the cut the rest of the way through her. A front-half mount's all I'll be able to save. Her hips and tail and hind legs, the skin hanging in useless shreds from the splintered bone, I set off to the side on a dishrag.

Her eyes won't close. Dogs' eyes never do. Even when you pull their lids down with your own fingers, they slowly open again, but I try a long time, easing them down as far as they'll go and holding them in place, until finally she at least looks like she's fighting sleep. I turn the water hot as it'll go and spray her down with the sprayer, squirt dish detergent on and lather her up, working the suds into her fur to break apart the slicks of blood and digestive matter. It takes a good five lathers, each one running paler pink and brown down the drain, to get her clean. I dry her with three separate bath towels and lay her on the counter, sit down at the kitchen table and rest my cheek against it, close my eyes for a couple minutes. I haven't even started, and already I'm exhausted.

My body's heavy when I push it up from the table. My hands shake as they sweep my paring knife across the honing steel, a couple swipes each side, and press the blade into the thick, soft skin at the bottom of her belly. It slides right through. She splits open easy, bursts almost, light shuddering cold along the blade as it cuts clean up to her breastbone, subcutaneous fat welling into the cut in little yellow globules like fish eggs. The stink that bubbles up with them is worse than the smell of any wild animal I've ever cut open, thick and putrid like she's rotted a week in the sun. I breathe through my mouth so I won't smell it.

The little bit of blood left in her surges into the cut, forms a lip along the edge of her skin, and falls away as I peel it back from either side of her belly, either side of her rib cage. It comes off easy, the knife running in long, smooth strokes across the seam where it joins the body, the fascia between them thin and pliable as the inaudible pause between syllables. That's all that holds her together, and it's barely more than nothing. Underneath it, her torso's wrapped in a cocoon of white fat an inch thick. I get some cornmeal from the pantry, sprinkle it over her to soak up some of the juices. The bone and socket of her shoulder pry apart with a wet crack, the ligament tearing, and her forelegs fall loose, one, then the other, heavy inside the skin. I work it up her neck, over her face, her eyes two blurry dark spots beneath the membrane that binds their lids to her brow, like something trapped under ice, until the blade drags across the bone of the socket, its scrape shivering up my arm, and the membrane snaps away.

What's left of her, when the knife cuts through the cartilage of her nose and her skin falls into my arms, is a feral pink and white mass, the shredded convolutions of her intestines spilling out of her unfinished belly, her teeth endlessly bared and waiting to snap. Her eyes, without their lids, have none of their stoicism, none of their graveness or nobility. They leer out in wide-eyed shock at a world where every glint and movement is a terror. It's the skin and the skin alone that makes any of us worthy of love or kindness. Underneath it we are monsters, every living thing.

I fill a stockpot with water, shake in some baking soda, and set it to boil; I drive the bones of her forelegs from their thin, tight sheaths, snip through her toes at the last knuckle with my kitchen shears, scrape her ears back from the stiff blades of cartilage inside them, bits of flesh wedging under my thumbnails.

The water breathes a whispered, rushing sound, though nothing stirs inside it. Clusters of tiny bubbles cling to the sides and bottom of the pot, against their own weightlessness. I saw through her neck with my bread knife, cut the tongue from between her teeth, her eyes from their sockets. The first tiny bubble detaches from the side of the pot and drifts upward. I lose it somewhere in the water, in the gash of light across its surface. With a grapefruit spoon I scrape the brain from the inside of her skull, as down the stringy walls of a pumpkin, to make sure I get every last bit.

This is what it takes to hold on to something. To keep the things you've loved. The water flexes and warps; bubbles swell as they rise to its surface, driven upward by their own emptiness, and break open into the open air. I ease her skull into the pot.

Steam billows hot and damp on my cheeks. It coats my glasses, feathers the hard lines of the counter and turns the sink and the pot cloudy and luminous, crowded round with fuzzy halos like the kind that coronate headlights passing across your windshield at night, and slowly fades away. A cold current ripples through me, starts all my arms and legs to shaking. Have to squeeze my eyes shut and hold on to either edge of the stove to keep myself upright. When it passes, I rummage up an old needle from the hutch in the hallway, use it to dig her flesh from my nail beds. Its point scratches white lines on the undersides of my fingernails. Cornmeal's crusted in spots across the backs of my hands like open, running sores. I scrape them away.

I set all the pieces of her onto one towel, pinch the corners together so it makes a little knapsack, and carry it against my chest, heavy and soft, into the hallway. Frank's still in the bed, asleep. I carry her outside, back to the dead patch, and lay her on the ground. The mower I drag to the shed, over the lip of the door, and back along the path he's cleared, if the overturned empty paint cans and fallen rakes and the weedeater lying on its back are any indication, by just shoving the mower forward through everything in his way. I return it to its proper, bowed place on the plywood floor, drape the oil-stained towel over its handle, and pick through tool-boxes and tackle boxes and loose piles of rusty wreckage until I find, in an old plastic coffee can full of doorknobs, two hook-and-eye latches and an old padlock, the rusty key still inside it, the metal around its body corroded in spots, dark rusty centers edged with light bluish-green. The latches I drop into my shirt pocket, a cold weight against my chest, and slip the nub of a pencil in after them; the padlock I hook in my belt loop. I take his drill, heavy in its plastic suitcase, from a hook on the corkboard wall, heft a shovel out of the old metal barrel he's got them in, and set them outside, the floor bowing and bouncing so bad with each step it feels like I'm walking on a trampoline. The door's been open so long, the frame's warped without its reinforcement, so I have to heave with all my might to drag the door into it, flakes of rotten wood splintering away where their edges scrape each other. I wrestle the hasp closed, hook the padlock through it, shut it with a loud click, and tuck the key into my sock.

I jam the shovel hard as I can into the dirt beside her, but it's packed so cold, drawn shut by so many little roots, that the metal edge bounces right off, barely makes a dent. She'd want to be buried, I know she would. She'd like the ceiling of dirt like a coffee table always over her head, the feel of it compact around her like Frank's legs on either side of her skull, squeezing it tight. I strike the earth over and over, the metal ringing cold and hollow and so hard it knocks my fingers off the wooden handle, and all I manage to do is scrape up a few little shavings. Can't even lift my leg high enough to stomp down on the shovel. I throw it against the fence, pick Daisy up, and carry her back across the lawn, out the gate, and into the woods. The yard heaves itself a little wider with every crossing, as if it were driven outward by some internal impulse, by the endless need to escape itself.

It's night now, and cold. I wish I'd brought a jacket. And a flashlight. Can't hardly see the ground I'm stepping on, almost fall down a couple times for thinking it's six inches higher than it really is. We don't go too far out, just enough that she won't bring the coyotes too close to the house. I can hear them tittering in the distance. They'd about gone extinct for a while there, but now they've made a comeback in every single county of the state, thanks, I'm sure, to the tireless, devoted paperwork of the Fish and Wildlife Service.

When we're far enough out, I lay her between the roots of an oak tree, and then I stand here, just looking down at the bundle, trying to think of something to say. One branch, swaying in the wind, creaks like an old door opening. My palm still rings with the shudder of the skinning knife, of blade grating bone.

She'd want to be closer to the house. Not out here in the woods by herself. Close to Frank.

'You took good care of him,' I say. 'Real good.'

The stars, carved into the dark sky, glint. I try to pull three or four of them from the whole vertiginous mass and hold them separate, hold them apart, to see them only in relation to one another, and give that relation a shape and a story and a name: the Twins, descending from

Olympus, scraping across the sky on their way to the underworld.

If he could name just one of them. If he could name just one of them, it would be all right. I could let it all go, Daisy and him and our whole life, I could let it all go quiet and easy, if I could hear him tell me just one of them. That's the last thing I would ever ask.

The coyotes laugh their wild, hysterical laughter, as if they've never heard a funnier joke. Ursa Major doesn't look a thing like a bear, and Orion's Belt is just three stars in a line. It could be any three stars. It was always too clear to me that there was no real pattern between them, only some tricks sailors made up to guide them home. That doesn't make the sky a map.

Still, I tried to see. But I never could.

★ ★ ★

I plug the screwdriver into the outlet in the hall and drill two holes into the molding of the bedroom door, on the outside where he won't see them, one halfway between the doorknob and the top corner, the other halfway to the bottom. He stirs awake, sits up in the bed. I push the bit into the wood slowly, hold it trembling in place until the trembling stops and I feel it spinning in emptiness. Sawdust trickles into a tiny mound on the floor. The smell of it muddles the air. Into each of the holes, I screw the eye of a latch, twisting it in by hand until it lodges inside solid wood and I can't twist any more, and then I shove a thin drill bit through the eye, use it as a handle to wrench the eye horizontal, driven so deep into the frame it can't tear loose.

I jam the bottom hook into its eye, pull the door almost shut, and trace a circle around the spot where it meets the wood. It shines pale silver for a moment before the thread of the drill tears it away, bores beneath it. The door's tougher, more solid than the molding was, creaks loud and pushes back against the bit. I bend over and brace the door with one arm.

'What're you doing?' Frank says. Doesn't even twist himself around enough to see.

'Sanding down the doors,' I say. 'Where I painted the paint on too thick.'

He makes a face like this is a real interesting, real intriguing bit of information.

With all my strength I bear down on the drill, bracing my elbow against my hip to drive the bit into the wood. It catches, squealing, and twists the drill near out of my hand, sends a hot crack running through my wrist and along my forearm. I stand up straight, take a deep breath. I put the drill in reverse and pull the trigger. It winds itself out.

'I'll get up soon,' Frank says, as if this ought to comfort me. 'Just as soon as I recuperate.'

I reach overhead and drill the top hole, the bit spinning toward my palm flat on the other side of the door. If I pushed it all the way in, its full length, it would break through the wood and pierce my hand, tearing the muscle, and shuddering splinter the thin bones inside. I screw each hook into its hole, feeling for the moment when its point reaches the solid wood and its

263

thread lodges inextricably inside. I pull the door shut, snug in its frame, and push the hook of each latch into its eye.

'Recuperate,' Frank says, slowly, as if sounding the word out to deduce its spelling, his voice blunted by the closed door. I lean against it, rest my forehead on the cool wood.

In the kitchen, the pot rattles with an insistent tap: Daisy's bottom jaw, probably, come unhinged by the boiling, buffeted against the side by the force of water erupting from itself.

'Recuperate,' Frank says. 'Recuperate. Re-cu-per-ate.' But no matter how hard he tries, no matter how he turns the word over and stresses each syllable, testing for weak spots, he can't find any place to break it open. No matter how hard he tries, he can't pry the thing apart.

19

I used to go through a bale of excelsior every month, big as a refrigerator and packed dense, but now they don't even carry it in the supply catalogs. Now you can only get it from the craft-and-hobby store, in tiny bags as if it were shredded iceberg lettuce: 'American Moss,' they call it, though it looks more like dried-up curls of crabgrass than any kind of moss, and use it as bedding for gift baskets, a rustic nest in which to tuck gourmet cheeses and handmade soaps, or else dye it green for the grass in children's Easter baskets — though they rarely even do that anymore, the watery-eyed lady with her blond hair braided into a long, fat braid, whom I asked to check the stockroom to see if there were any extra bags back there, informed me: most parents prefer plastic grass in their Easter baskets these days. Cellophane.

'The cellophane you can reuse,' she said, 'year after year. I highly recommend it.'

'Excelsior's perfectly durable when used properly,' I said. 'Mounts wrapped with excelsior have stood in leaky hunting lodges and musty basements for a hundred years without a spot of mildew.'

I rip a handful from the tangle of it, stray curls drifting through the air. It's real resilient, hard to bunch together, tries to expand into shapelessness the moment you ease your grip like grass springing up after your lifted bootsoles, but I spray it with water to help it condense, and slowly my hands remember how to hold and shape it, the loose tufts tightening into muscle through the same instinct by which muscle contracts. I bunch it into long, stringy bundles and bind them tight to the wire bones of her forelegs. I can only do a little bit at a time before the twine burns my fingertips, before my knuckles start to throb from pulling it tight. If you let it loosen, even a little, the muscles turn shapeless and shambling.

The sputtering drum of urine on plastic resounds through the house. I bought him what the package calls a 'portable male urinal,' but which I am fairly sure is nothing but an iced-tea pitcher with a screw-on lid. The burbling gets higher and higher pitched, then trickles into silence.

I press the leg on the counter, spread both hands on the top of it, above the elbow, and bear down with all my weight to flatten it out. Dogs' legs are real flat, not all round and hammy like people's legs.

'Wendell,' Frank shouts. 'Wendell.'

'What?' I yell. 'My jug's full.'

'Do you have to go more? It didn't sound like you had to go more.'

'It's full.'

'Hold on to it a minute. I'm busy.'

They ought to make them bigger. It doesn't hold hardly anything.

On the tiny black-and-white television I bought for the counter, Debbie's short little lawyer leans casually against the wooden bar in front of the jury and goes on, real friendly and jovial, like they're just having a get-to-know-you chat over a beer, about how her parents never loved her, and how her father touched her when she was a girl, and how the baby's daddy left her soon as he found out she was pregnant, and how she was working double shifts at the Pancake Palace to keep Little Larry fed and clothed while the truckers harassed her and the ugly girls kept stealing her tips, as if any of that is some kind of explanation: as if any explanation, even an actual one, could make that boy one bit less dead.

'Wendell,' Frank yells. 'My jug's full.'

I get my little hammer from the back of the silverware drawer. The latches are so thin, and they fit so tight, I can't pinch them good enough to pry them open by hand, have to tap the hook up from underneath with the hammer, real gentle so it doesn't bend the thing and real quiet so Frank won't hear, then grab it in the claw to yank it the rest of the way out. I leave the hammer propped between the molding and the wall, and pull up the dish towels I keep shoved into the crack at the bottom of the door. He never stops talking now, but the towels soften the edges of his words, blur them into one long smear so that, if you work hard at not listening, you can't separate one from the next.

The smell hits me soon as I open the door, thick and smothering with excrement and urine and stale skin. After just a minute or two you get used to it, but every time you leave and come back, it's as new and strong as if you've never smelled it before. Frank's lying on his right side, facing the door, with the urinal tucked against him in the crook of his elbow. His toilet, a metal frame with a thick, padded seat hinged atop a white plastic bucket, sits right against the side of the bed, its back braced against the nightstand. Liquids in the urinal, solids in the toilet, that's the rule. I took one of the arms off so he can drag himself onto it without having to turn around, and fastened all the feet to the floor with wood screws so he can't tip the thing over. He's left the lid open again, and he's forgotten to screw the cap back on his jug.

I don't look at him while I reach for it. If you look at him, if you make eye contact or acknowledge his presence in any way, he'll start to talking. Instead I act real interested in the television I got us for in here, sitting silent — he keeps it muted all the time — on a folding tray at the foot of the bed, the defense attorney strutting back and forth across the glass bulge of the screen. I like to turn all the televisions to the same channel, so you can walk from one room to the other and see the same program continue unbroken. Makes the place almost seem to hold together.

'One of the soldiers with a spear pierced his side,' Frank says, holding his jug up in toast, 'and forthwith came there blood and water.' The liquid inside, such a dark gold it looks like maple syrup, sloshes around so bad a little spills across the brim and spatters the floor.

'What's that supposed to mean?' I say. 'You got blood in your urine?'

'And he that saw it bare record,' he says, 'and his record is true.' He smiles, and his top teeth slide slowly down, pink plastic gums drawing away from the paler gums underneath. He cracked one of the clasps forcing them on, I know he did, and now every time he smiles or says more than two words, his top dentures drift downward. I can't look at anything else for watching them, and I can barely pay attention to a word he's saying. Which is one little blessing, I suppose.

He shuts his mouth, and his lower jaw knocks the top one back into place with a loud clack, but soon as he starts to talk again, it resumes its slow downward slide.

'My jug's full,' he says.

I snatch it out of his hand. He's holding it by the handle, of course, so I've got to grab it around the side and feel the sickly warmth of his urine radiate through the plastic.

'Then don't let it get so full before you call me next time,' I say. I slam the toilet shut. 'And close the lid when you use the commode. I don't want your mess smelling up the bedroom all day long. The smell gets into the sheets.'

'I been calling you a little while,' he says.

'I mean don't fill it all the way up. Leave a little room.'

'It's been sitting there all day. Wasn't nobody stopping you from taking it earlier.'

'You need to drink more water. Looks like maple syrup in here.'

At least he hasn't had an accident. About that one thing, that one last thing, he's real fastidious.

I take the jug to the bathroom and pour it into the toilet. It takes so long to empty, air bubbles squeezing in the opening, urine glugging out, that I have to rest against the sink. He's already asleep again when I set the container on his nightstand. The thud of the plastic startles him.

'Just resting my eyes,' he says, and rears back in the pillow a little, as if seeing me here is just the most delightful surprise, his eyes bright and blank and huge in his gaunt face. The weight's running off him again, faster than before it seems, lifting to the surface every cord in his neck and string of gristle on his arm once buried in muscle and fat, pushing them right up against the skin. Any further and they'd cut through. He looks like something children would see in their dreams and wake up crying. The pouch I sewed for him hangs over his side of the mattress, jammed full of fruitcakes. I haven't had to restock it in days.

'Roll over,' I say.

He looks up at me, weary.

'When was the last time you did it?'

He shrugs.

'Then roll over.'

Every hour, before bedsores open him up, eat his thigh into some weeping cavity. They say every two hours, but I'm not taking any chances. I've seen the pictures on TV, in those nursing-home exposés. I pull his shoulder to get him started. He turns cumbersome onto his back, grabs the mattress, and struggles to lift himself sitting. The pillow that was between his knees I shove under his thighs. Keeps the pressure off his hips a little, the bones from boring their way through the skin. It astounds me, sometimes, how weak it is. I tug out the waistband of his pajama trousers and dust each hip with zinc powder. It cools the burns on my fingertips, red and raw, and still it feels like I don't have any skin there at all. Every rustle of fabric, every brush of the breeze is agony. I thought so much twine had passed between my fingers that the calluses would never fade, but just a few years of ease and the skin goes right back to delicacy, as if that whole life of hard work hadn't made a bit of difference, hadn't left a single mark.

'What time is it?' he says, sitting forward suddenly, panicked.

'You're not going to your mother's.'

'We have to be there by eight,' he says. 'She's waiting on us.'

He tries to get up, but I push him back against the bed.

'She's waiting,' he says, wriggling in vain. I could hold him down one-handed if I had to. 'She's waiting.' Tears fill his eyes. 'I need to — '

'You're not going anywhere.' I press him against the headboard until he stops squirming. Then I rip some paper towels from the roll on the nightstand and push them around the floor with my foot to wipe up his urine. I pull a fruitcake from his pouch.

'Here,' I say, tearing open the plastic. The cake's heavy and damp and dense, feels like somebody's dead arm. Condensation's beaded like sweat on the inside of the wrapper. 'Eat.'

271

He stares out the window. Clouds haul themselves crumbling over the treetops. The light doesn't fall around them so much as hold itself absolutely still, tense, and try to endure their passing through it.

'Fix me up a chair on the porch, will you?' he says. 'So I can watch the birds?'

The goldfinches are still winter's dingy yellow-gray, but every day the sun burns down on them a little bit longer, and their feathers, like the leaves, draw in a bit more of its light. Soon they'll be full of all the brightness they can bear, until their tiny bodies tremble and whir with it and they have to fly off north to more temperate climes and let it fade away.

I shake the fruitcake in front of his face. 'Eat,' I say.

He turns his head away, as if the sight disgusts him.

'You don't need to buy any more of those,' he says. 'I'm tired of them.'

'I don't care if you're tired of them. You have to eat.'

'I don't want it.'

'If you don't want it, you have to tell me what you do want. What do you want?'

'Nothing,' he says, and jerks away from me.

'Eat.' I shove the fruitcake at his mouth. He keeps it clenched shut, just like I knew he would, and I smear it across his lips, trying to force in just a crumb, I smear it all over his cheek. I throw it in the toilet.

He stares at me in shock and wipes his mouth on the back of his hand. I stop and straighten up, correct my posture and take myself some deep, cleansing breaths like the lifestyle gurus on TV say to do whenever your anger starts to spiral out of control and threaten your most cherished relationships. I unhook the handles of the plastic bag lining the toilet, tie them together, and set it on the hallway floor.

'Leave the door open,' Frank says. He reaches out and pats the empty air between us. His fingernails are long like a woman's. 'I can't get it back open when you close it.'

I shake open another bag and fit it into the toilet.

'Please?' he says, a little quaver in his voice.

'You need to trim your nails.'

I close the door and latch it.

The grass is halfway up my shins already, the stars-of-Bethlehem lifting their purple-tinged heads, grown up all over his garden so you could never tell it had been anything but common, useless earth, and the pear trees are in bloom with that sweet, rotten odor that tricks even the flies, who swarm about their clusters of tiny white blossoms as if they were bodies burst open. The early-evening light sags, thick, too heavy and clogged with the mess it's picked up in the sun's slow drag across the sky to hold itself up any longer, a net thrown through the air to catch all the dust and dirt it can before falling down on us, every night, full of refuse.

The traces are almost entirely gone now, her blood diluted and pounded by rain into the dirt, the last little pieces of her flesh pecked away by scavengers. Every once in a while I catch another buzzard spiraling slowly down over the trees and hurry out quick as I can, shouting and clapping my hands. All that's left, the only remnants, are little fragments of bone scattered in the dust, so small and dried out they could be pieces of wood splintered from the root. They could be bits of rock.

I throw the bag into the huge county trash can, the one I am somehow, inexplicably expected to be able to tip back and keep perfectly balanced on two precarious wheels while simultaneously pushing it down the gravel drive without the whole thing falling over and crushing me. The bag lands with a dull smack, and I slam the lid shut so hard it bounces back up again, loud as a gunshot. A big flock of starlings scrambles up from the boughs of the oak across the fence, crying one cry from a thousand different throats. They flap so fast and disorderly their wings slip on the air, and they don't get anyplace, just rearrange themselves over and over above the tree, one filling another's spot soon as it's vacated. There are so many of them, fluttering and dipping, their frantic wings blurring the sky, that it almost seems the birds don't move at all, that it's the sky itself that bulges and buckles around them, like water on the cusp of boiling.

What it must have felt like to push his body beneath it, to feel the water resist and then give way, open then close around him, to watch it rise over his cheeks and stream into his nostrils, to hear it rush into his mouth and instantly strangle the sound of his crying. How blissful it must have felt when he finally stopped kicking, finally stopped churning the water up and splashing it all over her, in those few seconds, those few, quiet seconds before the full import of what she'd done set in. What a relief it must have been. No more wailing, no more crying in the middle of the night. Only silence and stillness.

They look like tacks, the starlings, pinning the sky against some emptiness straining to push through, some emptiness always just behind it that swells and shrinks and stretches it thin. Slowly they get themselves under control and settle back in the branches, one by one unfastening the last bit of pale sky. It falls from the waiting darkness and heaps on the horizon.

It's just that I miss him so badly.

The grass and the trees are still and quiet. Silence seems to move outward from the house, through the walls, through the glass of the windows, smothering everything. I walk toward it, toward the heart of the silence, and there at the very center of it, the very center, is Frank's voice, murmuring low and serious, and so soft with tenderness and patience I have to turn my head away and take a deep breath. As I get closer, the sound of it swells, thickening, until all it takes is the slightest pressure of attention to shape the endless, edgeless noise into discrete words, like cells beneath a microscope, slowly dividing.

'It'll get warmer,' he says as I open the back door. 'You've just got to get used to it, that's all. Just move around a little. Get your blood going.'

Inside, the growing dark stretches the floors,

pushes the walls away. I undo the latches.

'There you go.' His voice turns tender and warm. 'There you go. That ain't so bad, is it? Now lay back. That's it. Spread your arms out and lay your head back. That's it, that's it, you're doing great.' He stops talking just as soon as he sees me.

I perch on the edge of the bed, facing him. The only light in the room comes from the television. It's a relief after all that thick evening light. Television light's better, clear and thin and cold, like the moon's, reflected onto you by good-looking people who act much more wild and passionate and commit a bunch more murders than anybody I've ever known.

I feel hot and feverish. I feel like I'm burning up. I press his hand to my cheek, the deep, whorled grooves of his fingertips cool against my eyelids. I slip his hand under my collar, against my chest. He watches me warily.

The refrigerator grumbles, the bathroom faucet drips into the bathroom sink. It's wearing away the porcelain, looks like rust underneath. The walls groan with cracks straining to part the panels. Feels like the whole place is coming undone.

'It's all right,' I say. 'Go ahead and talk. You might as well do it while somebody's actually here to listen to you.'

He chuckles. 'You think you're the only one to talk to around here?'

'I'm the only one you've had to talk to around here for fifty-odd years,' I say. 'And I sure don't see anybody else in this house.'

'You'd better get your eyes checked, then.'

'Who do you think you're talking to?'

'Think?'

'Who *are* you talking to?'

'Lorraine,' he says, in shock and outrage that he'd have to tell me.

'Who in God's name is Lorraine?'

'Our daughter,' he says.

'Our daughter.'

He looks at me with a mixture of confusion and downright, genuine pity.

'You'd better go to the doctor,' he says. 'And soon. Your mind's going.'

I drop his hand. Poor circulation, that's all it is, all it's ever been. Just his hands and feet not getting enough blood. They're too far away from his heart.

'We don't have any daughter,' I say.

'I'm getting real tired,' Frank says, 'of you telling me what is and what isn't.'

'And just how old is our daughter supposed to be?'

'You don't know how old your own daughter is? She's six. There's no 'supposed to be' about it.'

'Well, then,' I say, 'if you'd care to explain the biological principles which brought her into this world, I'm sure I'd be interested to hear them.'

He crosses his arms and sets his jaw in a hard-clenched line. 'Not with her around,' he mutters, real low so she won't overhear. 'She soaks everything up like a sponge. She may look like you,' he says, louder now, 'but she got my brains.' He taps his temple and grins at an empty corner of the room, with on his face the brightest look of earnest, canine devotion. And then, as if in response to something said, he raises his eyebrows in a way I've never, not in all these years, seen before: as if they were the lid of a box opening, and inside was the most marvelous surprise.

'There's not anybody else,' I say. The words get trapped in my throat. Feels like I'm pushing each one through a screen, comes out grated and raw and split into its crude component sounds, grunts and squeaks and chokes barely overlapping into syllable. 'There was never anybody else.'

He stares at me, real suspicious in the shifting glow. It flickers over him, digging shadows into the wrinkles of his forehead that well up and overflow and vanish.

'There wasn't your mama cooking us dinner, and there wasn't a little girl. There was just you and me. Just the two of us, alone. That's all there ever was.'

He laughs a cold, condescending laugh. His eyes shine, not with tears but something else, something permanent, a viscous wave that never recedes. The television coats them in a silver glaze.

If he looked up, through the water as it closed around him, how strange the world beyond it must have seemed, his mother's dark shape always shifting, strings of light always melding and dividing, nothing ever just as it was.

I open the closet and drag the footstool over to his side. It's only a six-inch lift, but standing on top of it feels like I'm swaying back and forth way up high in the atmosphere, where the air's too thin for your lungs to grab ahold. My own arm moves in the television light like something from a silent movie, strange and jerky, as I grope behind his crumpled blue baseball cap and shove aside a stack of sweat-stained undershirts he never let me throw away and take down the little cedar box, just big enough to hold a pair of shoes, full of all the pictures we took that first summer.

I wipe the dusty lid with my shirttail as I carry it to the bed. The latch is so old and stuck in its place I have to sit down and wedge one of my keys underneath it to pry it up. 'Here,' I say, 'here, you look and tell me if you see anybody else,' and hold it out as I open the lid. Inside it, crumpled fruitcake wrappers are piled high and loose. The light gleams in trickles that run along their wrinkles, washes dull across their smudges of grease. One, on the very top, spills over the side of the box.

I dig through them — for the pictures, for his medals, for his mother's rings — push the wrappers to one side and the other. The box's unfinished bottom scrapes my fingertips.

'Where are they?' I say.

'Where are what?'

The corner of another wrapper sticks up from the box of tissues on the table beside us, right out the slot, where I'd have plucked it the next time I needed to blow my nose. I tug it free, gummy and warm like he'd just now taken the cake out. The creases are neat and sharp, the plastic sticky and slick at the same time.

'Sometimes,' I say, 'I wish you'd died out there that day.'

His face — what's left of it, what hasn't wasted away and disappeared, devoured by his own body just to keep him alive another useless day or two — hardens into something grim and immovable.

Wouldn't it have been easier on all of us? Wouldn't it?

'Don't you move,' I say. 'Don't you dare go anywhere.'

I look for them all through the house. I open every container, I throw wide every drawer. I pull the books from the shelves and the mirrors from the wall, I turn inside out every pocket of every jacket, every pair of pants. I dig through every one of our trash cans until my hands are sticky with garbage juice, and all I find, all I find is fruitcake wrappers, as if they were pushing themselves through every little gap in his memory, through every crack in the earth and torn-open word. I unzip the covers on the couch cushions and jam my arm inside and pull out whole wads of them from the corners.

'All right,' he says from the bedroom. 'All right. You've got to relax, now. Pretend it's your bed. Pretend you're just lying down for a nap. That's it, that's it. You're a natural.'

Not once, not one single time have I caught him hiding one. And still, when I've opened every tiny door and unscrewed every lid, when I've pulled open and pulled apart every little part of this house you can pull open and there can't

280

possibly be any more, still they seem to emerge from nothing, from places they weren't just a moment earlier, glinting like stars pulled out of the darkness solely by your looking for them: one balled up in the beak of a pheasant on the wall, another rolled impossibly tight and thin and wedged in with the line of compounded dust and fur between the floorboards in the hall, so tight I have to lean down with one hand on the china hutch and pick it out with my fingernails, another almost entirely submerged in the soil of a dead poinsettia we should have thrown out three months ago, only its torn plastic edge breaking up through the dirt and curdled leaves. I yank it out. Crumbled soil spills across the floor.

He would have been a good father. He would have loved that girl more than anything, and she would have loved him. Any child would. I try to will his words into shapelessness, to loosen my attention so they'll spill out through their burst borders, but I can't. I have to listen to every single one.

'Now, what I want you to do is look straight up at the sky. Don't look around, just straight up. You see all that sky? There's just as much of it underneath you. The sun's in it, and the clouds, everything. Remember? There's just as much of it underneath you, and a sky that big has got to be able to hold up a little girl like you. Don't you think?'

He sounds young again. He sounds the way he did that very first moment, open and friendly and warm, excited to overflowing with all those

281

best parts of himself, all those things he gave up along the way, left heaped and gleaming on the side of the road so what was left would be light enough to carry: the Frank he'd wanted to be, the Frank he could have been, if not for me.

'Don't be scared,' he says. 'There's no reason to be scared. I'm right here beside you. I'm not going anywhere.'

I carry the wrappers to him, every single one, the wide, loose mass of them crumpled into hard, wrinkled lumps in my hands, and dump them in his lap. They unfold themselves bit by bit, like something living, like something waking up. And he sits there, just sits there in the bed with his head bowed, with his lips moving silently.

'Are there any more?' I say.

He looks up at me, his eyes bright and fanatical and bewildered.

'Harvey?' he says.

'I'm not Harvey. I'm Wendell. Harvey's dead. They're all dead.'

'You're my brother, ain't you?'

I turn on the lamp beside the bed. It shrinks the room to normal size, pulls the walls in from the dark deserts they'd wandered off to. I grab him by the shoulders and pull him close. 'It's me,' I say. 'It's Wendell.'

'Ain't you my brother?'

'No. No, that's just a story. It's just a story we told.'

'You ought not go off like that,' he says. 'Without telling nobody. Mama's been worried sick. You ought to've at least wrote a letter. Let us know you was alive.'

His face softens. 'It's good to see you,' he says, holding back tears. 'I missed you.'

Something opens in my chest, sudden and wide and aching.

'Are there any more?' I say. I have to whisper it to keep the words steady.

'Any more what?'

I grab him by the back of the head and tilt his face down toward the wrappers. He peers at them as if they're very far away.

'That ain't how you're supposed to do it,' he says. 'You were supposed to let Lorraine find them.'

'Are there any more?' I shout.

He recoils a little and folds his hands primly in his lap. 'Nope,' he says. 'Nope, I do believe you've got them all.'

The opening swells, fatted, pulling in just a little more of the light, a little more of the space around its edges: the void of time. Not a river, or a turning wheel, but the empty, ever-widening hole of the sun when you look at it too long: all those years, everything we loved, everything we gave up, finally disappearing.

I grab him by the arms and pull him close. 'Whatever life it is you think you remember,' I say, real slow and clear, shaking him a little with each syllable, 'whatever life it is you think you had, I don't want to hear one more word about it. You understand? Not one more word.'

He nods, wincing. I'm squeezing his arms too hard. The skin's already starting to bruise, the blood gathering into plum-colored pools beneath it, pinched against the brittle bone. All I'd have to do is squeeze a little harder, and it would break. For a moment — it passes quick, real quick, before the impulse could even move from my chest to my hands, but for a moment, I want to. I want to see him cry.

'I'm sorry,' I say.

I take his hands, gently, carefully. They rest on his lap, limp and still, wrappers scattered around them, while mine shake and shake and shake, as if the tremors had somehow passed from his fingers into mine.

'I'm sorry,' I say. 'I'm sorry.'

Slowly, so slowly she doesn't even feel it, he pulls his arms out from under her.

20

I keep track of the time by his pill caddy. That's how I know what day of the week it is, and how much longer I've got to go until the week is over. Each evening, after I've taken him his last blood thinner and cholesterol pill and antidepressant, and told him they're candy to get him to take them, and he's chewed them and grimaced at their bitterness, I leave the green plastic compartment labeled with the day of the week open and empty so I know it's done, covered in its residue of chalky dust. The next one waits tiny and cramped and shut tight.

Each morning, I take my shower, and make breakfast, and put a glass of nutrient shake by the bed, and put in a load of laundry. I keep the TV off and the curtains drawn. I don't know why. Before lunch I put the laundry in the dryer, and after lunch I fold it and put it away. Then I go in to check on him. He sits propped in the bed, alternately staring at nothing and nodding off to sleep. I sit in a kitchen chair beside the bed and play my solitaire video game until I start to do the same. I try not to. If I fall asleep, I'll lie in bed awake for hours later in the night, listening to his loud, ragged breaths, but I can't help it. I'm tired. I sleep hunched forward in the chair, with both hands folded atop his cane and my forehead atop my hands, until eventually I slacken enough that the cane falls to the floor with a crack and my whole body slumps forward. That keeps me from getting any good rest. I pick the cane up and do it again, usually four or five times altogether.

After my nap, I unhook the bag from his toilet and take it to the trash. I dump out the contents of his urinal and wash it in the bathroom sink, with yellow rubber gloves and a soapy sponge, even when there's nothing in it. I turn on the televisions, I open the drapes. I'm not sure why. It doesn't change him, doesn't wake him up or make the day any lighter. Doesn't seem to be any reason, any point to it at all.

But it's important to stick to your schedule. It keeps the days moving one to the next. Holds them up from inside, like a good armature, so they don't collapse in on themselves. Saturday nights I dread, though, every chamber thrown wide open: dumping the pills into my palm, dividing them out among the waiting days, and closing each one up again.

In the afternoons, I work on Daisy, a little bit every day. I smear papier-mâché across the roof of her mouth and drag the tines of a big two-pronged fork down each side from its vaulted peak, I press cold wads of it into her eye sockets. The eyes are almost flat on the back, just a little concave curve to them. The others stare blankly up from their cubbies in the tackle box, the bobcat's pupil a narrow slash like the slice of a razor blade through pale amber, opening up the darkness inside it, the pheasant's a perfect black circle fringed with a thick corona of dark blood vessels like the crudely-drawn rays radiating from a sun painted on a cave wall. It's hard to get good dog eyes, so I had to use coyote. They work well enough, I suppose, they've got the big pupil, and the pale brown iris leaks its color just a little past its black border and into the white, the way a dog's does. I angle them to the side, in the opposite direction from the one her head's turned, to look out from between the corners of her eyelids.

On the television they're waiting for the judgment. The screen is split between the marble courthouse steps, slick and shining with rain, and the empty seats of the jury box. Fourteen hours now they've been deliberating.

Once a week, on Sunday evening, we make the trek to the bathroom. He swings his legs over the side of the bed, leans forward, and grabs ahold of the cane with wobbling arms, struggles to heave himself onto its one narrow point. The skin on the back of his neck is creased in deep, crisscrossing fissures like the dirt of a dried-up creek bed. I grab his elbow and haul. It takes us a little longer every time to get him standing.

He keeps one hand on the wall and with the other pushes his cane squealing and smudging black scuff marks all the way across the hall to the bathroom, never breaking contact with the floor. I have to help him raise it over the lip of the door, and keep one hand on his back, hunched and bony, to make sure he doesn't tip over backwards.

I take him to the shower and help him out of his clothes, sit him down on the plastic seat I bought and turn on the water, put the soap in his hands and close his fingers around it, but he doesn't clean himself at all. After a few minutes, the soap slips free and falls to the floor with a loud thud. Not that it matters much. Sitting under the spout like that, you can't lather yourself up properly for the water washing the suds away. While he's in the shower, I change the sheets. He never would turn the mattress like I told him to, and now he's left a crater in the foam that never fills itself back in. I feel it in my sleep, the downward pull tilting me always toward him.

I try think of it all as charity work. Just showing the common decency you'd show to any orphan or invalid, any injured stranger on the street. It's easier that way.

When I come back, he's just sitting there, his hands in his lap and his head down like his neck's too weak to hold it up, the water pouring over him, the soap plugging the drain so a flood rises over his feet. He looks up at me like he's being punished. Sometimes he knows who I am, sometimes he doesn't. It's worst in the late afternoons, usually, and the early evenings, right as the sun goes down.

He doesn't talk near as much now. Hardly talks at all. I'd thought it would be a relief.

I smear clay across her brow and forehead, my thumb leaving its imprint in little spiny ridges, pull her face back over her skull, and mold her features through the skin: pinch a lump of clay into each eyebrow, gather it into the ridges of good chewing muscle alongside her skull's bony crest. The insides of her lips I brush with glue, pull their corners toward her ears until her jowls have just the right curve and the loose edges of her bottom lip, dark and scalloped like some creature you'd find at the bottom of the sea, fall perfectly away from her gums. All along her lips and eyelids, I drive insect pins through her skin, through the clay, until the point strikes bone. They're the thinnest you can find, meant to fix the moth's wings to the lepidopterist's black velvet without crumbling them to dust, don't leave even the slightest hint of a mark. I set her on the vent in the kitchen floor, to harden and dry.

At five, I cook some dinner, which I eat by myself at the table. After dinner, I take him in some food, hold it out to him on a fork. I try to slip it into his mouth in the moments when he's far away, so he'll chew and swallow it by instinct. I wash all the dishes I can by hand until it hurts too bad, and clutching each plate through the slippery suds feels like somebody's pushed a sharp wire down each of my fingertips, along and against the bone, and trying to bend a finger means you've got to bend that wire, too, and you never know when it might snap and tear out through the skin.

The hours after dinner are the worst: those empty, quiet hours that instead of passing seem to just grow wider and wider, like bubbles rising to the surface.

I turn off the faucet and listen while I dry my plate: for a snore, for a mutter or a laugh, for the patter of a little girl's feet.

I sling silverware into the sink just to hear it

clatter. I throw the cabinet doors open and clang the pots and pans.

The pill caddy says it's Thursday, and Thursday night's the night I stay up late to go to the grocery store. I'm too afraid to leave him here awake, so I sit beside him in the dark and watch the news on the tiny screen and wait while he stares at something in the far, far distance, over the news anchors' shoulders: at the buildings of the downtown skyline projected behind them, at the tiny yellow squares of lit windows where, here and there, you can just make out the blur of a shadowed figure caught in the moment the picture was taken, someone hunched over his desk, someone looking out toward you in the midst of pulling down the blinds, never able to draw them all the way shut.

And there's Debbie Drowner, all dolled up in her prairie dress and blue bonnet, weeping big, glassy tears that roll down her rosy cheeks and drip onto the not guilty headline as it slides across the bottom of the screen in an endless loop. She falls to her knees on the courthouse steps, raises her hands to the sky, and thanks God for His infinite mercy.

I turn the news off and sit in the dark, listening to him breathe. Each inhale gurgles thick and wet. It catches in his throat, and for a few seconds there's silence, absolute silence, and the whole house is still, waiting. Then the choking noise as it breaks apart, the heavy wheeze of breath barely scraping through it. I half expect salt water to spill from his lips.

Tomorrow, there'll be dead boys floating in

lakes and pools and bathtubs all across this country. Just you wait and see.

After a few minutes, I creep to the door, check one last time for the ripple and gleam of eyes open in the dark, and sneak out of the house. The grass has got so tall, thigh-high and waving in every breeze, that I found some people in the phone book to come cut it, called up every landscaper there was listed, and these boys came the cheapest. And they give you a first-time customer discount on top of that, and you don't have to pay them or talk to them at all while they're here — I just gave the woman on the phone our address, and she said she'd send them out next week and mail me an invoice. I don't even have to be here.

I put the car in neutral and let it roll down the driveway, the wads of catkins gathered on the gravel muffling the tires' rumble, before I start the engine and drive through the teeming dark. Feels like it's trying all the time to spill into the headlights, to dent the bumper and crash its antlers through the windshield.

But I like it inside the store. Look forward to it all week. It's nice and cool, and the floor's polished so shiny and slick the reflections of the fluorescent lights burn away the lines between the tiles, and the lights themselves send a sort of numbing buzz washing over and through you. And the air is perfectly blank. All this food, and it doesn't smell like anything at all.

That's the best part. I'm tired of remembering. I'm tired of being reminded.

I should have started going to the grocery

store at midnight years ago. There's hardly anybody here this late, and no children at all, so I don't have to worry about maneuvering my cart around their exposed toes while they simper over boxes of sugary cereal, though I am forced to listen to some nocturnal couple, neither of whom could be older than twenty-five, arguing over whether they need the low-fat or the no-fat cheese. I push my cart away from them fast as I can, back toward the produce aisle and all its waxy skins. Used to be, you went to the grocery store for some cheese, you ate whatever they happened to have. Now everybody's got so many choices, two-percent or low-fat or no-fat, cheddar and Swiss and foreign names I can't even pronounce. They think they get to decide everything: who they love, how much money they're going to make, how many children they'll have and how smart those children will be, when most of them can't pick out their own clothes without looking like a clown or a streetwalker or some combination of the two. You don't get to choose. Not anything that matters.

Sometimes now it seems like somebody else's life. Like something I imagined.

The lights above the produce bins flicker, and hidden speakers rumble electronic thunder. A fine mist sprays from nozzles in the wall, coating the zucchini and peppers and parsley. They sweat and drip with the rain. When I close my eyes and listen, the storm almost seems real. I can see the flashes of lightning through my eyelids.

The produce doesn't taste like a thing, though. It truly doesn't. Every tomato looks seared clean, each blemish cut away and cauterized, every bruised, out-of-season peach big as a diseased heart, and just as bloodless.

I stay in the store a long time after I'm finished shopping, push my cart up and down the aisles, piling things in it, changing my mind and putting them back, until the skinny boys loading the freezer cases from plastic-wrapped pallets of waffles start looking at me like I'm some sort of criminal. The house is hushed and still when I get home, and when I carry the bags from the den to the dark kitchen and turn on the light, it feels like I've stepped into a whole other house and time, crossed from one place to another the way you do in dreams. None of it seems real or solid. One shouted word could dissolve the whole place, and me with it.

Before bed, I set the dishwasher to run, with the couple bowls and pots I didn't get to earlier. I can hear it from the bedroom, and the hum and chug help me sleep. First I get a knife and scrape some leftovers from the plastic containers they sit and spoil in at the back of the refrigerator: chicken salad, deviled eggs, green beans. I haven't learned yet how to cook for one. Even when I tried, I couldn't do it. It felt all wrong. And I never eat the leftovers. That would open too big a chunk of time when I should have been cooking, and the biggest danger of all is an empty space in the day. It's easy, then, for the whole thing to start collapsing inward, for the emptiness all around it to break through and rush in and join the emptiness inside.

The knife scrapes a little too loudly against the

plastic. I stiffen, and pause, and wait for everything to shatter.

The dishwasher's racks aren't half full, even with all the containers, but I pour the powdered detergent into the cup, and close the door, and turn the dial to run it anyway.

You just go on living. You don't have to have a reason.

21

The truck grumbles up the gravel early, right as I'm about to take my shower. You can hear it even from the back of the house with the bathroom fan whirring, these old walls are so thin. I check the curtains in the living room, in the bedroom, make sure they're drawn all the way shut, and watch from the crack between them at the window over the sink as two young men wade their way through the gleaming, waist-high grass. They haul all the old stakes out of the garden — free of charge — and pile them against the fence.

I turn the water on hot as I can stand, so it hurts for the first minute or so and leaves my skin tender and pink — that's the only way I feel clean anymore — and I've just stepped into it, haven't even started to shampoo, when I hear beyond the thundering drum of drops in the basin a loud, cracking crash. I'm already hurrying out of the shower, toweling off, tugging my pajamas back on, before the crash turns into a clatter from the kitchen and the sound of wood splintering, but by the time I get there, Frank's already out the back door. He's left it wide open: shouldered his way out of the bedroom so hard the latch hooks have bent and ripped from their eyes, yanked out the silverware drawer and spilled it all over the floor in finding the hammer, and used the hammer's claw to tear the doorframe away from the deadbolt, and now he's staggering across the yard, fully dressed, rumpled shirt and pants hung loose from his bones like empty skin and one raised finger jabbing admonition at the boys hurtling heedless around on their riding mowers, so fast and reckless you'd think they were in a race. I grab his cane and head out after him, yet again.

He marches right in front of one of the mowers. It would serve him right to get run over, and the boy at the wheel doesn't look like he's entirely ruled out that particular course of action, grinds the thing to a halt so close the clippings spray Frank's shins. I wade through the grass, still glistening and stooped with dew, and by the time I emerge into the stubbly strip they've already cut, the cuffs of my britches are dark and damp. Heavy, too. Feel liable to pull my pants down.

Frank's still holding the hammer. It knocks softly against his leg as he walks around to the side of the mower.

'Frank,' I say.

He waves me back inside. 'You get out of here,' he says to the boy. He's a real unsavory-looking character, has dark stubble like patchy undergrowth all across his cheeks, and the hair on his head shaved down to the same length. The sleeves of his shirt are cut away to show the curved furrows between his ribs and the damp tendrils of hair curling from his armpit, stuck to his side with sweat. The line between the tanned skin of his neck and arms and the paler skin of his chest is so stark and sharp it hurts me just to look at.

He shoves his hands into the pockets of his orange basketball shorts, pulled taut over his thighs so you can see every muscle's delineation, and pulls out a scrap of paper. He reads out our address.

'That's here, right?' he says.

'It is,' I say, and Frank scowls at me, warning and fearful and, if I'm not mistaken, a little bit threatening.

'It's all right,' I tell him. 'Come on, let's go inside. It's all right,' I say to the boy.

The way Frank glares at me, I'm surprised the grass between us doesn't shrivel up. 'I ain't going in the side of anything,' he says. 'Not until I get all these hoodlums off my grass. Go on.' He shoos the boy with his hammer. 'I know how you people operate. Just show up and start cutting anybody's grass and then tell them they owe you. Get out of here.'

The boy gives me an impatient widening of the eyes, like he's asked me a question and can't believe how long I'm taking to answer. Grass clippings are stuck to his bare knee. Without even glancing down, he wipes them away, but their green stains his skin. Behind him, his oblivious partner's still hurtling back and forth across the yard, gathering up vast swaths of grass in his huge, curved blades. A dozen tree swallows dart and dive all around him, gorging themselves on the swarms of exposed insects. A couple bear down like they're about to attack him, graze right across the brim of his baseball cap, but he's wearing big earphones and reflective sunglasses and makes no sign of knowing that anybody in the world exists but himself.

Frank squints at the padlock on the shed door, gleaming in the light. 'Somebody's locked me out of my own shed,' he says. 'Who put that lock there?'

'So do you want me to come back later or something?' the boy yells at me over the whir and grind.

'You don't need to talk to him,' Frank says to the boy. 'You need to talk to me. He don't even — '

'Look, I just need somebody to tell me whether to mow this yard or not.'

'Yes,' I say.

'No,' Frank says.

The other mower blows up from the dead patch a billowing cloud of red dust. Its top disperses hazy through the air; its heavy bottom sinks back to earth, spreads even across the dirt.

'Get out of here,' Frank yells. 'You too,' he says, flicking the hammer at me. 'Get.'

'You need to calm down,' I say. 'Everything's fine. I called them.'

'*You* called them? On the *phone*?'

'We'll come back later,' the boy says.

'Don't you go anywhere,' I say.

'You don't even live here,' Frank says. 'He don't even live here,' he says to the boy. 'He's my brother, in town for a visit. He don't even live here, he's just — '

'Frank,' I say. 'They don't care. Nobody cares. It doesn't matter anymore.'

I touch the back of his hand, lightly, to try to

pull him back here, into his own body standing in his own yard, but he snatches it away from my fingers with the quickness and violence of reflex, lifting the hammer overhead.

'He don't live here,' Frank says, desperate. 'He don't.'

The boy grimaces. He's staring at the crotch of Frank's britches. A tiny dark spot speckles the fabric next to his fly, like a drop of rain just landed.

'Frank,' I say.

'He don't live here,' Frank says.

The hammerhead draws languid circles against the sky. The dark spot spreads slowly across the front of his pants.

'He's sick,' I say to the boy. 'That's all.' I wrap my fingers around the hammer and pull it down from the sky. Frank lets me. The boy's eyes widen.

'Come on,' I say. 'Let's go inside.'

Slowly, silently, the stain drops a tentacle down one leg.

I hold Frank's cane out, the handle toward him. Reluctantly, dazed, he accepts it. I take another step toward him, and to maintain the distance between us, as if it were an unbreachable law of physics, he takes one step toward the house, my nearness swelling the empty space between us like the darkness between the stars when he shrugged his shoulders.

'So do you want us to keep mowing or not?' the boy yells.

I drive Frank away, step by step. He won't pick his cane up, keeps trying to just push it through the grass like it was his walker. It tears up the yard and gets lodged in the dirt, so he has to twist it all around to work it loose, and then he goes and does the exact same thing all over again.

'Pick it up,' I say. 'It doesn't have wheels, you know.'

He stares at me like I'm speaking another language.

'Do you see any wheels on it? Pick it up.' I yank it out of the dirt.

By the time we get to the bathroom the front of his trousers is drenched all the way down one leg.

'Clean yourself up,' I say. 'Fast.'

'I believe I've got to use the bathroom,' he says.

'You're wearing diapers from now on. I'm going to have to go to the store in the middle of the day and get you diapers. Now clean yourself up.'

I leave him there while I shove the hammer in the drawer and slam it shut, kick forks out of my way, and snatch my wallet off the table in the hallway and pull out two twenty-dollar bills. I take them out to the back patio and wave the boy down. He drives his mower right up to the concrete edge but doesn't cut the engine off. The whir of the blades flutters in my ears. Makes me dizzy.

'Here.' I press the folded bills into his sweaty palm and close his fingers around them. His body radiates warmth sure as the motor does.

'I'm sorry about that,' I yell. He gazes

longingly over my shoulder at a spot far away from me where he'd rather be.

'He's sick,' I say. The boy tugs the hem of his shorts down to cover his grass-stained knee. A little bit of me mourns its loss.

'Just don't buy drugs with it,' I say.

He turns the mower and retraces the path he cut through the grass.

When I get back inside, Frank's leaning in the door to the hallway, resting his head on the molding. His eyes are closed.

'What are you doing?' I say. 'Get back in the bathroom.' I grab him by the arm of his shirt.

'You shouldn't have called them,' he says.

'Come on.' I pull him toward the shower. The roar of the mowers rattles the window glass. 'Get your pants off.'

He tries to undo his belt, but it takes him so long fiddling with the leather, trying to slide it out from under the buckle with his palsied fingers, that I have to knock his hands out of the way and do it myself, open his belt and unzip his zipper and yank his pants and underwear down to his ankles, like a child. His rumpled shirttail hangs over his privates. The whole room smells of his urine, sharp and ammoniac.

'What if they tell somebody?' he says.

'They're not going to tell anybody.'

'You shouldn't have called them. You shouldn't — '

'Sit.' I point to the plastic chair. He waddles over and slowly lowers himself into it, his legs hanging over the edge of the tub, and proceeds to do nothing but stare anxiously out the window, even though you can't see a thing

301

through the cloudy scallops of frosted glass but vague shadows passing.

'Can you clean yourself?' I say. 'Or do I have to do that too?' I close the toilet seat and sit down. 'You could have killed somebody. You know that? Or yourself, more likely. That boy could have knocked you flat without even trying. He could have mowed you down. How'd you even get out there?' He didn't have his cane, didn't have a wall to hold on to. And I know he didn't have an amateur detective's clue where that hammer was. I made sure of that. 'How'd you even get out of the bed?'

He crosses his arms, staring at the damp, dark plaid between his legs, and doesn't say a thing.

'Give me your foot.' He has to pull up on his knee to lift it. I set his shoe in my lap and undo the laces. 'Pull.' It takes us a good minute of wrenching and tugging before we manage to pry the thing off. I peel down his long, soggy white sock, slide it over the hard yellow talons of his toenails. Little black grass seeds are caught in its stitches.

He sits forward, grabs my wrist. 'You don't know who they are,' he says, his voice low. 'You don't know who they are, or who they might know. You understand me? They could be anybody. They could be the foreman's sons for all you know, they could be the police chief's brothers. They could be — '

'They're not,' I say. I pull my wrist free and press my hand to his chest, push him back into the seat, but he sits right forward again. I try to hold him back, but he's too strong. 'Just calm

302

down, just relax. Everything's fine.'

'If anybody finds out,' he says, 'if anybody finds out, they'll — '

'They won't. Nobody's going to find out.'

'How do you know? You can't — '

'I checked. When I called them. I asked where they were from, and who their people were, all of it. They just moved here from New Jersey a couple months ago. They don't even live in town. They don't know anybody.'

'You promise?' he says.

'I promise.'

'You can't call people to the house.' His voice is hoarse now, shaking and tight to hold back tears. 'It's too dangerous.'

'I know,' I say. 'I know. I won't do it again.'

His heart's pounding too fast. It feels like a hummingbird in his chest.

'It's okay,' I say. 'It's okay. We're safe.'

He stares at me a long time, waiting for the terror to subside, then nods and slumps back in the chair, pulpy and sunken, a papier-mâché imitation of himself that might cave in at any moment. I heave his other foot into my lap and pry it out of his shoe.

'You're tying your laces too tight,' I say. 'It's no wonder your circulation's so bad. The blood can't hardly get down in there, and it sure can't get back up.'

I shimmy his pants and his underwear over his feet, doing my best not to touch the wet spots, open his shirt from wet tail to collar and slide its sleeves down his arms, gathering them as I go, peel them over the thick knobs of his elbows and wrists. The black lines of his tattoos are faded and worn. The birds on his chest sag earthward, their wings slipping on the air, and the sky on his shoulder is wrinkled in some spots and stretched pale in others, distorting the stars fixed in it, tugging at their edges until they ought to crack open and burn away the tangle of animals beneath them, and boil the ocean those animals all seem to be melting into.

Bent over the lip of the tub, I run some hot water into a washcloth, lather it with soap, and clean him from the feet up, scrubbing as hard and as fast as I can to scour away that sharp, cloudy smell. A bunion's bent his big toe so far that it's crossed under and lies completely beneath the smaller one beside it, and his socks have worn all the blond hairs away from his calves, left them smooth and shiny. Just below each knee, all the way around his leg, their elastic's dug a deep, pink channel into the skin.

He's quiet while I clean him, looks politely away with a resigned distance in his eyes. Every breath he takes is labored, wet and ragged. The skin of his thighs hangs wrinkled and loose in those places where it used to strain to hold in the brunt meat of him. I lift each fold, spread flat across the plastic seat, to wipe its underside.

He puts a hand to his top teeth and pushes up. 'These dentures are driving me crazy,' he says.

'I didn't think you'd noticed.'

'It'd drive you crazy, too, if your teeth started sliding down every time you tried to talk.' He reaches far back into his mouth. 'Can we get some glue or something?'

His voice sounds like his voice. His eyes are focused, the light falling into their pupils instead of skimming frictionless across them, as if they're actually seeing what's in front of them for the first time in months. I pretend not to notice.

'Frank,' I say, lifting the fold of his belly. Beneath it, his underwear's stamped a damp, puckered band around his waist. Looks like an intestine, or pizza when you've pulled the cheese off. 'Where did we meet?'

'Out in front of your shop,' he says, sounding annoyed. 'When you were done peeping at me and decided to come out and act like a normal human being.'

'I was not peeping. I was just standing there in my own place of business while you flopped all around with your huge head outside my window.'

'My head,' he says, 'is perfectly proportional to the rest of my body.'

I laugh as I run water into the washcloth. I'm afraid to look at him. I'm afraid he'll be gone again.

'What sort of a question is that, anyway?' he says.

My hands shake something awful as they fold the washcloth and lay it over the lip of the tub. His chest looms beside me, pale and pocked as the surface of the moon, chipped out of some cold, brittle rock that hovers always out of reach but never stops tugging at the tide. I grab his hand in both of mine. I don't believe we'll have many more chances to say anything that matters.

'Do you ever wish,' I say, 'that you could have

305

done things different?'

He looks at me a long, long time, trying to gauge whether to tell me the truth. I watch the lines on his calves, waiting for their blush to fade, for them to fill their emptiness from underneath, but nothing changes. Nothing moves.

'I think — ' he says. 'Sometimes I think I would have liked to be a teacher. Helped some kids. Made their lives better. I believe I would have liked that.'

'You would have been a good teacher. Or a detective.'

'I would have been a lousy detective,' he says, laughing. It seems to hurt him.

'I wanted real badly sometimes,' he says, 'to be a part of the world.'

My vision blurs, as if that haze around a winter moon my father always promised us meant snow, even though the snow never came, had settled about his body.

'Do you wish you could have had children?' I say.

He looks away, now, at the pile of his soiled clothes on the floor. The mowers are gone. The house is quiet.

'Well,' he says. 'Nobody gets everything they want.'

'I didn't know.' I squeeze his hand. 'I really didn't, or I — I would've — '

'Ain't a whole lot you could've done about it.'

'If you'd wanted to, if I'd known it would've made you happy, I — '

He rests his hand heavy on my thigh, as if to

hold me down. 'I knew what I was giving up,' he says. 'That day they put my mama in the ground. I knew I was giving up my family, and friends, and having children. I knew I was giving up my chance at being anything too great.'

It's a long time before I manage to say, 'You never told me that.'

He shrugs. I pick the washcloth up and squeeze it dry. The water runs out, leaves it wrinkled and stiff.

'I wish I'd — I know I wasn't always as good to you as I should've been,' he says. 'I know I could be difficult. But I was just so scared. All the time.'

'Of what?'

'That they'd take you away from me.'

Feels like there's a fissure, a cold fissure running along my breastbone, up into my throat. Like plates beneath the earth's crust, pulling it apart.

'Was it worth it?' I say.

'I reckon it was.' He smiles a sad, solemn smile. I hang my head down, so he won't see me squeeze my eyes shut.

'You think I'd have spent all these years cleaning up your mess if it wasn't?' he says, smirking.

'*My* mess?'

'You ain't the cleanest man I ever met.' He shifts in his seat. 'Can we hurry this up? My rear end's starting to fall asleep.'

I run more water into the washcloth, work suds into it until they bubble. I clean his privates, hanging heavy and wrinkled. I do it slower and softer than before, careful. When I touch them, they rise a little, then fall again, like a wounded animal heaving a shallow breath: like the first bird I ever held in my hands, a bluebird, its neck snapped by its own image grown larger and larger and finally made solid in glass, lying on the porch of my parents' house a year before I hopped onto the train that carried me away from it forever, when I was sixteen years old and wanted desperately to die. If you could just hold one, I'd thought, if you could just keep it still, you could find the source of its lightness. I lifted it from the ground and cupped it in my hands; I felt its life gutter and go out. I was surprised by the brittleness of its wings. There was no grace in them at all.

'You know what I've a taste for?' Frank says.

'What?'

'Some of your good yeast rolls. You got any of them?'

'I'll make you some,' I say. 'I'll make you anything you want. Anything but fruitcake.'

'Fruitcake? I don't even like fruitcake. It's too sweet.'

I start to cry. Have to hold on to his thighs to keep myself steady.

'What's wrong with you?' he says.

'Nothing.' I blow my nose into a wad of toilet paper. He frowns and brushes little bits of it from my whiskers. 'I'm fine.'

'Are you sure?'

I nod.

'Good. Make sure it's a big batch. I'm so hungry I could eat a horse.'

'It'll be a while,' I say. 'They have to rise overnight.'

'Can't you hurry it up?'

'No, I can't hurry it up. These things take time. You think I can control the gaseous properties of yeast?'

'Lord,' he says. 'There's no need to be so sensitive about it. It was just a suggestion.'

I turn on the hot water, cup it in my hands, and pour it over him. His skin dries out if you don't rinse the soap off it good. The water runs between my fingers and onto his thighs, over his knees, down his legs to his feet, the rivulets catching here and there on stray, wiry hairs, in the pink lines that lash his legs. I scrub them, massage them with warm water, don't take my eyes off them until he starts to shiver and I have to throw the towel over his shoulders and help him out of the tub, and still they linger there on his skin, carved into his calves like the imprints of grass blades.

* * *

I leave the front door open so he can watch the birds. He sits in his recliner all afternoon, binoculars hung from his neck, twisting around to look at the goldfinches streaking bright and fast through the branches like the sun's glare on a passing car, the cardinals like spots of blood dappling the leaves, the tree swallows, their blue cowls iridescent in the light, flying wild in pairs above the trees, across the yard, wheeling one way then dashing another with no apparent reason, mirroring each other's every scoop and swerve so that the distance between them, though they climb and break and plunge, never changes.

★ ★ ★

It's evening. In the limbs of the trees, hidden birds sing the fevered sun to sleep. The sky's turned a pale pink as the light fades, but it's white just above the treetops, like sunburnt skin the branches have pressed into and let go, watching, waiting, for the color to rush back in.

I only leave him long enough to mix the sourdough. I fed the starter and set it in the windowsill to bubble in the sun all day long, just like you're supposed to, but something's gone wrong with it. I stir in all the flour it calls for and then some, a little at a time, and mix it and mix it, but it never will stiffen into anything you could rightly call a dough. Maybe it's too humid in here, maybe the starter's gone bad, I don't know, but I do know that if I add any more flour, they're liable to end up hard as bricks. Finally I just give up, shove the bowl in the oven and turn on the light.

'How's it coming?' Frank says when I sit back in my chair.

'Awful. The batter's like pudding. I won't be surprised if it doesn't rise at all.'

'You say that every time.'

'I do not.'

'You do. And then they turn out fine.'

'No, you just tell me they turn out fine. And

310

then I never know what's wrong with them so I can fix the next batch.'

'That's because there's never anything to fix.'

'Well, there will be this time. I added so much extra flour, they'll probably — '

He throws the lever on his chair to put the footrest down. The force of its back slamming forward bestows him enough momentum to stand up. He sways back and forth a minute, then shuffles toward the hallway.

'Where are you going?' I say.

'Out back,' he says.

'Again? For what?'

He shrugs. 'Just want to make sure everything looks all right.'

'Hold on,' I say. 'I'll go with you.' I haul myself up out of the chair and follow him down the hall, open up the back door. I leave the light off so he won't see the splintered doorframe, so he won't see Daisy. I got all the pins out already, but I still need to rub some corncobs into her fur, fluff it out a little, and mold the caulk in her elbows into their bony points, and snip off the little beads of it that have burst through invisible tears.

The yard and the trees and the kitchen tile are coated in a thin wash of darkness like black wax, brushed liquid from a heated tin onto a lip, onto the hairless bottom edge of an eyelid, quickly cooling and hardening into a shining, translucent shell. I turn the patio light on as we go, and the surrounding night thickens, as if crowded together to make room for it.

'Well, I'll be,' Frank says, stopping in the

doorway, and peers right down at her, still sitting on the air vent, as if waiting in utter dejection for a treat. 'Daisy. I didn't know you'd kept her.' He leans against the doorjamb to steady himself while he picks her up.

'You weren't supposed to see her yet,' I say. He carries her outside, into the light. 'She's not finished.' The oils from my hand have smudged her eyes, clouded them with cataracts. I wipe them with my sleeve.

'It looks just like she was alive. Don't it?' He sounds wistful, and only a little sad, as if he's looking at a picture of somebody who died a long time ago, somebody he loved very much but hadn't thought of in years. He puts his arm around me and pulls me close. I rest my cheek on his shoulder. It's warm to the touch, burning with stars.

'Just exactly like she was alive,' he says.

I suppose there's a little mercy left in the world after all.

'What happened to her legs?' he says. Where they should be, the skin's drawn over her excelsior stump, fur ruffled over the tiny brass tacks.

'You'd fed her so much, her skin was slippery as a black bear's. Kept on losing my grip, tore it to smithereens trying to get it off.' Her belly looks all right, if I do say so myself. Drapes heavy and soft off her ribs, and flattens in a pool against his hand just the way it did on the ground.

'A black bear,' I say. I press my ear to his chest and listen to the thunderous rush of his heart as it opens, the thunderous rush of his heart as it closes. 'The fattiest animal known to North American man.'

He smiles and nods with deep satisfaction, as if this had been his plan all along. He kisses her on the nose, on the short, soft fur of her muzzle. She looks away in shame. He holds her at arm's length for a moment, studying her, then carefully sets her down on the very edge of the circle of light, her front half illuminated, her rear end in darkness. From that angle, you can't see the direction of her eyes, so she seems to be looking over her shoulder, at the woods beyond the fence. 'There,' he says. 'Now you can't even tell.'

He starts across the yard. I pull his elbow, try to slow him down. 'We'll get grass all over our shoes,' I say, but he grabs my hand and squeezes it tight, as if against somebody trying to pull us apart, and keeps on walking, and I go with him, picking my way over the mounds of clippings they've left strewn all over while he shuffles right through them toward the trees, their trunks nothing but accretions of darkness, their fissured bark the darkness's weathered, wrinkled skin. We walk to the very furthest ledge of grass along the bare patch, stand side by side for a long time without saying a word. He squints at the ground, then bends down, one hand on his knee, and runs the other over the edge of the lawn, feeling for evenness. The blades of grass, bending, brush across his palm. He shuffles along the fence like that, while I heave back on his elbow the entire time to make sure he doesn't lose his balance, until finally he manages to find one little tussock that sticks up a little higher than the rest.

'I knew they wouldn't do it right,' he grunts. 'Didn't I say they wouldn't do it right?' He grabs a handful of grass and rips it free. 'That's better.' He pushes down on my hand to slowly raise himself up again.

'I believe I'm going to head on to bed,' he says.

'Already?' I say. 'It's early.'

'Maybe for you. I'm wore out. Feels like I've been working all day long, even though I ain't done a thing.'

'It's so nice out. I could put us some chairs on the patio.'

He leans his head back to look up at the stars in the clear, cold sky, so many of them the sheer number's enough to make you dizzy, enough to knock you down. Still, there used to be more. Before we strung up all our lamps to keep them at bay, to drive them like wild things back into the night.

'Naw,' he says. 'That's all right.'

He kisses me on the corner of the mouth, whiskers tickling my lips, and turns to go. His stubble's soft now. Used to scrape me till I was sore.

We walk back across the yard. In the patio bulb's bright light, enormous moths flutter in circles, their outdriven shadows fracturing its glow as their wings, so fragile just the light itself ought to blast them into dust, catch it and hold it close to the curve of glass. They knock endlessly against the bulb, trying again and again to break through into the light's blinding heart, to wrap their wings around its glowing filament and absorb every last bit of heat until it burns them to ash. Somewhere out in the woods, deer are rushing, wild blood pounding in their antlers, each pulse laying down the next layer of sediment before it recedes, slowly hardening them into bone that echoes the shape of the veins that carry it there, which look themselves like the bare branches of trees. In the winter, they'll fall beneath the weight of the snow, two more dead limbs on the forest floor.

I open the door and try to lead him in, but he pulls away and turns around and looks out over the yard one more time, with his hands on his hips, scowling: at the grass washing clean and smooth all the way out past the fence, where it dissolves into the shade of the trees, and at all those places we tried our hardest to make it grow but never could, and at Daisy, weary and tired, turning her head away so we won't know she's watching.

'Not bad,' he says, nodding. 'Not bad at all.'

He heaves a deep, slow breath and shuffles toward the open door. I hold on to his hand, squeeze it as tight as I can, and walk with him into the dark house.

Acknowledgments

Thank you, first and foremost, to my family for their unending love and support.

Thanks to Emily Forland for her belief in the book and her great skill in shepherding it; to Rachel Mannheimer for her masterful guidance, sharp edits, and generally being an absolute joy to work with; to Alexa von Hirschberg for her expertise, enthusiasm, and care; to George Gibson, Laura Keefe, Laura Phillips, Marie Coolman, Megan Ernst, Nancy Miller, Patti Ratchford, Steven Henry Boldt, Theresa Collier, and the entire Bloomsbury team in the United States and the United Kingdom.

Thank you to everyone at the Iowa Writers' Workshop; to the great people of Highlander Center; and to John McNally, whose artistic and professional guidance for the past decade has made a profound difference in my life.

Thanks to my friends for being the best people in the world, and especially to first readers Chris Plating and Sarah Karon for the advice and encouragement I needed at just the right time.

Finally, thanks to Raymie, without whom I would not know nearly enough about love to have written this book; and to Liam, for watching over me nearly every day as I worked on it.